Praise for *The Williamson Turn*

"P. F. Kluge is a national treasure. His prose is irresistible, and his storytelling is masterly. That's why a new book by him constitutes an event. *The Williamson Turn* is a novel that's a voyage on many levels, including a passage into ourselves, whoever we may be, and the final port of call is pure wonder."

—Joseph Di Prisco, author of *The Pope of Brooklyn* and *Subway to California*

Praise for *The Master Blaster*

"Kluge paints an entertainingly sardonic portrait of the newest part of America, which he presents, more generally, as being emblematic of 'where America ends.'"

—*Library Journal*

"This title is recommended for large popular collections for its interesting character development, plot twists, and 'gotcha' ending."

—*Booklist*

"As the Master Blaster says of Saipan: 'Americans dream of islands. Islanders dream of America. This is where the dreams converge.' Delving deep into his rich setting, P. F. Kluge patiently lays out a tale of intrigue and ignorance worthy of Graham Greene."

—Stewart O'Nan, author of *Wish You Were Here*

"When four lost souls arrive on the same night flight to Saipan, they wager who among them will last the longest. Fear, violence, sex, and money blow like trade winds across this *Fantasy Island*, a microscopic petri dish of greed and race sweltering in the American Pacific. Kluge is among our finest novelists, and he flexes his muscles over this postage stamp of territory. Like all the greats before him, he saves his best line for last, in this his greatest book."

—Tony D'Souza, author of *Mule*

"That voice—jaundiced, seasoned, amused, and vibrant as it is—gives *The Master Blaster* added allure. This is not a young man's book; it's the work of a writer who has seen the world, literally and figuratively, for a long time. *The Master Blaster* is tinged with thoughts of mortality, but they are offset by a bon vivant's occasional flash of gratitude and beauty."

—Janet Maslin, *The New York Times*

"Kluge, a professor at Kenyon College, is knowing and ski shifting story lines...*The Master Blaster* is an ode to our fresh start. It's also a sly history lesson about colonial powers and native misrule. It's an exposé, seeded when Magellan discovered the archipelago in 1521. It's a love poem to Saipan disguising none of its warts."

—*Cleveland Plain Dealer*

"All of these characters along with the Master Blaster have their own narrative threads and Kluge's weaving is intricate and in many places brilliant. Prose and dialogue snap and crackle." —*Boston Globe*

"Kluge's novel follows an increasingly entangled plot as it alternates among the quartet's voices, with interruptions by diatribes from an anonymous local blogger, the Master Blaster, self-appointed guardian of the island's soul. From the often amusing clutter of all these voices, Kluge not only crafts a first-rate mystery, but also demystifies the ways our personal histories and ambitions seem inevitably to debunk even the noblest of our myths." —*Shelf Awareness*

"The Master Blaster is the operator of a bitterly critical blog based on a real site that calls Saipan America's biggest welfare client. The revelation of the bloggers identity is a book-dropping stunner."

—*Akron Beacon Journal*

Praise for *Eddie and the Cruisers*

"An excellently crafted book. The dialogue is sharp, the book is packed with exquisite description and a surprise ending."

—*Sunday Journal and Star*

"*Eddie and the Cruisers* seems at first glance to be only a smartly written novel about nostalgia for the music of the late 1950s. It quickly proves, however, to be a remarkably good suspense story, full of vivid characters and some hilarious dialogue." —*St. Louis Post-Dispatch*

"A warm, entertaining, and highly evocative story of youth, music, and growing up in the 1950s." —*The Philadelphia Inquirer*

"Sparkling dialogue, wonderful characterizations, and a plot which dazzles." —*Enterprise Sun*

"[A] good mix of everyday blues with old-time bebop." —*Booklist*

THE

WILLIAMSON

TURN

THE

WILLIAMSON

TURN

a novel

P. F. KLUGE

a vireo book • rare bird books

Los Angeles, Calif.

Publisher's Cataloging-in-Publication data
Names: Kluge, P. F. (Paul Frederick), 1942-, author.
Title: The Williamson turn : a novel / P. F. Kluge.
Description: First Trade Paperback Original Edition | A Genuine Vireo Book |
New York, NY; Los Angeles, CA: A Vireo Book; Rare Bird Books, 2017.
Identifiers: ISBN 9781945572463
Subjects: LCSH Foreign study—Fiction. | Travel writers—Fiction. | Voyages
around the world—Fiction. | Interpersonal relations—Fiction. | Life change
events—Fiction. | BISAC FICTION / Literary.
Classification: LCC PS3561.L77 W55 2017 | DDC 813.54—dc23

For my wife, Pamela Hollie, companion on all voyages; for Dan Ehnbom and James Godfrey, fellow professors; and for the students in my writing class who wrote their way around the world and into this novel.

We shall not cease from exploration and the end of all our exploring will be to arrive where we started and know the place for the first time.

—T. S. Eliot, "Four Quartets"

Thou hast committed fornication: but that was in another country; and besides, the wench is dead.

—Christopher Marlow, *The Jew of Malta*

I.

MANAUS AND RIO DE JANEIRO, BRAZIL

WILL POST KNEW FROM the start that the *MV Explorer* was a "smoke-free environment" and he'd been quite prepared to find a secluded corner of the ship. Once he saw the tiny scrap of deck outside his cabin, he guessed he could gamble on sitting there. He didn't like his chances, though. No matter how late the hour, there was always someone around, passengers or crew. And his private deck was flanked by other private decks, belonging to faculty colleagues who would ask him, in the nicest possible way, to desist: "Thank you for not smoking."

Thank God, then, for the designated smoking area on the fifth deck. Someone wisely granted that absolute prohibition wasn't practical. Some of the ship's officers smoked cigarettes, maybe that was it. So there were nicely-crafted wooden boxes, filled with sand, hanging at intervals from the ship's railing. Often there were other smokers, students and older passengers but not faculty. Fine. People got used to seeing each other and over time, their shared addiction united them in a kind of freemasonry. Instead of passwords and handshakes, it was bummed cigarettes and borrowed lighters and very occasionally the gift of a cigar, leading to a discussion of the fine points of cutting and lighting. It soon got to the point that if no one was out there when he pushed through the wooden doors, he felt some regret. There was another problem, though. Unlike cigarettes, cigars took about twenty minutes, maybe longer. You couldn't walk around and it didn't feel right to stand there at the railing that long. There were lounges and deck chairs all over the ship. Not here. He asked about whether chairs could be provided. His request was "under consideration," he was told. Meghan Shepard, bearer of bad news, wiggled her fingers to make quotation marks when she said it.

Well, he thought, *when you're on a three-and-a-half-month voyage around the world, you ought to be able to sit and consider the sea.* As a precaution, in Dominica he'd bought a molded plastic chair. A few nights ago, he'd carried it down to the fifth deck, set up in a corner, out of the wind, lit a Hoyo de Monterrey, and—no denying it—been very happy. Sometimes, things came to him when he had a cigar, unexpected things; it was as if they'd been circling overhead, waiting for a time and place to land. Now he studied the Amazon—there was a moon—and he felt the river hypnotizing him. He saw the river, mud banks, fields, and forest, a familiar mix by now, but tonight the river cast a spell, shifting, changing, advancing, receding. You could see one side of the river, then the other—dueling banjos—clouds and moons, and Post was happy to watch the elements arrange and rearrange themselves.

Do something a little different on a ship, especially a ship—a floating university—with a cargo of faculty, students, administrators, and you acquire a label. That chair made him a character, a Marx, half Groucho, half Karl. The cigar man. People chatted him up, ship's officers nodded, senior passengers told stories, students wondered whether Cuban cigars were worth it. Every time he carried his chair back and forth he got smiles and salutes. Some of his own students found him there, but even better were the student regulars, listening to music, joking, blowing things off. Not so diligent, some of them. Some had already bailed on global studies; they asked him what he thought of the course, which everyone was required to attend. This was a test, almost a trap. If he trashed the course, the dean would hear about it. If he praised it, he'd be written off. So he shrugged and said, with a straight face, he was so busy he could hardly get there. He was pressed: would he ever attend? And he said yes, of course, he'd let them know. After that, they relaxed around him and, if he missed a night, they asked where he'd been. He heard gossip about professors, which ones were "trying too hard to be popular," which were "past sell-by date." One night they'd be singing, another they'd be learning sign language. He got closer to them, like a Peace Corps volunteer working his way into a rough and skeptical village. He sat in his chair and felt that things were turning out well.

"Excuse me," someone said. Post turned to see a young man who was not a student, though he might pass for one. Passing as a student was probably in his job description, for this was one of a number of "living and learning coordinators," staffers who befriended and reported on students. Pals and guardians.

"Yes?" Post said.

"Can we talk?"

"I don't see why not," Post replied. And an inner voice added: *I don't see why.*

"Someplace else?"

"This cigar has fifteen minutes left in it," Post said. "It cost me fifteen dollars. And…" he gestured at the fifth deck kids, "these are all exemplary human beings."

"Okay, then. It's about your chair."

"This little chair of mine?"

"We think it sets a bad example. If you start bringing furniture out here, the students might do the same. It could get out of hand."

"This furniture, as you put it, belongs to me. I don't see any other furniture out here. On the seventh deck, around the swimming pool, you'll find quite a lot. It's almost impossible to weave through all those basking bodies. Probably unsafe."

"It's the idea of the thing. You set a precedent. We think the chair has to go. Even if it's just you, especially if it's just you, it sets a double standard."

"No, no, it sets a *different* standard. They are students. I am faculty. And who are you?"

"My name is Josh Farrington."

"And you are a…what?" Post acted more puzzled than he was. "Let me see. A life-long leaner? Those are the adult passengers. You are not an adult passenger. You're one of those…"

"A living and learning coordinator."

"Yes. A coordinator of students. But I am a faculty member and you and I are not colleagues…or companions. You report to the dean of students. I report to the dean of the faculty…"

"Don't you see the problem?" Josh Farrington said in an incredulous tone.

"I see a problem all right. But not the one you see."

"All right then…" Farrington said, backing away.

"A final question," Post called out. "Suppose I were in a wheelchair. You have a wheelchair passenger on this ship. Would you bar her from this deck? That agreeable, lively lady, Mrs. Carla Hutchinson. Would you dump her out of her wheelchair?"

"You don't *need* a wheelchair."

"I need a chair."

Farrington nodded and walked away, down past the lifeboats, through a door that led to the dean's offices. Would anything come of it? He'd made an enemy, no doubt. Yet Farrington had come after him. So be it. He regarded the students, the regulars. They were smiling at him. Thumbs up. "Badass," one of the girls said. He returned to his cigar and couldn't help feeling pleased. He was one of the fifth deckers now, the cynics, the goof-offs, the jokers, the sort of kids you'd find in a high school detention hall. On a voyage that took itself so seriously, he felt at ease among this irreverent minority.

¤

To HER GREAT REGRET, Meghan Shepard arrived early to lead a field trip around Manaus and found herself on the edge of a conversation at the ship's railing that didn't particularly include her.

"Okay," said Will Post. "It's the longest river on the planet and certainly the biggest. You sail in, it's like entering the belly of a beast. At first you're impressed. But it keeps coming and after a while…I wonder what my kids will write…boring! It's like going to the moon. Big deal. 'One giant step for mankind.' And then you're standing on a ball of rocks and dirt and dust. Here it's brown water, fallen trees, tin-roofed shacks now and then. Fishermen who don't wave back."

"The flatness got to me," Harold Beckmann agreed. "I missed mountains. I studied clouds, imagining that they were mountains. Did you ever play that game when you were a kid?" Post nodded. Beckmann rattled on. "It's all so horizontal. As if it were missing a dimension. I recall something from Thomas Mann to the effect that there are two kinds of human beings…"

A past-ripe professor and a journeyman travel writer, talking as if they were in bed together. *Give me a break,* Meghan thought. *How long could they go on?*

"The verticals and the horizontals," Beckmann said. "The verticals ascend. Scale heights. The horizontals repose. It's the difference between *The Magic Mountain* and *Death in Venice*, roughly. Which are you?"

"Some of both, I guess," Post responded.

"Spare me. That's what students say when they can't answer a question. You might as well shrug and say 'whatever.'"

"Okay. Vertical. Mountains, clouds, big sky. That isn't to say…"

"Yes, of course, we all have horizontal tendencies. More of them the older we get."

Meghan's horizontal impulses urged her to return to her cabin and take a nap. Her idea of hell would be a cross-country road trip with these two. Then, though, Beckmann acted as if he'd just noticed her. Meghan was certain he'd been aware of her all along and didn't mind ignoring her. Now he acknowledged her.

"It's remarkable," he said, "to find an international seaport so far from the sea. Hundreds of miles. I wonder if it will feel like a port?"

"What's a port supposed to feel like?" she asked. A snarky response, for sure. Beckmann must have heard the edge in her voice.

"That tang in the air. Sailors. Ships loading and unloading." He wasn't bothered at all. "Also a sense of being outside or at least on the edge of the law." Now he paused, with a smile that seemed to say, *Keep swinging and I'll let you know when you connect.* "I want to thank you for leading the city tour."

"I said I would and I will."

"Well, again, thank you. I'm off to Rio."

What an asshole, Meghan thought. When her proposed class failed to attract enough students, she'd been invited to pair with Beckmann as an adjunct professor. Another name for teaching assistant. It was unbearable. The old man was erudite, thoughtful, and way out of date. She couldn't cooperate and she couldn't compete. But before moving into Leo Underwood's office, as an assistant to the dean, she'd volunteered to join Beckmann on a field trip around Manaus. Anger mixed with relief when he told her she'd be doing it alone.

Meghan was heroic, collecting tickets, checking off names. Someone wanted to sell their ticket, someone else wanted to go back to the ship for an umbrella or a camera, or to use a bathroom. Big cameras, tiny bladders—those were the constants of group travel.

"Hey, guys," she shouted. "The bus is parked down the road. We'll take a little walk, see some sights along the way."

"How far is it?" asked one student.

"Ten minutes' walk," she said, after consulting a yellow-shirted guide who stood next to her.

"Will there be an ATM along the way?"

"Ask the guide."

"Where's Melissa?" someone asked.

"Here," someone called out.

"Not that Melissa. The one from the fourth deck. *That* Melissa."

"Do you see her here?"

"No."

"Then we'll leave without her. Sorry. It's past time."

They filed off the deck. Everyone had backpacks, water bottles dangling on the outside. What was inside? What would they need for a three-hour tour in a bus? Out they marched. At the front of the terminal, they turned onto a street lined with stalls, cooked bananas, cold sodas, automobile parts, T-shirts, and a hundred yards of stalls with women's undergarments, flimsy panties, tight, punishing sheaths, brassieres with holes for nipples that reminded her of how headlights fit into the front of automobiles. Nipples and headlights. Both had high beams.

Two yellow-shirted guides led the parade past Eiffel's barricaded masterpiece—not a peep out of them—but Meghan insisted on a fast pace. The guides were in front and Meghan and he walked in back, at the end of the parade.

"Why didn't you wait for me?" a breathless girl inquired. Pink-faced, sweating, angry. "I was only five minutes late."

"How could we know it would only be five minutes?" Meghan asked. "Thirty people were waiting. And you weren't there."

"I paid fifty-four dollars for the tour."

"And your point is?"

"I'm very upset."

"Go ahead, please," Meghan said. "You haven't missed a thing."

The fish market was stunning, the size of a football field, with aisle after aisle of fresh freshwater fish the size of sardines, the size of dolphins, red meat and white, plain as catfish or dappled as Japanese carp. It was a fish market, an art gallery, a butterfly collection that could have held her for hours. Even better, the fish sellers—the scalers and cutters—and butchers were friendly. They knew that no tourist was likely to cook a fish, so there was no need to hustle. Money was off the table, shopping was out of the question.

"I don't get it," someone said. It was Melissa, making up for lost time. "What are we doing here?" Was she speaking to another student? To herself? Or aiming a comment at Meghan? "It's hot and it smells," she added. How did anyone begin to talk to someone like this? Did it help to quote T. S. Eliot, that the first and best way to explore a country was to smell it? Meghan could imagine her retort: "It *still* smells and it's still hot." Raised to assert herself, no doubt. You go girl! What mattered to her? Souvenirs more than memories, probably. "What are we doing here?" she repeated.

Some of the students got it. They lingered, watched the fish mongers work, photographed exotic fish, posed in front of ugly ones. Did the use of cameras signal interest? Enthusiasm? Or was it a self-protective reaction, like waving a cross in front of a vampire?

"What are we doing here?" That ditzy girl's question turned into something deeper when Meghan applied it to herself. Her Fulbright Fellowship in Bucharest, Romania, at the Department of American Studies of the National University had just been for a year. Soon after she arrived, she began applying for jobs back home, visiting and tenure track, college and university, public and private. American Studies was her field and her thesis, "Exile and Return: Patterns in Filipino Immigration," interrogated the experience of people who came to the US to become citizens, generally prospered, raised families, and sometimes returned, usually in their old age, to the country of their birth. Her thesis resonated: it could be applied to any, many, possibly all groups who came to America, but for reasons of access, cost, and language, she had chosen the Philippines. Not a voguish country, she had to admit. Apart from World War II battles and occasional coups, it didn't attract much attention, popular or scholarly. But, she told herself, the place had been under US control for half a century—a virtual colony—and between the two countries flowed currents of affection and resentment, loyalty and cold-eyed calculation. Perfect.

In Bucharest, Meghan planned to revise her thesis and turn it into something publishable, even popular. A new spin on a classic story: *America, Love It and Leave It.* The book was there, she just knew it. Meanwhile she needed work. A dozen applications went out. She waited for answers in Internet cafés, noisy, slapdash places, with neighbors playing video games, shopping online, or downloading pornography. They had better luck than she did. That's when she remembered Semester at Sea.

¤

How, HAROLD BECKMANN ASKED himself, *has this place escaped me?* Even before they landed in Rio, he felt a pang of regret. Will Post claimed that all of the world's great cities were on water, but few combined beaches and mountains, verticals and horizontals, aspiring and reposing. On the bus from the airport to the hotel, the Semester at Sea kids exited along Copacabana Beach where they were scheduled to breakfast at a kiosk and then off on "a one-hour bike ride along one of the most famous beaches in the world." But by this time, midmorning, the sun was pounding and the famous beach was hot as a griddle. Off they went, God bless them. The trip was entitled "Rio Like a Native." Beckmann had already decided against an ascent of Sugar Loaf, a call on the giant Jesus who overlooked the city, a samba lesson, a percussion instrument class. After depositing the students, the bus proceeded to a hotel a few blocks in from the beach. Beckmann knew the middle of the day wasn't his time; he went up to his room, showered, read ten pages of a novel he sensed he was not destined to complete on this trip, and fell into a delicious nap. When he awakened, hours later, he was ready to explore Rio on his own. But as he walked through the lobby, he saw the students in chairs, on the floor, waiting for a tour to begin, answering as their names were called. He kept walking. Then he heard his own name. Oh God, he'd forgotten—the tour he'd signed up for, then had second thoughts about but had not gotten around to canceling. He could cancel now; he could keep walking as if he hadn't heard. But there was nothing to be done. When they called his name a second time, he dutifully answered, "Here," and headed for a bus.

Poor people live in low places; wealthy people claim the high ground for their mansions and castles. That was how the world worked. Rio was different. About 1,200 favelas—poor communities—claimed the slopes above the city, above the beach. They were easy to see from down below, interrupting the green flanks of the mountains with patches of wood and metal. *They had a view of the world, all right*, Beckmann thought, as the bus negotiated one hairpin curve after another in low gear. He wondered what they made of it, of sunrise and sunset, ships coming in off the sea, planes landing. They had guns and drugs as well: the favelas were notorious. But a handful of favelas had been cleaned up. "Pacified and integrated" was what the guide said. "A model for other favelas." And—this was hard to fathom—an attraction for visitors. "Poverty tourism," according to Will Post. The bus stopped at the very top of a hill. The Dona Marta Favela began where they stood and went straight, and steeply downhill, with a sidewalk diving through layer after layer of small houses jammed together and holding on to the hillside for dear life. It was as though all the poor dwellings they'd seen in Manaus had been swept into a bag, brought here, and emptied out on the hillside. The sidewalk was solid, new, and had a railing: a benefit of being pacified and integrated, no doubt. The visitors passed houses, peeked into windows, doorways; they watched and they were watched. They saw people watching television, sitting in doorways, playing cards outside bodegas. But there was no conversation, no exchange. A silent procession, that's what it was.

There were seven hundred steps from the top of the favela to the bottom. They didn't know this when they began; what began as a challenge turned into an ordeal, especially for the older passengers. Beckmann was in the middle of the line and, before long, he was taking one careful step at a time, telling himself, *now this step, now the next*, the way a mortally ill patient says *one day, one day at a time*. Then, just ahead of him, he saw one of the kids step out onto what was the roof of the house below. White slacks, white shorts, white hat: he recognized the kid. Sleepy, nonchalant, indifferent, he'd come down late to the hotel lobby, last on the bus, and he had a digital camera in his hand, which he pointed everywhere. *Pick your shots*, Beckmann thought: new life for an old saying. But the heedless student stepped further out onto a sheet of rusty corrugated metal. The roof started to creak and groan, you could see it sinking beneath his feet, someone's dwelling on the edge of collapse.

"Get off the roof, you asshole!" Beckmann shouted. "That's someone's house!" Just in time the kid jumped back, went under the railing, and returned to the sidewalk without a word. Beckmann stood there, dumbfounded. It wasn't the kid. It was what he'd said—what he'd shouted—for everyone to hear. "Get off the roof, you asshole." What on Earth had gotten into him? He wasn't a man who shouted or cursed. And yet he had. Abashed, ashamed, he returned to concentrating on each downhill step.

Then he heard a commotion in back of him. "We got a problem here," someone shouted. He turned—carefully, unsteadily—and saw a woman sitting on a step. One of the kids, a girl, was giving her water, another wiping her forehead with a paper towel. The woman at last arose and started walking, thanking people left and right. The descent resumed and one of the girls, the one with the water bottle, caught up with him.

"She got more than she bargained for," she told him.

"We all did," Beckmann said. "Aren't you in my class?"

"You bet."

"You stepped up nicely. What's your name?"

"Jody Phillips."

"Wait," he said. "There's something else…"

"About what?"

"About you," he answered.

She waited for him to continue but he suspected she was ahead of him somehow.

"I have it now. There was an endless meeting during orientation back in Nassau. Someone was asking us all to close our eyes and imagine something. Something wonderful, instructive, I forget. I kept my eyes open. So did you. Our glances met. And then…you winked at me!"

"So I did," Jody Phillips admitted. "Guilty as charged." And it was all Beckmann could do not to tell her what a delight he'd felt at that moment, a connection, out of nowhere with a handsome girl.

How many years had it been? Surely, it meant more to him than to her. Still…

"Good moment for you, up the steps," Jody said.

"How so?"

"Calling that kid an asshole." She winked at him again.

"Oh, please," Beckmann said. "That wasn't me. That was a momentary lapse. Who is he? That fellow…"

"The asshole? That's Bobby Rummel. And don't worry, you weren't wrong. Spoiled. Rich. Lost. In global studies while bar graphs and pie charts dance on screen, he's exploring porn sites. Believe it or not, a lot of people find him charming. Girls, I mean."

"Sorry. How charming?"

"More hook ups than a trailer camp," Jody Phillips said, smiling in the hope he would understand. He wondered if she spoke from experience.

"Oh well." He glanced back uphill. The woman was walking on her own, almost going out of her way to demonstrate that she was just fine now, commenting on things they passed, then even waving a "hello" in his direction.

"Do I know her?" he asked Jody. A senile-sounding question, he admitted.

"Edith Stirling. She's one of the life-long leaners who's been sitting in on your class."

"Of course!" Semester at Sea admitted adult passengers to classes, if space was available. Some shrugged the offer off; others had missed registration, waiting until the last minute to book passage. That was when last-minute two-for-the-price-of-one deals were offered. But some senior passengers definitely wanted in. Of those, some stayed, some did not. There were issues. These senior citizens raised their hands, contributed to class discussion, and—sometimes—just wouldn't shut up. When a professor aimed a question at the regular students, the old-timers could be counted on to answer. Beckmann had four regulars whom he quite liked. Yes, Edith Stirling, a thin, stylish woman who—though she hadn't lingered to chat—laughed at his jokes. If a class had clicked, she gave a thumbs-up as she breezed out of the room.

At the bottom of the steps, there was a problem with the buses. They weren't able to park at the bottom of the favela. They'd been forced to park elsewhere. Downbeat and tired, the visitors waited. Was the trip worth it? What had it meant?

"Excuse me, Professor." It was one of the living and learning coordinators. "Junior assistant scoutmasters," Will Post called them.

"Yes."

"I gather you were in an altercation with a student."

"I wouldn't call it an altercation. He acted badly, in a way that could damage the program."

"Did you call him an asshole?"

"Yes."

"Well, I have to tell you his name's Bobby Rummel and he's very upset. I may have to write it up."

"Feel free," Beckmann said, feeling anger flare. Odd. He was known for his gentle nature. He could not remember losing his temper in public, ever. Oh, he had put on a vexed expression when it served a purpose. But never, never had he had an out-of-control moment until today. And he was not ashamed.

"Do what you must," he said. He read the young man's nametag: *Farrington, Joshua.* And snapped his fingers as if he were just remembering something. "I think you should know that if I am attacked, if I am charged, I will defend myself. And, may I add, I know an asshole when I see one."

He watched Farrington walk off to where a group of students were sitting at a kiosk. Among them was the fellow he'd called an asshole. Their eyes met, locked into a staring contest that Beckmann wasn't going to lose. Then Bobby Rummel walked over toward him. *This,* Beckmann thought, *would be a dreadful moment.*

"Is it Beckmann? Professor Beckmann?"

"Yes."

"I was out of line. No hard feelings."

"I was a bit out of line myself. No hard feelings."

"So…" Rummel hesitated. *What now,* Beckmann wondered. "Could I have your picture?" he said. He motioned for a buddy to take his camera. "I mean with you."

He didn't seem upset at all.

¤

AT LAST, BECKMANN HAD three and a half days to himself. The students did their tours, Beckmann was on his own, up for early coffee, then out to Copacabana Beach for sunrise. One of the few disappointments of the ship was that there was no way of walking all the way around it on the outside deck. Now he had miles of beach. The view down the coastline was almost endless. The sidewalk had a pattern, a wavy pattern that copied the sea, beckoning him onward. On the inland side were hotels, Riviera-looking palaces. Copacabana! A name out of the past, a name out of song lyrics, movies, a name for nightclubs, yet here he was walking fast, enjoying a breeze that was still cool, nodding at customers—old men mostly—taking coffee at kiosks. Old men and old dogs. He felt wonderful but at two miles he turned and headed back, sweating now, in charge of himself but not as buoyant as he'd been at the start. It didn't take long for the beach to broil, pink and orange sunlight surrendering to hot white light. He returned to the hotel, came late to the hotel buffet—bacon, a croissant, and half of a lemon-squirted papaya. Then he hung out a do-not-disturb sign, stripped down to his underwear, and took a nap.

Afternoons were for reading and lecture notes. He'd prepared material on Brazil, though he wasn't an expert. Here in Rio, new ideas came to him, things he might try out in class, ideas that wouldn't have come to him if he were not here. He asked himself if all encounters between colonists and colonized were not inherently sexual. That ought to get the students' attention. Colonies and empires began with a show of power, warfare followed by brutality and exploitation. In short, rape. But there was more: idealism, naïveté, a wish to organize, modernize. A missionary impulse. That was part of it. And if the beginnings of it all were mixed, what about the endings? The legacy? The religion, the language, the buildings left behind, the blood, bureaucracy, and law? The memories? How were the foreigners regarded after they left? Or if they stayed? What about nostalgia? What about regret? What sense of accomplishment, of loss? Did hate endure? Or a bit of fondness? Yes, you could talk about rape, you had to, but romance was part of it as well. What about previously brutalized colonials who moved legally or not into their erstwhile exploiters' homelands? Algerians in France? Indians and Pakistanis in England? Indonesians in Holland? What about the European stayers-on in liberated colonies? Ah, so much to measure, so much to learn. How much simpler would life be if everyone stayed home? Simpler, yes. But better? That was worth talking about.

In the late afternoon, and it had better be late because it took a while for the Copacabana beach to mellow, he set out again, walking more slowly and reflectively than before: morning was *allegro*, afternoon *penseroso*. He paused at a shady park with dozens of tables where men and a few women were playing dominos. Some players were raucous, joking and baiting—commenting on every move. Others sat mute, concentrating. Bystanders moved from table to table, following the games. They came here every day, he was sure, some retired, others dropping by on their way home from work and he wished that there was something like this, something informal and reliable, in his life back in Ohio.

He crossed over to the beach, which was by now well into its golden hours. Again and again he stopped to follow games that were underway, foot-volleyball, beach volleyball, beach soccer. And the players, fit, young, tanned, oiled, and agile. What nonchalant grace! Like nothing he'd seen. Hard not to wonder about them. And envy them. Oh, if Thomas Mann had only come to Rio, put *Death in Venice*'s Gustav Von Aschenbach on this promenade, the world would have read *Death in Rio*, for this place could be the making, or unmaking, of anyone who came here.

The sidewalk was busy toward the end of the day. Bikers, rollerbladers, walkers, and joggers passed by. He sat at a kiosk that sold fresh coconut juice, piña coladas, and beers. Regular customers outnumbered obvious tourists. He drank a beer and studied the volleyball players; bronze, sinewy, attractive. *This is where, this is how Von Aschenbach would have sat, deeply involved in a game he couldn't quite grasp.* He ordered a second beer that he did not especially want, because he felt he ought to pay for sitting in a place that so contented him. Contentment had overcome him, he admitted, from the moment he stepped on board the *MV Explorer*. Most people on the ship were oh-so-busy. Meghan Shephard's disembodied voice recounted dozens of meetings, options, suggestions, invitations, warnings, and requirements. Silence was a vacuum which the program abhorred. But he'd stayed calm—yesterday's shout of "asshole" notwithstanding.

He arose, not without wondering what it would be like to stay here after dark. Doubtless, the beach turned into something else, sexy and dangerous. He was done, his time was past. He walked back to the hotel, but in no rush. He stopped once. Right where the beach met the sidewalk, he found a sand castle that was the size of an automobile, a place with walls, moats, towers, a startling piece of work. And, he supposed, an invitation to vandalism. It could be trampled in a minute. Ah, but now he saw that the place had a protector, a dark man in shorts and a T-shirt, sitting in a chair where he—or someone—would spend the night. At his feet, a plastic jar invited contributions. Listening to a radio—it sounded like a soccer game—the watchman paid no attention to him. Beckmann found a ten-dollar bill and dropped it in the bucket. The watchman barely noticed. Could he have missed that it was a ten-dollar bill, not a one? He gave Beckmann a tiny nod and signaled that he was now entitled to take a photo of the sandcastle. He mimed the aiming, the snapping. "No thanks," Beckmann responded. Then he pointed at his eyes, at his head as if to say, *I count on myself to remember.* That got him a bit more of a nod and what he recognized as a word of thanks: *obrigado.*

As he left the beach and turned inland toward the hotel, he wondered what kind of figure someone like Von Aschenbach would cut in today's Rio. Mann's novella was set in a pre-World War I Venice, with Aschenbach attired in a crisp lightweight suit, threepiece, with a watch fob and a cane. *What about here? And now?* And—as if in direct reply he saw an older man standing nearby. The man, a dog walker, turned and looked back at the volleyball players in a farewell glimpse that went beyond an interest in the outcome. Aschenbach? But the man was practically naked. He was wearing a kind of thong, his genitals in a tight pouch like stones in a slingshot. He left nothing to the imagination, the sag of the belly, the cleft in his butt. Aschenbach in Rio. Not pretty.

¤

THAT NIGHT, BECKMANN REPAIRED to a poolside bar at the top of a hotel and ordered an Irish coffee. It was a drink he loved and for reasons he didn't understand, it tasted best in warm weather. Also, like many other retro dishes—eggs Benedict or Caesar salad—it was hard to find at its best. More often than not you were disappointed: a cup of see-through coffee, a splash of whiskey, and a squirt of "dairy product" out of a shaving cream can. Still, he kept looking. He sat at a table near the pool, glancing down at the streets. The Irish coffee was taking time. That might mean the bartender was looking up the recipe. Or taking his time on something wonderful. He glanced at the bar. The man was just sitting there. What on earth was—or was not—happening? Had he called for help? What a botch this was going to be! Par for the course, these days, the misses outnumbered the hits and, one recipe at a time, the world was going to hell. But no, the elevator door opened and a waiter brought out what was—yes!—a pot of freshly-brewed coffee. So coffee was taken care of; the whiskey was next. That left the whipped cream, and if it were canned, he'd have the drink in front of him by now. It must be fresh whipped cream, stirred, poured, smoothed one layer at a time. He turned away, walked to the railing, looked down at the street. On a corner, women stood outside a bar. They were dressed in skimpy skirts and halters, neon green in the case of the woman he was watching, how she glowed in the dark. She saw him, standing eight floors above, and waved to him, from what felt like a world away. Would some of the ship's passengers find her tonight?

Now he saw the bartender approach, carrying a tall glass in a tray. "Irish coffee," he said. Beckmann gave him a grateful nod. "Irish coffee," he responded. That was it. Two men who knew what was real and what was fake. *If I ever come back*, Beckmann thought, *I will not find him here*. The coffee was strong, the whiskey too, but the miracle was the whipped cream, cool and firm, sealing the top of the glass. He probed gently with a spoon and tasted. Perfect. The least he could do was spend enough time drinking as the bartender spent preparing.

"Hello, Professor," someone said. "May we join you?"

It was the two women from the favela, the woman who'd been distressed and the girl who'd helped her: Edith Stirling and Jody Phillips.

"Of course," he said, starting to arise.

"As you were," Jody ordered. "You seem to be having such fun. Are you sure there's room for us?"

"On one condition. You join me in one of these Irish coffees."

The women sat down. Edith was totally restored, it seemed. Tall, attractive, bright eyed, good looks combining with a kind of shrewdness. And Jody was totally at ease. You just knew that she'd grown up with a couple of brothers.

"How are you?" Beckmann asked Edith.

"It was just a spell…the heat, mostly," she replied. "And the steps."

"Well, thank you both for taking pity on a professor, drinking alone."

¤

HE WAS A HISTORY professor, sixty-five years old, a venerable, almost iconic character at a small Ohio college. Forty-plus years and counting. Counting up? Counting down? Counting out? New people kept coming while old friends died or moved. Every year added to Beckmann's seniority, yet narrowed his range of acquaintance. Every year brought him closer to the front of the faculty processions, the front row of chairs on stage at commencement, watching a parade of twenty-two-year-olds receive their diplomas, four hundred kids, but these days he knew that he wouldn't be around to greet them at their twentieth reunion, perhaps not even their tenth. He wouldn't know how their lives turned out.

He'd been at home—at home alone—writing comments on papers and giving grades, which these days were A minus or B, or rarely C plus. He looked forward to his sabbatical next semester. The college's provost had asked him, in the nicest possible way, just in passing, whether this might be a "terminal sabbatical."

"Terminal sabbatical." Good title for a murder mystery. In his college it meant a year off at half pay or a half-year at full pay, all designed to invigorate a worn-out professor. But a terminal sabbatical was employed to ease—or induce—retirement in a past-ripe professor. A sabbatical from which you did not return. He'd made no plans, he replied, one way or the other, and left it at that. Plans had gone out the window when Anna died, for all plans had involved them both. Planning for one was like cooking for one. Sometimes, he pictured himself nearing the end of work, of life, like someone standing in line at a checkout counter, contemplating work or retirement, in the same way a shopper would confront the choice between paper or plastic. Then, the phone rang.

"All right, it's been a long time, Professor, and that's my fault," Julia Shannon said.

"Never mind," he said. Students were unpredictable. Sometimes the ones who camped out in your office, hanging on every word, at least until they received their final grade, disappeared. And others, relative slugs, remembered you forever. "I'm happy to hear from you now," he continued. "I wonder why." It was way past the time when anyone would want a letter of recommendation, thank God. After three years, no one cared about your transcript. Julia's last phone call had been…what?…a dozen years ago? She was then at the University of Virginia, heading up some sort of job search, and wanting back-channel information about a candidate. It did not surprise him, now, to hear she was an administrator.

"Well," she said, "I have an offer for you. But before I get to that, could I just say something? For what it's worth, I often think about you. I admire you. And, for the longest time, I wanted to follow in your footsteps."

Well then, he thought. *I guess that particular ambition is behind you.* He listened to an account of a career that was prospering, a marriage that was over. He remembered Julia well. She was smart, with an unerring instinct for what it took to get an A. The way a sommelier sizes up a diner's taste and wallet, the way a courtesan assesses how a client can be quickly serviced, Julia Shannon knew what a professor wanted to hear in class and read in papers. She served—serviced?—any and all her professors that way. And you never knew what anything meant to her, what she loved or hated, how she wanted things to be.

"About my offer," she said. "Are you ready?"

"Of course not," he said. "But I'll certainly listen."

"Okay. There's a program called Semester at Sea. A sort of floating university. It goes around the world in a hundred and five days, with classes every day at sea and field trips and other stuff in about ten ports. Faculty is about thirty, six hundred students, and a clutch of senior passengers. And I'm on this faculty liaison committee with Semester at Sea. And...cards on the table...I called your department. I thought maybe you'd retired. And...oh my God...I'm sorry about your wife..."

"Thank you. So am I."

"You have a sabbatical next semester. Should I stop now? Or should I proceed?

"Stop now," he said. "Do not proceed."

"Oh, I'm so sorry..."

"I'll take it."

"Just like that?"

"Yes."

¤

"THE GRAPES COME AND GO," Will Post said, while contemplating the fruit on offer at breakfast. It was the first meal he'd had on board for days. "The grapes come and go," he continued, "but the plums stay around forever. They came upstream, they'll follow us back down. I asked about the oatmeal, could they thicken it up a little. They told me if they thickened it, they'd have to have somebody nearby to stir it. So…how are you?"

"Happy to be back on board," Meghan said.

"What was it? Hold it! It's coming back to me. An eco-friendly jungle village rainforest experience. See…I'm winging it here, spider monkeys, alligators. Fish for piranhas, maybe eat them. Homestay with locals. And I believe there was a service component?"

"You're good," Meghan admitted.

"I trade in tourists traps."

"Okay. Some students picked up rum on their way to the boat. They rode on the roof of the cabin. They took pictures. We arrived at a rickety village. No one spoke English. Some of the kids tried Spanish but that doesn't get you far. So we nodded and signaled and made faces and laughed. It was frustrating. We ended playing with the kids and taking photos… Oh, God, Will. I can't do this… If I see one more student holding some kid in her arms while someone takes a picture… It's like sitting in Santa Claus's lap…"

"It's okay. You saw the river, right? Saw people, how they live and all?"

"What happened to your neck?" Meghan asked. "I haven't seen a hickey like that since high school."

"'Thinking globally, acting locally,'" said Post, quoting a slogan of the voyage.

"Pathetic," Meghan snapped and walked away.

There, Post thought, *goes the end of something: a shipboard acquaintance that lasted two weeks into the voyage.* They'd met back in Nassau, the night before sailing. They shared a meal, fish (grilled not fried), rice (yellow not white), sweet plantain. The first thing that impressed him about Meghan was that when a waiter parked two cans of beer on their table, she asked him to come back with two glasses, chilled. Next, she emptied the beer slowly into a tilted glass. "These guys pour like they're emptying a can of motor oil into a clunker," she said. Then she talked about the voyage, this odd, wild one-off of students and faculty, field trips, classes, hook ups, breakups, breakdowns, and glorious fun. She was happy to be back, she was overjoyed, it was written all over her. Back at the hotel, they sat on a verandah outside his room, evaluating some top-of-the-line sipping rum. *Enjoyable on the verandah*, she said. Then she wondered if it could be enjoyed in bed. And this morning she walked away in anger. "On a trip around the world anything can happen," she'd told him that first night. It sounded like a promise. Now it was more like a warning. And it applied to her. No course to teach, no partnership with Beckmann. Now she worked in the dean's office. There was more. Their cabins were right across the hall from each other and they'd made a game of rushing from one room to another with little—sometimes no—clothing on. But that had stopped, all of a sudden. No explanation, no "we've got to talk…" Maybe she believed that sex was great when you were…well…sailing, when you were on a roll. But when you were down, though, it turned sour and nasty. That's what she thought, he guessed, and he supposed she was right. Still, he missed her, missed telling her about what he'd done in Manaus, which was a kind of travel, a kind of reporting that he'd never done before. The fish market started early and so had he, dressed in the dark, pocketing a chocolate croissant he'd smuggled out of the dining room the day before. It was still dark when he hit the street. All the stalls were shuttered: no interest in flimsy underwear before dawn. Inside, the floors were wet, the counters were bare, a couple of puzzled workers smiled at him. With its sinks, tables, scales, knives, chopping blocks, it resembled a morgue that was awaiting the victims of a catastrophe. Then, while he stood watching, the fish came, in pallets and baskets, in plastic sheets, out of lorries, off of fishing boats pulled up on the riverbank. How could any river have so many fish? Seeing the Amazon was nothing compared to seeing what came out of it every day. Fish on ice, fish swimming in pails, fish alive, dying, dead. No triage in this ward, though. He walked the aisles carrying a pen and a pad, just to suggest that he had a reason to be here. Some vendors pointed to this fish or that fish, gave a thumbs up: expensive? exceptional? endangered? They signaled a fish that was recommended for pregnant women, impotent men. As the first customers appeared, he watched the inspection, the arguing, the bargaining. Could a slave market have been much different? When a buyer walked away, he saw some fishmongers smile, or roll their eyes, or mutter. Will Post lingered. He noticed little restaurants—stalls, really—outside the market. He took a seat at an oilcloth-covered wooden table. He pointed to someone else's plate. He'd have one of those. His table overlooked a passage that led to the river: a street, a sidewalk, an alley, a sewer littered with garbage. Some ragged-looking men sat on a stoop. As he drank a beer and waited for his fish—a sure sign it was being cooked to order—one of the men from the alley climbed up to the restaurant and approached a table where some people had just finished eating. One of the diners left the table to pay. His place was taken by the alley man, who brushed the leavings off of every plate into a bag and went back down the steps. Post's fish arrived. He went at it with his fingers. He'd heard the old line that fish—especially salmon—was what you used to convey sauce to your mouth. Here fish was the thing, the only thing. Forget bread crumbs, deep fryers. With the fish came *farofa*, toasted manioc flour that reminded him of couscous. When he was done he ordered another beer. And another fish. That was when a woman sat down at his table and started to talk about fish, about an allegedly aphrodisiac fish, which she urged him to try. Looking at her, Post sensed he'd be needing it.

On the second morning, part of him doubted that the Amazon would accomplish the same thing two days in a row. But it did. Back in the ship he'd found a Brazilian immigration official and asked him to write, in Portuguese, "your best fish." With it, he moved from counter to counter. Some people shrugged him off, in a way a restaurant waiter might insist that everything on the menu was great. Others had suggestions. But when he was about ready to choose, a fishmonger put down his knife and escorted him to another man's counter, pointed to a large fish, and walked away. Post then took his purchase—it looked like a rib roast—to yesterday's restaurant, handed them the fish, and signaled that he would pay what they asked. He got a nod and a beer. The guys in the alley were in for a treat. He mused about the fish that was often served on the *MV Explorer*, a tiresome fish called hake. A kind of codfish, he discovered. Lovely phrase. He sat back, thinking about tourist food. Buffets with chafing dishes and artificial labels. Menus with words like "authentic," "native," "local," "exotic." Photographs of the food. Look around a room: if it was full of tourists, something was wrong, the price or the food. Sometimes both. He'd gotten it right today. What arrived was a fish with the substance of beef, the succulence of pork, and delicate meat attached to a bone that you'd expect on a rack of lamb. He was already looking forward to tomorrow, a last lunch at the fish market. Lunch with a legend, the world's champion circumnavigator.

¤

LEO UNDERWOOD, EXECUTIVE DEAN, sat in an office he'd thought he might never see again. It had been taken from him and now it had been restored. He glanced out at the Amazon and agreed with the consensus that it was really something. Now it was time for a bit of tradition he'd been postponing since Nassau. At the end of every voyage he left a little something behind, hidden away on purpose, a business card at the back of a drawer, a memo taped to the pipe underneath the sink, and most recently, a used Q-tip at the bottom of the television set. He felt for it with his fingers. It was gone. Nothing escaped the Filipino stewards. No one carved their initials on this tree! But outside, he had his monument: a plaque that named this office after him, and included the names of dozens of donors honoring his presence over twenty-five years. What was the word again? Eponymous? He was the man who gave his name to this office. And now he was back on board. Like Colonel Sanders walking into a Kentucky Fried Chicken outlet.

This return was a surprise. He'd served as dean fourteen times, moving—like a cavalry officer whose horses are shot out from under him, one after another—from ship to ship. Where were they now? The *Seven Seas*, the *Ryndam*, the *Universe*, the *Universe Explorer*? Dismantled for scrap on some toxic Bangladeshi beach, scavenged and cannibalized, yet here he was, back on the biggest and fastest ship of all. This ship might survive him. But you never knew. Years ago, people would have bet on the *Queen Elizabeth I*. At launch in 1938 and for a half-century afterward, it was the largest ship ever built. In 1970 it was sold to Hong Kong Harbor tycoon C. Y. Tung, early sponsor of the Semester at Sea program. *Seawise University*, that was the ship's new name. But when its conversion was nearly complete, it caught fire in Hong Kong Harbor. Well, *caught* fire didn't quite get it. The fire caught the ship, not the other way around. Maybe an insurance fire, maybe communist agents, maybe disconsolate shipyard workers. Charred and capsized, it lay on its side in Hong Kong Harbor. Later, some of it was dismantled but its keel and boilers remained at the bottom. *You never knew what did or didn't last,* Leo reflected. Himself included. Fourteen voyages around the world was a record that no one would ever match. That didn't mean, though, that he didn't want a fifteenth. Yet, until recently, he'd thought his time had past. His presence on board was, he admitted, self-dramatizing, theatrical; he was a legend at the center of the stage, microphone in hand, decades of stories to tell. The faculty, inevitably, came to resent him. At the end of every voyage, there were complaints: he was anti-academic, anti-intellectual. And then, with the shift of academic sponsorship to the University of Virginia, he sensed that Semester at Sea wanted a new look. What, then, became a legend most? Timely (or long overdue) retirement. How he'd missed it! He got invited to alumni meetings, dockside fundraisers, just long enough to hate leaving when the ship headed out on the longest possible voyage. Oh, he'd had his share of trips. No one could match him and no one would catch him. But that didn't stop him from wanting more. Who wouldn't want more? And then, just as he was about ready to admit that he would never again be permitted to do the job that he did best… "the best man in the best job in the world," he got a phone call.

"What's up, kiddo?" Leo had asked when Anna Cather called from Charlottesville. "How's your life, your career, your killer good looks?" An ebullient question which she could respond to flippantly or seriously. The unasked question was, what do you want and why?

"It's been too long," she said.

"You've got that right."

Then she told him she wanted to visit him. He waited for more, waiting long enough for her to know that he knew she was withholding something. But she offered no explanation.

"You remember the way to the house?" he asked.

"By heart," she replied.

¤

HALF AN HOUR AWAY from a meeting that might be awful, Anna Cather felt as if she were entering Leo Underwood's field of force, the same feeling she used to have when she was on a ship under his direction. She hadn't visited in four years and she felt guilty about it. "I visit my parents because I have to," she once told him. That was when she still had parents to visit. "I visit you because I want to." He'd been the dean of her first voyage. It wasn't love at first sight. He talked a lot, and a lot about himself; he was the star of every story. The captain, crew, and faculty were bit players. And then one night, outside Penang, she was in a car that another student had rented—against the rules. They were heading back to their hotel in Batu Ferringhi, a tourist beach. Some ports required effort, demanded serious consideration. Penang was for fun. One other passenger had just remarked that there wasn't much education going on in this port and someone else—was it the driver?—said the same was true of the ship, and Anna, joining in and congratulating herself on her cleverness, added that on this voyage, education was available but not required. Then the car clipped a bicycle, knocked it over, and spilled a young girl and a basket of unsold mangoes on the side of the road. In no time the police were there, almost as if they'd been waiting just down the road. They didn't bother with the girl; she'd only scraped her knee and kept apologizing as if it were all her fault. The cops shooed her off. Then they escorted the Semester at Sea students to a police station, took their car keys, and locked them in a cell. No interrogation, nothing written down, no instructions or explanation. They heard the police talking at a desk down the hall, laughing. Their lucky night, it seemed. Then, Anna got frightened. The ship was sailing. They were due on board in two hours and departure was scheduled for 3:00 a.m. The ship would leave without them and—oh, God—their passports were on their ship. "Excuse me!" Anna shouted. "Could someone come here? We really have a problem!" A policeman appeared, one of the cops who had brought them in. He wasn't tourist-friendly. "We really need to get out of here," Anna said, like a kid who really, really needed to pee, which was also true. "Are we under arrest?"

"No," the officer replied, "not at the moment under arrest," in that crisp English you hear from educated foreigners. "You're being held. We could arrest you if that would clarify things."

"No, no," Anna pleaded. She suggested that the US Embassy be called. But, she was told, the US Embassy was in Kuala Lumpur and at this hour of the night, a phone call would be useless unless she wanted sympathy from a Marine guard. But they were passengers on a student ship, Anna explained: Semester at Sea, a friendly sail-around-the-world voyage.

"We know your program only too well," the cop replied.

Did they want a bribe? Anna wondered. Maybe not. Maybe they wanted an apology and a little respect. "Could you call the ship?" she asked. "They're leaving soon."

The cop smiled. "Anchors aweigh," he said. No doubt about it, he wasn't indifferent. He was hostile. Their eyes locked. "We have called the ship."

Anna asked when help would arrive. The cop shrugged and left. Dumb question, she had to admit. Half an hour later, she heard Leo Underwood's voice, growing louder as he walked toward them. He was laughing and the cops were laughing, too, with him, not at him.

When they were back on board, she followed him to his office, gave him a moment to settle in, and knocked on the door.

"I just wanted to say…"

"You're sorry," he interrupted, raising a Heineken to his lip, swallowing a third of the bottle and cheerfully belching. "Save it."

"I didn't come to say I'm sorry," Anna said. "I wanted to say I learned something. I learned that travel is hard as it is. And it's a lot harder when you do something stupid. There are people watching us and waiting for us to screw up everywhere we go. And we oblige them. So thanks."

"Hold it," Leo said. "Want a beer?"

"I'm not twenty-one."

"Okay." He handed her a beer.

¤

THE TREES MET OVERHEAD on the street that led to Leo's house. Cars with out-of-state license plates passed slowly by, leaf peepers paying their respects. The houses on Leo's street were stately places, two and three stories, brick or clapboard, with generous porches, tall windows, and widows' watches on their roofs. You could picture Mark Twain in one of these houses, sitting with a whiskey and a cigar, savoring the fall foliage. The turning of the leaves moved north to south at twenty miles a day, Leo told her, and she'd arranged previous visits to catch the peak. This time, though, she hadn't planned it that way, but she got lucky with the leaves. Luck with Leo Underwood was another matter.

The week before she took office as director of the Institute for Shipboard Education, the chairman informed her that Leo had sailed on his last voyage. He'd already been told. It was a *fait accompli.* "Deal with it," he said. She wasn't surprised. There had been complaints, especially from faculty. "A one-man show." The University of Virginia wasn't going to put up with it. The program was controversial enough as it was. One trustee told her, "We did what you'd've had to do. We cleared the decks. Favor for you. Favor for him, too, though he'd never admit it." She'd talked to Leo from time to time. He'd thank her for thinking of him—"not forgetting him"—and that was it. The distance between them remained. But now she was a hundred yards away, wondering which falling maple leaves would land on her hood and windshield, which would drift away. Then she got out and walked toward her reunion. She saw his front porch and was disappointed not to see him sitting outside. But he must have been waiting just inside because the front door opened and there he stood, watching her come up the steps, standing in front of the door as if he wasn't sure whether he'd let her enter.

"Hello, kiddo," he said. As always.

"I've missed you," Anna said, realizing some unexpected power in what she said. Something had slipped out of her life when Leo left the program and it was more than just a subtraction, it was a kind of death. "If I only had one thing I could say to you, if you kicked me out right now, I'd want to say just that. I've missed you."

"Thanks," he said. As if a deliveryman had just handed him a new telephone directory: the end of a conversation, not the start of a new one.

"The second thing I wanted to say…"

"There's more?"

"Is I really need a hug. I've got no one right now who hugs me." She advanced toward him, he opened his arms and drew her in, taking her back to the night he'd gotten her out of a Malaysian jail and become indispensable. Yes, she knew that indispensables came and went, the cemeteries were filled with them, but here he was. Yet the hug felt tentative and guarded.

"I'm out of practice with my hugs," he said. "Come on in. Or would you like to sit out here?"

"Maid's day off?"

"No more maid," he said. Then he gestured at the street, maples reaching down from either side, oaks turned stolid brown and hemlocks keeping their distance, green, evergreen, above the commotion. Anna followed Leo. She could tell he lived downstairs. A pillow and sheets and feather quilt lay on the couch, a half-open door revealed a closet full of clothes, and a table next to an easy chair showed a scattering of un-swept crumbs. Then they moved back to the porch.

"When you live up here," Anna asked, "do you take all this for granted? The way Pacific Islanders roll their eyes when a tourist oohs and aahs at a world-class sunset? 'Another damn enchanted evening?'"

"I missed it when I wasn't here, on autumn voyages." His voice trailed off in a way that signaled he was ready for her to get serious.

"I'm sorry about what happened…"

"It wasn't your fault. They axed me before you took charge."

"But I saw it coming."

"What could you do? It was over." He was moving briskly through her agenda: hug, leaves, dismissal, item by item, as if he needed so be someplace else. "I'll tell you this. I had a world record going around the world. That's not counting astronauts. They orbited. I sailed. I wonder, though. You think that ship'll be sailing another fifteen years? Do you have an opinion? Or a gut feeling? Hold on. Opinions are a dime a dozen. I want the gut feeling."

"My opinion doesn't matter right now," Anna answered. "Or my gut feeling. Do you want to be executive dean on the next voyage?"

The silence that followed was about five seconds on the clock. But it felt that time itself had stopped.

"Get out of here," he said, his voice so flat she wondered if he were telling her to leave. But then curiosity got the better of him. "What's going on, Anna? Is this a cruel practical joke? Has the Board of Trustees come to regret shitcanning me? Impossible, I know about administrators. They don't look back except to celebrate themselves. And they never admit mistakes. Well, this isn't happening. They fired me once. That wasn't enough for them? It was for me."

He leaned back in his chair, then pushed his way out of it. He was heavier than he used to be and, at the same time, a little smaller. When he returned, he carried two Heinekens.

"Listen," he began. "I get emails every day. Hard to read and impossible to reply. All those kids wanting to know how I'm doing. It's like when I remember my parents. They've been gone a long time. Forty years. If they were alive today they'd both be over a hundred. It's ridiculous to be in mourning after so many damn years. But that doesn't stop the memories from coming. And that's what happens with those kids on the ship. The years stretch out but the memories trail along. That's enough for me. I don't need more memories and I sure as hell don't need another voyage. But who's behind this?"

"Your guardian angel. Carla Hutchinson."

"See what I mean about memories? I'll be damned."

"Tell me about her," Anna said. "Lots of phone calls back and forth, but I've never met her."

"That's one fine lady," Leo said. "I should call her." About half his voyages, he said, had included Carla Hutchinson, the bride and later widow of an international banker. Was it the International Monetary Fund or the World Bank? Not sure. He'd learned and forgotten a dozen times. A fine, erudite gent named Dexter who let his wife run his life. How many times, when Carla asked about a tour or a restaurant or some shopping, Charles Hutchinson put down the book he was reading and, smiling, ask, "Why are we having this discussion?" He'd have been content if the ship circled the world nonstop. His wife—a looker, at least in the early years—was outgoing and sharp. His opposite, in many ways. That made for a lasting marriage. And after his death in a plane crash in Kenya, she kept coming on board. Only when Leo was executive dean. Leo was, she once told him, a male version of herself. She meant it as a compliment, he assumed. That didn't prevent him from suggesting she not be accommodated again after she came aboard five years ago, struggling with a walker. It was a project, getting her on and off the ship.

"I should have called her," he repeated. "I'm lousy that way. All those emails, they're like tributes, testimonials, but I can't respond. Not lately. I don't have much to say—anything good, that is—that would amount to much."

"Were you…" Anna paused, searching for a phrase. Lovers? An item? Or—the current favorite, probably derived from overnight arrivals at trailer camps—a hook up? Leo answered before she could choose.

"It was there for us, after Dexter died. Maybe before, but it never happened. Scared me, I guess, being so close to a woman who knew me better than I knew myself. Hugs. Lots of hugs. Hugs that are good in happy times, good in sad times, good before and after and in this case instead of sex."

"Well, I guess she wants another hug. And another voyage. With you. And she's offering a contribution of two million dollars if it can be arranged."

"Jesus, Anna. I don't know what I'd be letting myself in for. And neither do you." He was close, Anna saw. Not there yet. But she wasn't done.

"Oh, yeah, there's something else," she said. "This is in confidence. Okay? It's secret."

"Secret. Okay. You got it." And remembered… Was it something he had said or something he heard? He wasn't sure. *All secrets are meant to be told…eventually.*

"You've heard that our government listens to traffic on certain networks that might be used by terrorists? They do this without knowing who's talking or where it's coming from, at least that's what they say. Hey, Leo. I'm trusting you on this…"

"I know."

"I haven't got anything on paper. I'm just telling you that I got a phone call from someone who took a voyage, back in the day. Takes an interest. Sends a medium-sized check to the alumni fund."

"One of my kids?"

"I can't say. And I don't want you trying to guess."

"I won't try."

"I was told there's been some chat about a certain 'student' ship that sails around the world. A slogan was mentioned. 'We give you the world.' Our slogan. And then, a suggestion that the world ought to give something back. In the Straits of Malacca."

"Doesn't sound like a donation."

"No. And it didn't rise to the level of whatever level they need to set off alarms. Except this one friend of ours thought he should call me."

One friend. Former student. Anna was being careful. Nothing to even identify the sex of the caller. She was telling him what she thought he needed to know. No more than that.

"Listen, Leo," she continued. "You're the only person I'm talking to about this. No one else. Suppose I called a meeting. Trustees, staff, former deans, donors. Can you imagine the conversation in the room? 'Oh, by the way, it's probably just loose talk, but we hear there might be a terrorist strike against the ship.' They'd be gone. The word would be out. Do we offer a 'danger discount'? What about the company we hire to operate the ship? And the bank that holds the mortgage? We do anything like that, we might as well cancel the trip. And if we do that, we're finished, the whole thing's kaput. The university pulls out, the shipping firm backs off. We'd be dead. Even though…loose talk is probably all it is."

"That's my guess," Leo allowed. "So where do I fit in? We've been through the Straits dozens of times, without incident. And sure, the kids get worked up about pirates and they pass around reports of tankers and freighters that disappear. But still…"

"I hear you and I agree," Anna said. "But this isn't about pirates. This is about terrorists."

"It's still bullshit."

"But if word gets out… Well, you know about the Internet."

"Me and the Internet, we've never been introduced. I'm doing fine."

"Trust me, Leo, I need a calm, experienced dean. And nobody does it better."

"Thanks."

"And I wanted you to have another voyage," Anna said. "I'll feel a little better about you."

"So will I."

"Is that a yes?" Anna asked.

"Yes."

"Then stand up," Anna said. "I want another hug. That first one was kind of tepid."

"This one will be better."

She turned for another look when she was at the bottom of the steps. This was a calculated gesture meant to suggest that there was something she'd almost forgotten.

"Oh, I almost forgot. You remember Meghan Shepard?"

"Sure do. Sharp cookie. A student on one voyage and worked in the travel office—with you!—later on. Went off to get a degree."

"She got it. And a Fulbright in Romania. But that's ending and the job market is tight. So she's wondering about the next voyage. She's in the faculty pool right now but that may not work out. If it doesn't, we need a Plan B. She could do something for you."

"Well," said Leo, "as a rule I get nervous about people coming back too often. Getting familiar, comfortable… But in her case, sure."

"Okay, then," Anna said. She felt ready to choke up again. Leo brought that out in her. "I guess we're done. See you on the ship."

Five minutes later, Underwood sat in his rocking chair with a glass of rum. He rolled it around his mouth, even as he repeated, "Back on board!" How he'd missed it. He lived in a house that was too big for him. A generous cabin on a ship was far better. Simpler, but richer. He'd wondered about setting up as a cruise ship lecturer. He could do that. And he looked into freighter travel; there were people who virtually retired to freighters, one voyage after another. A storage locker was all the home they needed. But it didn't happen. He missed the program itself, knocking around the world with a bunch of kids. It was the voyage, not the travel. His interest in the countries visited was slight. All he knew were the ports. That was where trouble happened: arrests, accidents, illness, you name it. He stayed on the ship or close to it, left the big-ticket items—the Taj, Hiroshima, the Great Wall—to the students. And, God love them, the faculty. "See you on the ship." How he'd missed it! And the thing he missed the most, he had to admit, was that every voyage brought a different audience and all his stories were new. The ship! Voyage number fifteen, the terrorist threat? That was gravy.

¤

THE LAST MORNING IN Manaus, Will Post saw Leo Underwood enter his office, leaving the door open behind him. He walked to the door, snapped his fingers, as though something had just occurred to him. He leaned into the office, in time to catch the Dean of the Voyage settling into a chair with a tired groan. When Post knocked on the door, Underwood's reaction was hard to miss: annoyance at so early a visit, before he'd had his coffee. "I wasn't expecting you…" Post wondered if Underwood even knew his name. He didn't spend much time with faculty.

"I'm Will Post." He said. "I'm on the faculty. And I'm not coming here with a complaint or a problem."

"No problem?" Leo asked, leaning back in his chair and laughing. "You must be kidding. You're the guy who roams around asking questions. I hear you asked the captain if they had firearms on board."

"That's me. He wouldn't say."

"He couldn't say. Least of all to you." Leo pulled the ship's directory off his desk, capsule descriptions of passengers and staff, found an earmarked page, and proceeded to read. "'Will Post began his career as a freelance travel writer whose work appeared in *Condè Nast Traveler*, *Travel and Leisure*, and *National Geographic Traveler*. His adventurous, free-ranging reporting earned him numerous prizes and a reputation as a 'volatile, unstable, irresistible mix of Anthony Bourdain and Evelyn Waugh.' His two volumes of collected essays are *Wonderlust* and *Lessons Left to Learn*. He is the proprietor of a controversial website, 'Tourist Traps,' described by *The New York Times* as 'mad, bad, and dangerous to read.' He lives in New Jersey and other less-stylish places.'" Leo paused when he finished reading. "I figured you'd be dropping by. So, okay. What's up?"

"How about lunch. Off the ship?"

"Well, okay, I guess," Leo responded, getting up from behind his desk. But then, as soon as they stepped out on deck, he put a hand on Post's shoulder.

"Wait a minute," he said. "It's kind of important." Post followed him to where a woman in a wheelchair, attended by a striking girl who was her companion, was waiting for an elevator.

"Hello, darling," Leo said from behind the wheelchair.

"Same to you," said the girl pushing the chair. Tight shorts, halter top, and a hit-me-with-your-best-shot expression on her face.

"Not you," Leo said, pointing to the woman in the chair. "Her. We go back forever."

"It's about time!" Carla Hutchinson said. "Hello, old friend."

"I'll get her back to the cabin," Leo promised. "Safe and sound. Has she had her distemper shot?" Now he kneeled in front of the wheelchair, put his hands on her, and looked up at her face. Going, going, no way around it, but not yet gone. Still had life in her eyes.

"I know what you did," he said, "for me."

"Two troublesome characters for the price of one," she said. "I couldn't picture this voyage without you."

He wheeled her out toward the fifth deck where he stopped, braked the wheelchair close to the railing, and found a molded plastic chair for himself.

"I wonder, kiddo," Leo said. "You've caught my act so many times. Haven't you had enough?"

"Not quite," she said. "I wanted to be back here and I wanted you to be here. Not some strangers. And sometimes—just once in a while—I missed the kids on the ship. I'm sorry we didn't have kids."

"You and me?"

"Goodness, no."

"Just kidding." They'd flirted for years but he wasn't in her class back then. And now she wasn't in his. Still, all those voyages counted.

"No worries about me this time, Leo. No field trips, no shopping, no bus trips, all the commotion that made you recommend against my return."

"Ouch! You knew about that?"

"They told me. The people in Charlottesville. They hoped it would turn me against you so I wouldn't insist on sailing with you…" She paused and laughed. "Just be yourself, Leo. I wouldn't want you to change. I'm not sure you're capable of change. I could always count on that."

"Okay, girl. Now let's get to the seventh deck and tuck you in."

"Go tuck yourself," she responded.

¤

THEY'D SPLIT THREE BOTTLES of beer and a hefty fish and, though they were finished eating, neither of them was in a rush to go back to a ship that, even now, was filling up with passengers and problems. Underwood's cell phone rang three times before the fish arrived, rabies testing for a student who'd annoyed a monkey, a taxi driver's complaint about someone who'd vomited in his backseat, and—it never failed—a missing passport. Underwood shut off his phone and dispatched the fish. Before answering, he signaled for another beer. Then he sat back and considered Will Post.

"You know how often I get invited out by faculty?" he said. "Zero."

"Well…sorry."

"I'm not sure it's bad news exactly. But anyway… Thanks for this." He nodded to a man who'd come to collect…and eat…the scraps. Then he talked. It had been several years since his last voyage and, after a while, there was no denying that he'd been put out to pasture. He told himself he'd had his share. Fourteen voyages around the world. What a kick! Talk all you want about a junior year in Costa Rica, language and all, but this voyage gave you the world, no lie, it wasn't just a slogan. The academic side of things—speaking frankly here—was just okay, a little less than okay, a little more, it depended on the voyage. But the voyage never disappointed, never. Global studies—they used to call it Core—was a problem. A required course that never failed to fail. He was getting drunk, Post guessed. But not stupid.

"Great meal," Post said. "I'm glad we did it. And…I'm thinking of all our passengers who rushed through here…been there, seen it, done it…let them eat hake."

"I like that. 'Let them eat hake.'"

"So…why did they ask you back? You say you were out of style."

"Oh, hell…" Underwood said. "I thought you forgot the question. Thought the fourth beer would do the trick." He leaned forward and stared at Post. "I'm going to take a chance on you. And if you talk…I'll know. If I took a poll of 'who on this ship should I confide in?' it wouldn't be you."

"Got it."

"I mean it. You're faculty. That's one. You're a reporter. Two. And three…" He stopped. He wondered if he should continue. He was crossing the Rubicon. He was confiding in someone he didn't quite trust. *Who might*, now that he thought about it, *trust him?*

"It's *hush-hush*. 'Loose lips sink ships.' They heard something back in Charlottesville. A scrap of talk on the Internet somewhere, a warning that this voyage might be different. We might be in for a surprise. A problem for the so-called 'student ship.'"

"Where? Who?"

"Hey! My mom didn't raise any dumb kids. No follow-up questions. Okay. Just keep in touch. Drop in on me. Watch me work."

"Okay," Post said. "For now."

He nodded. He was getting more than he bargained for. All that love Leo had for the voyage. Or was it the love he attracted while on board? Anyway, this lunch would count as his good deed for the day. Or week. Hearing out the executive dean, and wondering, why is he telling me this? Was he looking for a friend? Or a writer?

II.

TAKORADI, GHANA

ECKMANN WATCHED THE STUDENTS filter into the main hall for Leo Underwood's "State of the Voyage" speech after leaving Brazil. Sure, this was a voyage, not a cruise, but they couldn't tell that from the way they dressed. He noticed short shorts on women, baggy pants on men, Mohawks for some of the men and braided cornrows for the women, obtained from Bahamian women who worked the docks back in Nassau. The kids were loud, too, and the women louder than the men, the word "like" embedded in every sentence. They wore backward hats and backpacks that made them beasts of burden. They might have come out of a Harry Belafonte song, carrying bananas onto a freighter.

"There's something I have to tell you," Leo began, quietly. Anyone would think he had bad news. "I was waiting for the right time. I'm tired of waiting. I need to say it now. It means a lot to me. And you. I've been around this program from the beginning. It amazes me that this voyage happened even once. That three or four ships may have come and gone, watching me grow up, grow old. It makes me proud and it makes me patriotic. That Americans keep going out into the world way we do, around the world! I want to thank all you kids, the old-timers, the captain and crew. The faculty. I hope it goes on forever. God bless America."

Leo stopped and there was silence, as if at the end of a prayer, a private moment that he'd vouchsafed for them.

"And now…" His voice was booming. "We're going to…Africa!!"

The place erupted in cheers. Even as he spoke, the Amazon—which they'd made so much of a week before—slipped away behind then, barely noticed. So…last week.

"You have to hand it to him," Beckmann whispered to Edith Stirling. "He really pumps it up. Every port is the latest and the greatest."

There was something of the relentless booster about Underwood, and his enthusiasm was complicated by the fact that he rarely ventured more than a mile into the places he drummed up. Tonight was one of a number of "State of the Voyage" speeches he'd planned, billed as an evening of "questions, comments and affirmations." He touted the upcoming "Sea Olympics" on a day when classes were canceled and replaced by fun and games for all, with student groups divided into teams that were called "seas." Orange, Red, Yellow, Black. Senior passengers—life-long leaners—competed as "The Dead Sea." Leo briskly declared that classes were going well, that students had a wonderful and respectful relationship with the crew, that the staff had settled into their jobs nicely and the accounts of service projects on shore were thrilling. A series of dinners for students wanting to interact with faculty was over-subscribed and the *Three Cups of Tea* discussion sessions were doing fine.

Now, a few tweaks. Sorry about the countless warnings during orientation. Sorry about the monkey bite. He wished students on field trips would go easier on their trip leaders. Too bad that so many rumors sprang up and spread. Please, come to him for the truth. Finally, he gave his opinion that 90 percent of the kids were great. They were going to make a difference in the world. Ten percent had some growing up to do. And, count on it, they were all going to be different, better people when the *Explorer* docked in San Diego. That, Beckmann had learned, was a constant message. You will change. You are changing. Haven't you noticed? It never stopped, this insistence on growth. Like dieters after two days of light meals, they were urged to agree that, yes, yes, magic was underway. An article of faith.

After "The State of the Voyage," Beckmann, Edith, and Will Post needed drinks. And needed to be silly. Was Zsa Zsa Gabor still alive? And Sister Eva? Was "Moon of Alabama" in the Threepenny Opera? Were Laurence Olivier and Danny Kaye lovers? Anything, please, but talk about the voyage, that's what they agreed. And then Beckmann—while deploring Underwood's "promiscuous enthusiasm"—surprised Post and Edith with some promiscuous enthusiasm of his own. He'd invited his class to consider what happened between colonizer and colonized as a sexual encounter. And they loved it, the room lit up. A comparison that might readily be rejected as dated, eccentric, sexist, caught their attention. A blind date. A bad date. They found a way of taking the measure of colonies and empires. It worked as a metaphor and as an analytical tool. What about intermarriage? Miscegenation? Was racial mixing evidence of an enlightened treatment, loose morals, or sexual predation? Did it—in Brazil, for instance—lead to an obliteration of racial differences or to a more nuanced racism? The students were with him, the talk was lively, the class went overtime. Another professor waited outside in the hall, annoyed. Beckmann had to apologize. Post and Edith exchanged shrugs and smiles. What was up with Beckmann, the erudite and forlorn widower, sitting back pleased at connecting with the kids? Now, Post had the moment he'd been waiting for.

"Ever hear about the Williamson Turn?" Post asked when Beckmann finished. A scoop, a discovery, a rumor. This was Post's stock in trade. His curiosity was endless. Had a certain professor repeated the same lecture he'd given a few days before? Was another professor—nicknamed "The Projectionist"—filling class time with movies? And another who was never seen talking to his wife. A third who'd somehow delivered the same lecture to the same class.

Twice. Were stool softeners included in cafeteria food? What was the procedure when a passenger died on board and grieving relatives declined the offer of a burial at sea? What then? The funeral was impressive, he learned, the ship sailing in a slow circle around the spot where the body slipped into the depths. But if family members insisted on interment back home, the deceased would finish the voyage down in a freezer. Space had to be made and the rumor was that copious amounts of ice cream started showing up at meals.

"The Williamson Turn?" Post repeated, lifting a glass of tonight's concoction at the faculty bar. Ghana Uhuru or whatever it was called. "I'll take your silence as a 'no.' Well, I talked to one of my sources. He insisted that no one on this program has ever gone overboard. Not at sea. A kid clowned around in port somewhere, fell into the water, got sent home. But not at sea. So what happens if someone goes over the rail, accidentally or on purpose? Are you fascinated? Well, if the person has been seen going overboard it's the Anderson Turn. They pull a U-turn, basically. If the person's out of sight—and it doesn't take long for that to happen—rough water, dark night, fog, it's the Williamson Turn. That's the turn for me. Puts the ship on a return course, going back to where the lost person might be found. There's a Scharnow Turn, too, and I gather that's when it's been a while longer."

"One question," Beckmann said. "Suppose we said good night after our post-prandial drinks. And in the morning, I did not appear for breakfast. Or…later…for class? My cabin is empty? What then? Eight or twelve hours later."

"You sound like you've thought about it," Edith said.

"I believe that everybody thinks about it," Beckmann said.

"That's why they have the Williamson Turn," Post declared.

¤

AT NIGHT, BECKMANN SOMETIMES visited the little bit of deck at the back of his cabin, though not for long. It was gusty out there. During the day the ship kept to middling, fuel-efficient speeds, fifteen knots or so, but when people slept it raced, and in rough seas the ship had a way of slamming down into the water that suggested a fat child belly-flopping into a pool. That was fun. He was still a kid in that respect: fascinated by violent weather. Post's discovery of the Williamson Turn got his attention. Fifteen minutes struggling in the water, choking, flailing. But what was that, compared to what his wife had gone through? You couldn't wait until the very end, when you were helpless, as helpless as his wife had been when she pleaded with him to do something. You had to be able to go over the railing. Suicide. The very word was vulgar. Operatic. There was no self-dramatization in him, no reproach to family or colleagues. Only irresistible logic: a few terrible moments—at no charge—in the ocean versus bankruptcy and painful months of medical care, followed by an overpriced funeral.

¤

AFTER BREAKFAST, POST WENT back to his cabin to pick up his smoking chair, carried it down to the fifth deck, lit up and reviewed the program for the Sea Olympics: hula-hoop limbo, tug-of-war, trivia, wheelbarrow races, three-legged races, dodgeball, basketball, crab soccer, tallest card tower, synchronized swimming, ping-pong played with spoons not paddles. It had the over-articulated tone of fun-for-the-kids-planned-by-adults. No school today. Enough! He had a pile of papers from his travel writers. Most of the first bunch, after Dominica, had been mediocre and perfunctory. Today, he hoped for better. Had all this talk about writing not blogging, writing for an audience, about inner and outer journeys, had any effect? He decided to read them on deck. A cigar would make the work go more quickly. He went up to the cabin for the papers, poured a third cup of coffee in the faculty lounge, and returned to the fifth deck, which was empty. No students. No chair. But on the fifth deck a couple of ship's officers stood smoking cigarettes.

"Have you seen my chair?" he asked the white-shirted, white-slacked, white-shoed ship's officer who'd told him what might happen if someone went into the drink.

"No."

"It was here, five minutes ago. I went up for coffee. I came back and…gone. Someone took it." *This,* thought Post, *was perhaps the most obvious observation, in or out of print, that he had ever made.* He felt foolish.

"You want us to make an announcement? Shall we attempt a Williamson Turn?"

"God, no," Post answered. He couldn't bear what would follow: questions, concern mingling with mockery.

Post made his way back to his cabin. On every deck, the silly stuff proceeded, with announcements every few minutes, a change in location for the wheelbarrow race, a new time for synchronized swimming. That was Meghan's Shepard's voice. It was as though someone who'd spent a half-dozen summers in some camp had returned, after college, after graduate school, after a Fulbright, to work as a camp counselor. He had a dozen papers in his lap, six from each seminar. Beckmann had warned him about paper grading. It was the hardest thing a professor did. You could lecture or lead discussions and they would sit there, taking notes, nodding occasionally, laughing at some cleverness and it would be fine; it could probably go on forever and at the end, they'd be friends. But no, happiness ended when papers were returned, commented upon, graded. Yet there was no avoiding it. Don't go picking through the pile looking for something that began decently, he'd been advised. That's like going straight for the shrimp at a buffet table. Close your eyes and reach in. Might be shrimp. Might be hake.

The first paper from a male student took him on a service trip to a village outside Manaus, where the reception was sullen, puzzlingly hostile:

> Somehow community services loses a little something when the village we were trying to help out expected us to build a $10,000 hospital in three days and all we could provide was a crappy job painting their school.

A misunderstanding, maybe a deception. Somebody had promised something that wasn't possible. Both sides got cheated. In a cafeteria, the writer finds:

> A woman who viewed us as cheap labor as opposed to people doing something out of the goodness of their hearts because we couldn't build her a Goddamned hospital…

Who was to blame? Was it the travel agents? The travel office? Yet the piece didn't end with the fiasco. The narrator goes into a kitchen and compliments a previously surly woman on her coffee. He flirts a bit. Does he have a girlfriend? the older woman asks. Yes, no, maybe, he responds. He cracks them up in the kitchen. He takes more coffee and somehow the trip is rescued. Next paper. One student found Manaus disappointingly "unprimitive" with:

> Vendors selling absolutely anything they could get their hands on: diamond earrings, cell phone chargers, beef pastries, old sneakers,

X-rated magazines, TV remote controls, thongs,
bikini bottoms.

The specificity impressed Will Post. Detailed description leading
to a nice comparison.

The market sprawled out in the street, like rows
inside a Dollar General.

This was getting to be fun. The kids, his students, were taking him
places he had not gone. They were his partners, his agents. They were
good company. He picked up another Amazon adventure. After some
preliminary chat, the writer made a confession:

We walked out of a grocery store with four bottles of
rum and two liters of Coca Cola. I had planned for
two days of drinking my own urine and making food
out of a monkey I shot with a blow dart. Instead I
got an overnight in a jungle lodge with an individual
bottle of rum and delicious home-cooked meals.
Hey, when traveling, the saying goes, 'be flexible.'

The kid was wise-assed and funny without being cynical. Good
tone. What turned out to be one of the best papers hit an unexpected
note. It recounted a visit to a remote village. In spite of the problems
Post had been reading about, the kid had come to like the village. But
on the day of her departure, she noticed that another boat had pulled
up to the village dock.

At first, I was dumbfounded. What was such a
boat doing in this out-of-the-way village? Then I
remembered there had been an "Acajatuba Village
Overnight: Group B" trip just below the trip that I
had signed up for all those months ago. My heart
sank—there was another group coming to do what I
had just done and they were already there. I felt as if

after a few short hours of hiking in the jungle I had
been replaced.

They figured it out, some of them. They had gotten what was there
for them to get: excitement and frustration. Then he heard someone
knocking at his cabin door. It was Beckmann. Beckmann rarely called
on him. It was usually the other way around; he'd be on the seventh
deck, knocking on Beckmann's door.

"Come with me," Beckmann said. "Right this minute. There's
something you have to see."

"What?"

"A feature of the Sea Olympics. It's called 'Dress Up Your Dean.'"

¤

AND THERE SHE STOOD, strolling around like a model on a runway,
waving at cameras, posing with students, standing in for Leo
Underwood. Meghan had been decked out as a "typical" Semester at
Sea student. Around her neck hung five cameras, on her shoulders an
oversized backpack with a blue umbrella, a water bottle, a Semester
at Sea photo ID, and a rubber ducky. Her jacket had three pouches,
holding two tubes of sunblock, a map, and a wad of Brazilian money.
Add a birdwatcher's hat, aviator sunglasses. Her face had been painted
pink to suggest sunburn and there was a dab of white sunblock on
her nose. A safari jacket, the likes of which you saw on embedded
journalists, and boxer shorts completed the outfit, along with muddy
hiking boots and a roll of dollars tucked inside her socks. Beside
her was a huge piece of roll-on luggage with an American flag and a
teddy bear.

"This is sad," Beckmann said. "Must we all be made clowns? Poor girl."

"I think she thinks Leo Underwood can help her out, after the voyage. He asked her…told her…to do this for him."

"That may be. Still…"

"Let's just say she's being a good sport."

"Someone, sometime, is going to pay for this," said Beckmann. "I guarantee it." He thought he caught her looking his way. *Maybe me,* he thought.

"She's trying to figure out what to do with her life," Post said. "She's young."

"I'm old. Still trying to figure things out, in my way. But it hasn't come to this."

¤

WHY DID HE DO this to me? Meghan asked herself. She lay naked on her bunk. Her clown show outfit was all over the floor, camera, goggles, cap, map, hat, and all. What had she done? Leo had always gladly played the clown, a pie in the face, a bucket of water of his head, all in good cause, dressing up as a pirate or as Poseidon when they crossed the equator.

Then she knew. Anna Cather had asked her to keep tabs on Leo, to stay close to him and report anything that seemed a little off. So far there was nothing much to report and her phone calls to Anna had been gossipy chat, full of Leo's quirks and foibles. But, two nights ago, she had mentioned Leo's odd connection, Will Post, the travel writer. When she finished the call and left the office, she glimpsed an unmistakable figure sitting out on deck, enjoying a balmy mid-Atlantic evening and almost surely drinking a Heineken. Had he heard her? Was this her punishment?

¤

"WHAT ARE YOU SMOKING?" a student asked Will Post. It was Tommy, a fifth deck ringleader who specialized in finding places to drink on shore. A Chinese-American based in New York. Post had overhead him declaring that he'd never gone—"not even once"—to a global studies session. That might make him a total goof off. But he had a cordial, thoughtful side.

"This," said Post, "was supposed to be a Cuban."

"Counterfeit?"

"Maybe. Or God knows what happened to it before I got it."

"You've got to be careful with Cubans," said the kid, holding out a Hoyo de Monterrey in a metal tube. "Try this."

"Well…thanks."

"I've got more, he said. "A lot more."

"I shouldn't accept a gift from a student."

"Don't worry," he said. "Go ahead. Enjoy that cigar."

"Why are you here? I can't help wondering. You don't go to global studies. What about your other courses?"

"Depends."

"It's up to you?"

"For sure. Listen, I don't need the credits. I've already got what I need to graduate. Anyway, my school doesn't accept credits from this outfit."

"So why come?"

"Same reason you came, Professor. For the voyage. I guess we're two of a kind. Except they pay you a little money, which you probably don't need. And my parents pay a little money, which they don't need."

Post extended his hand, fingers clenched into a fist the way he'd seen his students salute. Tommy reciprocated. Their hands met, knuckle to knuckle.

"Cigar buddies," Will said.

¤

Up at 6:00 a.m., drinking coffee in the faculty lounge, Beckmann and Post looked out at a foggy morning, gray mist, gray sky, gray water, all of which made it impossible to find the horizon let alone the continent beyond it. Still, there was a sense of something coming, a sense that the ocean was losing depth, that they were coming in to shore. Ships were out there in the fog, and oil platforms. Then they saw another shade of gray, which was the coastline.

Oh, the warnings about Africa! In the pre-port session before Takoradi, they'd all been asked to recite the commandments: don't get bit, don't get hit, don't do it, don't get lit, don't eat shit. There were corollary warnings. Always be aware of your surroundings. Never go anywhere alone. And now came Africa-specific cautions: don't buy drums with animal skins, cricket bats made of local wood, and—oh, my God—don't eat bush meat: monkeys that were grilled and sold along the road.

"I've never been here," Will Post said. "That should tell you something."

"No tourists, no tourist traps?"

"In Manaus, I had the fish market. Here I have the name of two restaurants, both founded and run by expats. Germans. Want to do lunch? With Edith?"

"I'll ask her," Beckmann said. They were regarded as a couple now, he noticed.

"I'll see if I can snag one of my students," Post said. "There are some good writers in class. They want to be travel writers. I may have a lot to answer for."

"I already do," said Beckmann, thinking of Meghan, dressed as a fool. Should he have insisted on keeping her as his teaching assistant? He wondered. Probably not. She didn't need his wisdom. She wanted his job.

He couldn't blame her. There'd been at least a dozen, maybe two dozen, students over the years who'd aced his courses, dropped by his office to talk and confide. They did everything he required and recommended and went on to graduate schools so that they could become—let's face it—something like him. And there was no place for them. They became teaching assistants, they became frequent fliers, shunting from one part time teaching post to another. And when he heard from them—or about them—he sensed that his admirers were bitter. He stayed around forever; there was no mandatory retirement age at his college. He could understand Meghan's anger. He wanted to sympathize with her, though not quite apologize. He doubted, though, that they'd ever get close enough for that.

¤

TAKORADI WAS WAITING WITH a hunger they hadn't seen before. Even before the first groups of field trips were summoned to the gangplank, drummers and dancers marched back and forth on the dock. Further on, a fleet of buses was parked with guides and drivers waiting beside them. Opposite the ship a tent city was being set up, loaded with textiles, jewelry, and carvings. The *MV Explorer* might look like a cruise ship but it was a floating university. These were students, not tourists. But the Ghanaians hadn't gotten the memo.

"Here's today's adventures," Will Post said. Below, the drummers paced up and down the dock, barefoot, sweating. "Okay. First thing, the usual diplomatic briefing. Then, there's an overnight visit to Winneba, which it happens is a sister city of Charlottesville's. Be still my heart! Delegates will be coming aboard. Then they go off with the kids, who'll be greeted by drumming and dancing from two 'warrior groups.' Go to a hotel, explore town on your own and the next day, meet 'market queens.' Next visit the 'University of Education,' students and faculty. Okay, then they go to a place called Essikado and meet a queen mother who 'plays an important role in traditional society.' Discussion included. Then a dance and drumming workshop and… the first of many tours of the slave castles. That last one, I'll do later."

"Me too…" Beckmann said.

"So we're having lunch… God, look at that!" The first students were on the dock, dutifully marching for the buses but, when they passed the market, a riot broke out. Vendors came out of their shops, dangling necklaces, flashing postcards, banging drums. A feeding frenzy.

"I heard the students at breakfast," Beckmann said. "It's Sunday. Where will they find money? And why do we arrive so often on Sundays? Lower docking fees? Keeping students out of trouble?"

"Well, Professor, I can tell you one thing and it's the surest thing you know. They take dollars."

¤

THEY HAD NO IDEA what they were getting into. Shortly before noon, Beckmann and Edith left the ship, followed by Will Post and a student named Darlene Tedrow. Post said she was a writer. But not to her face. She was shy, short, self-conscious. At first, acting like she'd gotten caught trespassing in the faculty lounge, she said little. Then again, what was there to say? First the vendors came at them, sensing adults would have money to spend. They wanted to talk, shake hands, trade names, make you feel rude if you didn't slow down. They offered gifts, embroidered bookmarks; you felt ashamed walking by. Remember my name, they pleaded, and asked for your name back. Hard to refuse.

Turning a corner and heading toward the gate, they all sensed—you could feel it—that they were making a mistake which no one quite had the courage to correct. Glaring sunlight, bad air, warehouses on one side, loaders, pallets, bags of cacao beans; on the other side, an oil rig towed to shore for repairs, a shower room and latrine for workers. And no end in sight. The road crossed a railroad track, the sun beat down, a U-turn back to the ship felt worth talking about. And Beckmann worried about Edith. This was worse than the favela.

"Are you okay?" he asked.

"Don't worry about me," she said. "Promise."

"Okay. But if you need us to stop in a shady place…"

"That's worrying," she countered. By now they were all sweating, not just necks and armpits. Rivulets of sweat coursed down their chests, soaked into their belts. Why work so hard to get to Takoradi, an uncelebrated second-tier city on a broiling Sunday? Why couldn't a student, that Darlene person, speak up? What was the point of being a student if you couldn't complain, make excuses or—the recent vogue—have "issues"? Post had said she was "sneaky smart." She had good eyes. And, alas, good manners. She marched without faltering and so they soldiered on.

They passed a weedy field in which dozens of railroad cars were parked, a graveyard of rolling stock, every one of which could have appeared in *Schindler's List*. What were they doing in Ghana?

At last, the gate. Groups of students flashed their passports and were waved through. And instantly swarmed. Meatballs in a piranha tank, they were pushed and shoved, tugged and cajoled by taxi drivers. The Beckmann-Post party was next. Best price, trip to beach, me-not-him, this way please, where you from, slave castle, fishing village, I have children, you want local food? "Pretend we're walking to town," Post said. They got ahead of the scrum of taxi drivers and headed across the street to where cars were parked. Nothing like an orderly line of taxis here. That hadn't occurred or, more likely didn't appeal, not when you could jostle and connive.

"How much to the Northern Star?" Will Post asked a man who was napping in the front seat of what might be a taxi. Another man came up from behind. "Where are you going?" he demanded. Post kept talking to the fellow in the car. Cut out the middle man. He repeated the name of the restaurant, said that lunch would be about an hour and then they would then return here.

"Forty cedi," the man replied.

"Twenty cedi," Post countered.

"Okay," the driver said. Post's instant pride at having cut the asking price quickly yielded to the certainty that it could have been cut by half as much again. "Ten cedi," someone shouted, but by then they were already in the car, passing fruit and vegetable stands, beer and soft drinks for sale. Some of the students had paused to contemplate postcards, postage stamps, baseball caps, straw hats. Others were walking toward town on a road that wound its way up a red clay hillside. Dust covered everything. It covered buildings and clouded windows, claimed the dashboard, and the arm rest, overlaid the seats they sat on, kicked up a cloud behind them and—this seemed worst of all—coated the branches and leaves of every tree, even the weeds that grew along the road. The whole place begged for rain. The students were looking for a hill, described in guidebooks as a nature park where monkeys abounded. That was from Darlene, reading from a guide. "'Widespread monkeys,'" she quoted.

"No monkeys today," said the driver. He added nothing. Were the monkeys nocturnal? Did they take Sundays off? Dislike white people? By now, they were in Takoradi, moving along a street of one-story buildings with most stores shut. A desultory place on Sunday.

"I hope the restaurant's open," Post said. He didn't feel lucky. The ship was looking better all the time. And there was a rumor that, on days when lots of students disembarked, the food got better.

At last, they found the Northern Star in a two-story building with a few tables outside underneath umbrellas. They headed inside, were pointed toward a table, and went one by one to wash their hands, to splash water on their faces and necks, to run wet hands through their hair and start to dread the forced march back to the ship. When they returned, their driver was sitting at their table studying the menu.

"I'll take care of this," Post said. Thinking globally, acting locally. That slogan. Or was it the other way around? He leaned toward the driver. "Excuse me," he said. "If you could meet us outside in an hour, as we said, that would be fine."

The driver returned the menu to the table and stepped outside.

"Can't blame him for trying," Post said. "Was I an asshole? Was this an intercultural situation or something? Anybody?"

"No," said Edith. "He took a chance. You never know. But no…"

"It's a four-cedi ride, anyway," said Darlene.

"Wow." Post nodded at his student. He'd liked her work, but she never volunteered in class or chatted with him outside. Now, after that line about the four-cedi ride, he figured she was comfortable. And now that Post was appraising people, he admitted that Edith Stirling was a handsome woman. Tall and graceful, her hair was coming back. Post-chemo? Beautiful, in a way, but everything about her felt tenuous. She'd won a battle, not a war.

They ordered beers and surveyed the room, with customers at just two other tables. The beer was wonderful, as necessary as the water they'd splashed over their faces and hands. And there was air conditioning.

"It's a German place," Beckmann decided. He'd noticed pears in bottles of brandy, a row of beer steins above the bar, soccer posters on the wall. In French, Spanish, Portuguese places, wine prevailed. This was a place where beer ruled.

"Prosit," Post said. And they touched glasses.

"Oh, my God," said Edith. "That first taste, that swallow…in a place like this, on a day like this. There's nothing like it." *She was amazing*, Beckmann thought, considering that brutal walk from the ship. Now she turned to Darlene. "How did you find out that a taxi to town should cost four cedi?"

"Blogs…from previous voyages," Darlene said. "There's a ton of them. What you should bring. Where to go. Where not to go…"

"Tourist Traps?" asked Edith.

"Global studies. To be avoided."

"Are you attending?" Beckmann asked.

"I need the credit. I sat through driver's ed in high school. My parents took out a loan so I could be on this ship. They wanted me to take a trip like this, and neither of them has ever had a passport. There's no way I'm going to have a bad voyage. Global studies? It's like a lifeboat drill. Put on your life vest, go to your boat station, raise your hand when your name is called. And leave."

"How are your courses?" Edith asked. *How considerate*, Beckmann thought. He had been about to ask the same question but decided that soliciting student reactions to other faculty members was bad form. But now he listened with interest.

"I've got a philosophy course—ethics—that's first rate. And a course in India—art and culture. A class in world poetry that's working out."

"That's three," Beckmann said. "And let me say that over the years I've asked a lot of students what they're taking and it never fails, they rattle off three courses rapidly. Then they stop. They have to think and it's 'oh, yeah, I'm taking…' and they name the fourth course, which is always a dud."

"Well," she said, laughing. "I'm in this workshop on travel writing…"

"Well then," said Post but he stopped when he saw Leo Underwood entering the room, pushing a wheelchair in front of him.

"Carla Hutchinson," said Edith. "She might be the smartest woman—make that the smartest anybody—on board. Including, by the way, us. "

When Leo had Carla squared away at the table, he walked toward them.

"Caught in the act," he said. "Alcohol on the table."

"But sir," Darlene said. "In pre-port, they told me never, never should I go anyplace alone."

"All right," he said. He turned to Post. "Is that guy outside your driver?"

"Yes."

"I need a word with you," he said, walking over to the bar. Post followed. Was this going to be some kind of a reprimand? Drinking with a student? A female? What else could it be? On a ship that had more Mickey Mouse than Disneyworld, he could not be surprised.

"I came in a van. You go back in the van. He can come back here and take me home when I'm done. Pay off your driver."

"Sure. But why?"

"There's that walk between ship and gate. First, that clusterfuck of hustlers, then the trek past railroad cars and oil rigs, warehouses and shit houses? The van will take you all the way in, right to the bottom of the gangplank. Your life-long leaner lady will be grateful."

"So am I. I owe you."

"Take your time finishing up," he said. After he left, they avoided further exploration of Darlene's ambitions. They enjoyed the dessert, mango strudel, coffee, and a small glass of pear brandy. Darlene passed on the brandy and kept staring across the room.

"Those two," she said, "are…or were…close."

"What?" asked Post. "How can you tell? You can't hear a word they're saying."

"It's not in what they say. It's the way they sit when they're not talking. The easy silence between them. Memories in the bank."

"She's right." Edith said. "I noticed how he touched her hand a moment ago. No hug. The lightest of touches… That's enough."

"Hey, Professor," Post offered. "You and I could have watched Leo and Clara all day and never guessed they were connected. Am I right?"

"Men are oblivious," Beckmann replied. "Women know things that we miss, in my experience at least." Then he glanced at Edith and Darlene. "These two are no exception."

Post studied Darlene Tedrow. Smart as hell, nondescriptly dressed, rarely made eye contact in class, never spoke unless called upon. But she could write. He'd been surprised when she agreed to this lunch. And today he noticed that she was attractive, in a petite and girlish way. Now he returned his attention to her.

"Before we got interrupted, I was wondering what you wanted to be."

"When I grow up, you mean?"

"I think you are grown up."

"Well then, since you asked," she responded. "I want to be a travel writer."

"Oh my God," Post said. Had it come to this? Another kid who hoped that somebody, anybody, would pay them a salary to go somewhere and write about it? What could—make that *should*—he say to this nice kid? She was talented and he didn't want to be an enemy of talent. "Who are your favorite travel writers?"

"Well, there's Paul Theroux and Pico Iyer. And you. Tourist Traps. But my special favorite… It's kind of an acquired taste…"

"Yes?"

"Amelia Bligh."

"I've heard of her," Post acknowledged and that was the end of it. But he couldn't believe that here, of all places, this kid had come upon his secret life.

¤

LATE THAT NIGHT, WILL Post walked the deck before turning in, asking himself how that little Tedrow girl discovered Amelia Bligh, finding more than she knew unless she knew more than she said.

Two years before, he was getting tired of Tourist Traps. The columns still paid well, though with the collapse of newspapers everywhere and the loss of outlets—which suggested clogged plumbing—its eventual demise was inevitable. He was looking for another voice, another angle, and settled on the voice of a woman, a new voice for a fashionable online market. Sassy, sexy, adventurous. The columns were an instant hit. They were occasional pieces that found their way to him in odd places, at random moments.

WOMAN WAYFARER

by Amelia Bligh

Is there anything like the sinking feeling you get at the approach of a trio of strolling musicians across a crowded dining room? Short of a rude command— and a hurt retreat—is there anything that can dent their faith that all meals are better with a soundtrack? Women have even more to fear. When the musicians arrive, the steak gets cold, the stakes go up. If, like this traveler, you prefer to eat alone—and you really, really don't mind—the jeopardy increases. Nature abhors that vacuum on the other side of the table. Never mind that you're enjoying an arugula salad, reading Joseph Brodsky, any woman dining alone is Eleanor Rigby.

He could picture her, not in a factual police identi-kit way but in bits and pieces, muscular legs from years of dancing, long musical fingers, an amused pouting mouth. He enjoyed her company. He liked seeing the world through Amelia's eyes.

WOMAN WANDERER

by Amelia Bligh

I love full-service gas stations. There's something mean-spirited about self-service. It smacks of penny-pinching introversion, sweaty-palmed self-abuse, and unappetizing box lunches. But there's more, much more to this. There's not a woman who won't agree with me. Full-service is sexy. When you pull into full-service you make a date with the horniest, hang-doggiest of high-school dropouts, the kind that are uncomfortable in bookstores, even the kind that stay open all night. It's too much like homework. But when a woman appears in a car, a passion play begins. Maybe it's because of the process itself, the empty tank in need of filling, the nozzle waiting to be whipped out of its socket—after a bit of probing foreplay—jammed into the body by Fisher. Next come those leading, sexually loaded questions. "Check your oil?" "Wipe your windows?" "Look under the hood?" All the while, we are being pumped so full, filled to overflowing, and oh, those last few stubborn squirts before the still-dripping beast withdraws.

He'd kept his name out of it. Strict instructions to his agent, his business manager. No biography. No interviews. It would take a break-in or a subpoena to find him out. He was keeping Amelia to himself. And now had this Tedrow girl found him out?

¤

THERE WERE WAYS OF getting to know someone, little secrets that Beckmann had learned over the years. Look at the books on their shelves. Open, if you dared, their medicine cabinets when you used the bathroom. And play Scrabble with them. Their strategy, their decisions to turn in bad tiles, their resort to geeky words that could only be found in the Scrabble players' dictionary, all revealed their character. Edith and he had been playing for weeks after dinner in the faculty lounge. But tonight, after that lunch in Takoradi, he pushed back his tiles as if confronted with an inedible meal. He had something he wanted to ask her, he said. But before that he had something he wanted to say. To share. He wanted to talk about his life. And his wife, Anna. And he'd been wondering about Edith.

After cancer had declared itself, after radiation and chemotherapy had already damaged her, there came a morning when their doctor had given her the best possible news. She was cancer free. She didn't believe it. Oh yes, they'd walked out of the office holding hands, making travel plans, foreseeing happy times. And yet. "Listen to me," she had told him. She said this was like when he'd been gardening all day. Weeding. You cleaned up the plot, you turned the soil. A brand new garden, prepared for another springtime. Virgin soil. Tabula rasa. Clean slate. But you knew better. The weeds came back.

"Now, may I ask you a question?" he asked Edith. "You said…it was in Rio, that you'd been in publishing. What did you do? For whom? Anybody can read about my so-called career in the ship's directory or on my school's website. More than you want to know. But…"

"I'm just another life-long leaner. Fair enough?" She sat quietly, pondering the letters that she'd drawn and from the look on her face, she might have been subject to an attack of vowels, two Os, three Es, and one U. An almost unplayable draw, unless you consulted the hated Scrabble dictionary. "I thought you'd never ask. My husband was Leonard Gallant."

"My editor! Oh, my God. Small world!" he exclaimed. "Leonard!"

"Yes."

"A wonderful man. Erudite. Courtly. Smart. Smart as I was. In many important ways, smarter. All of his writers must miss him. I know I do. It hasn't been the same for me since then…what…fifteen years ago?"

"Twenty. Five presidential terms. Seems like a long time. *Is* a long time. But sometimes it's only yesterday."

"And you worked with him? I'm surprised we never met."

"I kept my maiden name, you notice. And I was in a different department. Not editing. That was too close for comfort. I was in publicity."

"So…"

"Take a deep breath, Professor Beckmann. I'm the woman who did those reading guides that show up in the back of trade paperbacks. For instance, in your particular case, 'Do you think colonialism can ever be a good thing?' and 'The United States claims that it is not a colonial power. Please discuss.' And, you might remember this one: 'If the United States were to be colonized by a foreign power, which one would you choose?'"

"You're…her? That woman. I remember my responses. Words like 'barbaric' and 'simplistic!' And that was you?"

"That was me."

"I was such an…"

"Asshole? Is that the word you're looking for? I was on the favela tour, you'll recall."

"It's a word that has found me."

"Every other author collaborated willingly, happily. Answered my questions and came up with some of their own. Not you. '*Colonies and Empires* is complete. It says what it says.' At the end, you told me to do what I wished. Which I did."

"And now we meet…"

"When I saw your name in the faculty directory, I said I wouldn't do it. I'll cancel. That arrogant, distant, haughty man! And then I decided that I would do it. I wouldn't let you get in the way. In a way, I did it for Leonard. It's what he'd have wanted."

"I'm glad you came," Beckmann said. "We'll keep this connection a secret. And the day after tomorrow…"

"I know. We're 'doing the slaves.'"

¤

SMUGGLING WAS A COMPETITIVE sport aboard the *MV Explorer*. You smuggled fruit and cheese out of the dining room: the fruit in your pocket, the cheese in plastic bags slipped into a backpack or a valise. That was small-time stuff, intramural. The big game was bringing things on board the ship, past the guard at the bottom of the gangplank, past inspection and metal detector at the top. It wasn't about alcohol. That was permitted, for faculty. It was the food—the snacks—you needed to go with the drinks. Peanuts, potato chips, crackers, they were okay. But cheese, salami, sliced ham, fresh fruit, smoked fish, and luncheon meat were proscribed. Beckmann had found provolone in Rio that he distributed, one slice per person, per night, like communion wafers. Tonight, Post was countering with some pepperoni sticks and a bag of salted corn nuts that had been tucked away with the books that he'd shipped to Nassau.

"Hey, Professor." It was Rosa Sanchez, a fifth-deck smoker who had started sitting in on his writing sections. She wasn't formally enrolled. She wasn't a student. She was in Carla Hutchinson's employ so she herself qualified as the youngest life-long leaner. And by far the finest looking, already famous for her tight shorts and revealing blouses. She stopped traffic. Still, there was something good-natured about the way she dressed, taking her best shot and daring others to do the same.

"I was just going out," Post said.

"My bad luck," she said scanning his room. Students weren't supposed to be in faculty rooms, so you couldn't blame her for looking in at forbidden territory, though his towels, toothpaste, and laundry were like anybody else's. "I love corn nuts. Where's the picnic?"

"Here," he said, giving her a bag of corn nuts. "Good and good for you. Your body will thank you." And he couldn't help looking her body over, just as he was meant to.

"Actually," she said, "I brought you this." She handed him a class roster for one of his seminars. He'd spent twenty minutes looking for it, ransacking the piles of Semester at Sea papers that lined the wall. No matter how much you threw out, the instructions and guides and forms just kept on coming.

"Hey, thanks," Post said. "I was starting to panic a little. And thanks for sitting in."

"I've been wondering about you, Professor," she said. It was vague, deliberately tantalizing, and she knew it. "I'm not a regular student, you know. I'm taking care of Mrs. Hutchinson."

"I've seen you," he said, "pushing a wheelchair. I'm surprised they let her on board."

"This is supposed to be her last trip. She's had a couple of last trips already. She's a friend of the program, if you know what I mean. But anyway, it's not like I'm a regular student. Have I made that clear?"

"Yes." Post couldn't believe his luck. She'd come to him. Knocked on his door. And now she was coming on to him. Knowing what she wanted, what he needed.

"I was wondering if I could submit something I've written. I know it adds to your workload. Everybody else's workload too."

"You've got it," he said, taking the pages she'd offered. "And the corn nuts. I'd say you did all right."

"I can do better," she said, walking away.

Later, after dinner, he walked the deck, a last stroll before turning in. Evening in Takoradi, it wasn't one of those farewell scenes—"Sunset in Portofino"—that you'd see on a calendar. Directly across the pier, the second floor of a warehouse offered a few shops, including a "Duty-Free" emporium—an open-when-a-ship-is-in operation that surely had no connection to any other Duty-Free in the world. Next to it was a bar and there were tables left and right, crowded with students from the ship and a handful of Ghanaians, including women and some guys who looked like they worked the oil rigs. It was quite a scene: loud music, drumming, shouting, howling, empty beer cans rattling down the dock, empty beer bottles shattering. Part of him wanted to go over there, find some fifth deckers whose main research interest, on land or sea, was finding out just how much they could get away with.

"The horror, the horror," someone said and, from the way they said it, he could tell it was a faculty member. The words sounded quoted, ironically quoted, not felt. He turned to see a woman professor. He wasn't sure what she taught. Was it "Foods Around the World?" Or "Alternative Medicines?"

"What an embarrassment," she added, even as a couple bottles broke against the dock. "Ugly Americans."

"I suppose."

"Suppose?" She said it and was gone. No point in informing her that the ugly American had been the hero of the Lederer-Burdick novel. That was all right. What was happening now across the dock was something he didn't want to share. But there was Tommy, his cigar buddy. And the same Sanchez who'd returned his class list and pleaded to have her writing workshopped was on top of a table, a circle of drunks sitting around it, looking as if she'd just jumped out of a birthday cake, dancing, turning, waving and...how quickly she backed off from the railing...blowing him a kiss. Ugly American? Please!

¤

"DOING THE SLAVES." HAROLD Beckmann and Edith Stirling decided to sit at the front of the bus. Less trouble getting on and off was part of the decision but what mattered more is that they would not have to look at and reprimand the kids behind them. They were coming aboard now, and, no doubt about it, these bus trips that had seemed irresistible when they skimmed the field trip catalog back home were something they'd wised up to. A long bus ride, a loud local guide, by now they'd had it with that stuff. They'd prepaid ninety-nine dollars for today's outing and that didn't make them any happier.

"This will be a long day," Beckmann predicted. "But there's something I like about it. It's the way things used to be. There was a time when teachers and students did things together. Take walks, eat meals and sometimes—I know I date myself—have a glass of wine. Or sherry! And we have some of it—a lot of it—on this ship. I like that. The encounters. The way you cross paths, the way you eat together. The ship dips and rolls and shudders and we all feel it."

"GOOD MORNING EVERYONE!" their guide was shouting into a microphone. You couldn't not listen. You couldn't talk: that would be a discourtesy. But listening wasn't easy. It included the guide's shouting out a word in the local language, then commanding the students to respond in chorus, as if they were having fun, learning. After that, he offered scraps of history, politics, food and culture, delivered in a bullying, jocular fashion. He enjoyed his command over a visiting audience. When he ran out of things to say, some of the senior passengers gamely tossed him questions. The cost of a house, say, or a school uniform. After a while, he was suggesting that Ghana's first leader, Kwame Nkrumah, had been poisoned by the CIA. The ride down the coast was slow, prolonged by a rest stop at a gas station, where for a while it was unclear whether the same number of women who'd jammed into the restroom had emerged from it.

Still, they enjoyed the trip, just locking their eyes on the country they were passing through. In Ghana, there was always something to look at. The villages along the road were appalling and fascinating, crowded warrens of huts and shops that pressed against the edge of the highway and spilled inland and uphill in a vista of tin roofs, unpainted wood, packed dirt paths, gray water in open ditches, clothes drying on the ground, scraps of paper and plastic everywhere, peels and cores and husks. These were places that lived off of whatever came down the road, whatever could be induced to slow and stop. Rough places and poor, one after the other, but, if you believed what you read, in close contact with the Almighty. Every shop advertised its personal connection to higher power: Jesus Loves You Beauty Parlor, God the Provider Auto Parts. And, whenever the bus stopped, or even slowed, people were offering bottled waters, roasted peanuts, cooked and raw bananas.

"You know what?" Beckmann asked. When he spoke it was as though he'd broken a spell. It was that kind of ride. You zoned out and you zoned in. "We stopped for God knows how long to relieve ourselves and buy snacks at a gas station. We stopped because of clean restrooms. But suppose we passed such hygiene by and let the students off here? To be swarmed. To find a bathroom or a latrine, a ditch, a tree, a hole in the ground? To bargain for food? To walk those dirt lanes? Go into the village and through it? To be cajoled, accosted, huckstered and, maybe, befriended?" He could picture it. He could picture desperate I've-got-to-go students being escorted somewhere, their urgent need being shouted out to everyone they passed. And then they'd be led to some wretched place and while their new best friend waited outside—and a crowd of kids gathered—the SAS kids would sit and shit and if that wasn't living and learning, if that wasn't thinking globally and acting locally, what was? And they'd learn something all right, they'd have to remember it, and their cameras would do them no good.

"I think that some of them wouldn't get off the bus," Edith said. "And some of them wouldn't come back. And, of course, they'd all hate you. But I see what you mean."

"That's been the biggest surprise," Beckmann continued. "Again and again, we pass places where we ought to stop. And, yes, we visit places we should avoid. But let me be positive. I'm an aging American professor and I hate whisking through places that call out to me. Stop here and you could talk to the people about the names of their stores and what they believe. Sincere faith healing! Sit down on a bench. Keep your camera in your pocket. Ask about a toilet, yes! See if they'd be helpful. They're cautious, the ones who run this program, and they have their reasons. They err on the side of caution. But err they do… A flat tire on this road, a breakdown, that would be the beginning of a story. A blur becomes a picture, a frame that they can step into…"

"I'd be happy if the guide's microphone conked out."

"No difference. He's already shouting."

¤

AFTER TWO HOURS, THE SAS group arrived at Elmina Castle. Slave castle was a misnomer. Better to call it a slave dungeon. And a mob scene. As soon as the passengers alit, they were surrounded by new friends offering gifts, students collecting money for their schools or to buy textbooks, students wanting email addresses in the States, information about scholarships. Oh, if only a person could walk alone, into the castle gate, into a place that spoke for itself and conduced to personal reflection. But they traveled in a guided group, clowning and yawning and clicking cameras. The castle itself was the kind of colonial edifice Beckmann enjoyed, the oldest European building in the country, full of grace and space, of galleries, verandahs, spacious rooms, polished floors, open windows, and a view of the sea. It was built to last. The place was a pleasure, a guilty, very guilty, pleasure. The horror was down below and for once it made sense to be in a group, marched underground like meat stuffed into a sausage, into rooms that sweltered, suffocated, entombed. The men's dungeon, the women's dungeon, the punishment cell, the punishment hole. Go underground anywhere, into any roadside tourist cavern, you expected a cool place, a bit of a refuge from the world outside. Not here. The dungeons were brick-lined, tiny windows out of reach near the top of the room, the inside of an oven, darkly humid, and their brief visit was an insult, measured against weeks and months of starving, shitting, dying. Eventually, the students stood at "The Door of No Return," through which surviving slaves were manacled and marched down to the waiting slave ships. What to make of all this? Some students jumped into the punishment hole, waved to friends with cameras. More than ever, Beckmann was convinced that cameras dumbed down the whole trip; their purpose was to record, not reflect. But, to be fair, serious students were trying to feel what they were supposed to feel and have a few thoughts of their own as well. Not much time for that sort of thing.

"I don't get it," said the woman who worked in the ship's counseling center. "Look at this." She was outside the Door of No Return. Beyond and below were some mossy rocks tumbling down to a sandy beach.

"What is it you don't get?" Edith asked.

"Look at it," she said, gesturing below, beyond. At what? At a beach that was jammed, dozens of fishing boats pulled up on the sand like an invading fleet? At people fussing with nets and engines, sorting fish? It was noisy and filthy down there. And alive.

"This is a kind of sacred place," the woman said. "You walk through a chamber of horrors. Auschwitz in Africa. You step out of the Door of No Return. You get a carnival, a fish emporium, in a place that should be empty and silent."

"They earn their living down on the beach," Edith said.

"Life goes on? Is that your point? How am I supposed to process this? A junkyard? Why not build a Wal-Mart or a Jiffy Lube? It couldn't be worse than this."

"I bet they'd like that Wal-Mart," Beckmann argued. "You might not. I might not. But we are visitors. They live here." Thank God for the call to return to the bus. The woman, straining for a reverent movement, turned back. Once again, Beckmann would have sent the whole busload down there and he'd have led the way. Immersion in chaos. Something to be said for the reverent moment. Something more for hurly-burly exploration. But on this trip, neither side won. The bus prevailed, the schedule ruled, the guide never stopped talking.

One odd thing after another. The visit to the slave castle was followed by lunch at a resort hotel on a beach. It was a Semester at Sea pit stop. Buses headed from Elmina Slave Castle to Cape Coast Slave Castle crossed paths and shared lunch with buses headed in the other direction. They'd gone from off-the-charts cruelty to resort buffet. No guilt here, no need to process anything but fish, chicken, vegetables, and Heinekens for Beckmann and Edith.

"This next castle, I'm not so sure about," she said.

"Are you okay?"

"Fine. But I need a siesta. Just give me a shade tree and forty-five minutes."

What an appealing idea. A shady palm, a pleasant breeze, a safe distance from students who were out on the sand bargaining with Ghanaians for carvings and T-shirts.

"If we take a nap, we'll regret it. How about some coffee to revive us?" Beckmann was being sensible. It was hard.

"I don't want to be revived," Edith responded with a petulance that was youthful, healthy. "I want a nap."

"If they call the bus…"

"If we miss the bus, so what? We can take a cab. Better yet, Harold, take a room."

"We'll have to sign off the trip. You know the rules."

"Fine. Sign off for both of us."

III.

CAPE TOWN, SOUTH AFRICA

"**Y**OU'RE PUTTING ME ON," Will Post said. "They got married?"

"*I'm not kidding*," Sanchez insisted. She'd stayed behind after class. He liked that about her, being in no rush to leave. So many others watched the clock.

"Where?"

"In a village. A traditional ceremony."

"Did they know each other? Before the voyage?"

"Nope."

"Who married them?"

"Some village guy. A chief, a priest? Do you think it's legal?"

"I think it… What's the word I'm looking for…" He waited, as if he were rummaging through an invisible thesaurus for the right word. Then he had it. "I think it sucks."

Every port produced tales of student adventures and misadventures. Ghana had plenty. Taxi drivers who took students where they felt like taking them, shaking them down for money when they were stopped by cops, accompanying them to bar-brothels, proposing marriage. He'd read about a village visit that offered a naming ceremony. After being welcomed with dancing and singing, one by one, they stepped forward to receive a tribal name. A few hours later they were back on the bus, claiming to be deeply moved, as if they were part of the village, honored guests whose presence would be remembered. In fact, these names would last about as long as a fake tattoo. Silly stuff, but harmless. But this marriage was something else, a mockery of marriage, of travel, of study. Was he alone in his feeling? What about Beckmann? Life was about the accumulation of memories, he'd said a while ago. Was this the kind of memory he had in mind?

Leo Underwood's office door was closed but soon after talking to Rosa Sanchez, when Will Post knocked, he answered, just cracking the door open.

"Just a minute," he said. "Stick around."

He walked down the hall into a lobby with ship's officers on one side, Meghan Shepard's office on the other. On the wall at the back of a staircase, there were several boards on which photos of all passengers were posted. He found the married-in-Ghana pair, the newlyweds, a dark, dreamy girl and an amiable guy. There was a message here, he decided. On any given day, in any port, anything was possible. Shit happened. He wondered about looking in on Meghan, but then he heard the familiar *ding-dong* that signaled a salvo of public address announcements: volunteer groups making origami doves to take to Hiroshima, sending Valentines to Hershey Chocolate's unenlightened president, and protesting labor conditions on his company's plantations. Then, two students knocked on the door. Post knew them: the newlyweds. Underwood ushered them in and invited Post to follow.

"Well then," Leo began from behind his desk. And was promptly challenged.

"What's he doing here?" the male newlywed asked, gesturing at Post. His name was Drew, and Post wondered whether he should try to think of him as "the husband."

"I was just wondering if you're registered for wedding gifts at the ship's store," Post snapped back. The bride—Lisa—flushed.

"Post is here at my request," Leo said.

"Could we please get on with it?" Drew asked.

"Well…are you married? Simple question."

"It was just a field trip… Kind of an impulse thing."

"I'll ask again. Ask you both. Are you married?"

"Not really," Drew said. He glanced at Lisa, not sure they were on the same page.

"So it was a joke. Your joke. You're jokers. That's about the size of it. Do your parents know?"

"No need," Drew said. "What happened here…." He moved his hand, waving it all away. "…is none of your business."

"Here's how it looks to me," Leo countered. "This 'kind of impulse thing' you did leads up to an impulse of my own, packing you two off the ship in Cape Town. You demean the ship, turn a field trip into a clown show and you insult the country you were visiting."

"Low blow. Those villagers didn't act insulted. They thought it was a real hoot. And they made money besides. This is bullshit. We're twenty years old. What we do, if it's in St. Patrick's Cathedral or some Ghanaian village, is none of your business. Want to tell my parents? Please. You've got my home address. My father's first name is Ronald. You might put 'esquire' after his last name. He's a lawyer. Kind of likes publicity. Was there anything else on your mind today?"

"Get out of here," Leo said. The newlyweds left, not before Lisa turned back to them.

"Have a nice day," she said.

"Was that the way it was supposed to go?" Post asked, holding out a glass while Leo poured some scotch.

"Don't do this to me, Will," he said. "Don't do your inquiring reporter thing right now. The old days, I would have done something. At least that's what I tell myself. Kick them off? Maybe not? Talk to them? I just did that. You saw how it went. I used to handle these screwups. So this morning I called Charlottesville. Bad publicity, that's the worry. 'Semester at Sleaze.' 'The Love Boat.' That old stuff. I was told to handle with care. And I failed. It was their relationship, their decision, their business and how dare I… They're worried, back in Virginia. Keep the lid on, they say."

With that, Leo Underwood shifted his swivel chair so he was facing out to sea. All Post could see was the back of his head, hair thinning at the crown. What followed was a monologue that was indifferent to audience reaction and did not welcome interruption. Some of it was already familiar. Underwood insisted that a voyage was a great thing that benefitted superior students and redeemed screwups and troublemakers. For years he was judge and jury, now they had a committee. Every voyage, students were disciplined; every voyage, some were put ashore. That was something Underwood did well, handled by himself, until now. Okay, cards on the table, he knew that faculty resented him. "Anti-intellectual," they said. He denied that. But "anti-faculty" might be in the ballpark. He was drawn to screwups, he admitted, the ones who broke the rules, rented cars, went skydiving, closed bars, trashed hotel rooms. The trip meant something to them. It could change them, even if—*especially* if—they got kicked off. The screwups, the ditzy hair-flipping girls, knuckle-dragging guys, could learn more because they had more to learn. And nothing was more instructive than getting jammed up in a foreign country, mugged on a dark street, cheated in a bar, caught mixing pills and booze, oh Christ, there was no end to it. Learning opportunities, all of them. Losing your passport, your very identity! *True* global studies! They came to him. Some angry and hurt, others pleading or defiant. That's when he got to work. This was a youthful error that they'd put behind them, this was a chance to learn, to start becoming the person they were meant to be. By the time they'd left it was hugs and promises to keep in touch, which some of them did. He got emails, wedding invites, baby pictures. The program got donations, too. And yet. And yet. There were some who hated him.

"Last year," Leo said, "they trotted me out to an alumni gathering. Fund-raising, of course. Those things happen on the ship between voyages. Miami? New York? I forget. Usually, a bunch of kids seek me out, hug me, test my memory. Thank God for name tags. I was schmoozing with a bunch of them, just ready to head back to my cabin, when someone approached me, someone who'd been standing behind the people I'd been talking with. In his forties, I guessed, a thin, smart fellow, kind of aristocratic, a Dick Cavett or George Plimpton type, a mix of intelligence and entitlement. We always get some of those. 'Dean Underwood,' he says. But he doesn't offer his hand. Another thing, no name tag. 'Do you know me?' he asks. 'Do you know my name?' Put that way, there was nothing I could do but wait for him to introduce himself, tell me what voyage he was on. But he didn't. He just stood there, looking at me. 'Have we met?' I finally asked. 'You bet. And I came when I heard you'd be here,' he says. 'I came because of you. You put me off the voyage. You ruined my life!' With that, he turns and leaves, not waiting for a word from me. So I went after him. That was because there was always the chance that I'd done some harm. Nobody gets it right all the time. I knew what I'd say. 'Look, you came here. You've thought about this. And whatever you pictured me saying to you, tell me, I'll say it. Whatever it takes for you to be able to let go of this.' But the guy was gone. I'm pretty sure he'd left the ship. So whatever the fellow wanted, it wasn't an apology. He had something in mind for me."

"He just wants to give you a few bad nights."

"Then he succeeded."

When they came into the office from where they'd been sitting out on deck, Meghan Shepard was at Leo's desk going through email. She had a desk in another office where she made announcements.

"How's life in the Fúhrerbunker?" Post asked her.

"Moving on up. 'Today the fifth deck, tomorrow the world.'"

"Any word on my smoking chair?"

"We're working on it night and day, sir."

"Right." He nodded at Underwood and left.

"You heard what we were saying?" Underwood asked Meghan.

"I did. You left the door open. It wasn't my job to close it."

"It's okay, I trust you."

"You're okay trusting me," Meaghan said. "But him?"

"So? So what?" Leo thought she was miffed, jealous that someone else had his confidence. Well, he trusted her. At least he used to trust her. But he wasn't about to let her decide whom else he should trust.

"Bobby Rummel's waiting outside," she reminded him.

"Bobby Rummel. That's the kid that old Beckmann called an asshole in Rio."

"If you got put off the ship for being an asshole..." said Post.

"Yeah, I know. Man the lifeboats. And leave some room for faculty. Being an asshole isn't the problem today, though. It's about a complaint from a woman. For him, the wrong woman. Wrong and wronged. Bring him in."

Tousled hair, smiling face, familiar wised-up manner, Bobby Rummel seemed no stranger to expulsion from school. Nor had he dressed up for the occasion: white cotton shirt, wrinkled linen pants, leather sandals, just what he'd worn at the hearing which found him guilty of sexual assault on a woman who, Leo had to admit, had been one sharp, angry-looking lady.

"You know you're leaving the ship," Leo began. "I think it's the right decision. But I wanted to talk awhile before you're gone."

"I'm charmed and flattered," the kid fired back, and Leo knew this was going to be rough. Students, two or three or more, got deleted from every voyage, no more than were sent packing from prep schools, colleges, universities everywhere. For drug use, drunkenness, sexual harassment, vandalism, plagiarism, and so forth. But the loss of a voyage was different. There was no reenrollment, no return.

"How about a soft drink? Some juice?"

"Keep your soda."

"Is there anything you want to say?"

"Trying to make me feel better? Trying to make yourself feel better? You got my side of it. I had a partner in crime. An accomplice. Ready, willing, and, just between us, very able. I gave you a petition from fifteen students who asked you to keep me on board. Mostly women. So...would it do me any good to repeat myself?"

"No, it wouldn't."

"I studied you during my so-called...what? Trial? Hearing? Sub-judicial, paralegal whatever. You sized me up. And boy, did you size her up. That took longer. I felt a compliment coming my way."

"I guess there isn't much I can say to you," Leo said, surprised that he was giving up so quickly.

"That's it, huh? Kind of a letdown. I've heard what you do. Convincing kids that their life has changed, they've learned from their errors, and like everybody on this friggin' ship they're gonna be a better person. Me included. In spite of—no, make that because of—getting kicked off. Etcetera. Spare me that."

"Okay, Bobby Rummel. You get the last word."

"See you around," Rummel responded, standing up. "Save the hug."

Listening to them, Meghan wondered what Leo made of this last voyage. Anyone who met him marveled at his energy, his yarns, his practical wisdom and trademark hugs. His public persona remained intact. The voyage was all about him. But she saw anger, boredom, brooding, and, in her case, indifference. He was getting more pushback from the students he called in. They shrugged, they talked back, they called their parents who called Charlottesville and Charlottesville called him. "A frigging daisy chain," he called it. But she had to be careful. She still needed him. She needed him to support her just-discovered mission. Global studies. It might never have come to her if she had classes to teach. Or friends. But she was the dean's aide, the dean's voice, the dean's go-fer and stand-in. On this voyage, she was a pain and a joke. Thus: global studies. The hated course that everyone had to attend. It didn't work. It never worked. To call it Rubik's Cube would be a compliment. Something fatal and insoluble: pancreatic cancer, Lou Gehrig's disease. That was what she'd tackle. And if she came up with a solution and if she succeeded—half-succeeded—she'd have to be acknowledged. Rewarded.

¤

BECKMANN LAY IN BED, his sleep contending with an insistent bladder. A losing battle. As with roofs and basements, water always wins. He rose groggy but alert enough to sense something had changed outside. Had the ship slowed? Or turned? Or both? Hard to tell? He slid open the glass panel that led out to his bit of balcony. Looking left and right, he saw none of his neighbors at the railing. But what a moon was up there, out there, full and lonely. Full moon and calm sea. A perfect moment, his alone. From now on, he would mark his calendar, stay up late, or set an alarm. He'd missed too many full moons.

¤

"A KNOCK ON YOUR door at three a.m. gets your attention," Will Post said at 6:00 a.m. coffee in the faculty lounge, "and I have to admit I guessed right. Rosa Sanchez was banging on my door. Maybe I'd been dreaming of her?"

"A dream come true," Beckmann said.

"She was a wreck. A mess. Crying…and that's not her style," Post continued. "You know that woman she wheels around the ship? Old friend of the program, generous donor. All that stuff. Well, she went overboard last night."

"My God! Mrs. Hutchinson!"

"She liked sitting out at night now and then, Rosa tells me. Back of the ship. And last night was kind of beautiful."

"A huge moon. A whopper."

"So usually Rosa sits with her and they talk. They're a pair. They look after each other. But there were nights, lately, when in the nicest possible way she asked to be left alone. Couldn't blame her. Come back in a couple of hours. That was the deal. So Rosa goes away. Rosa comes back. And finds the wheelchair where she left it, against the railing, empty."

"Mrs. Hutchinson? Amazing!" Beckmann said. It came out as a compliment. "So what now?"

"Ah ha! Let me tell you." Post was full of the excitement that always showed up when he'd made a discovery. "It's the Williamson Turn! To try and find her. At least, to say we tried. It's protocol."

"It seems needless. Surely, she's found the death she wanted. Even if we/they found her floating on the water, what's the point of retrieving her? To have a funeral at sea and deposit her in the ocean a second time?"

"They tell me it's not such a great way to go," Post said. "Because at the end, whatever you think you want, your body has a will of its own. And it wants to live."

"How long do you suppose it takes?"

"I asked. Depends on the weather, the waves, the temperature of the water. Ten minutes or an hour. Like I said, it's a bad way to go."

"I've seen worse," Beckmann said.

¤

BEFORE BREAKFAST, LEO ASKED Meghan to announce that all passengers were required to remain in, or return to, their rooms until their presence—and Mrs. Hutchinson's disappearance—was confirmed. It was a formality. She was a goner. And Leo sat in his office wondering what he'd done to deserve this, on his last voyage. On his watch. And God, the phone call he'd just had with Charlottesville. You'd think he'd thrown the woman overboard. The length of the search; the need to get to Cape Town on schedule, so that students could catch expensive field trips they'd booked to game parks and nature preserves; the cost of extra fuel required to rush to port in time.

"Did you know Mrs. Hutchinson?" Meghan asked. "Did you like her?"

"Sure I know her. I know everybody. I even knew her when she had a husband. We had some fun nights on shore. Big on perfume, I used to kid her, what's the flavor of the day? Big fan of poetry, too."

His memory came out vehemently, annoyed that he had to be reminded of the woman who had caused him such a headache. The question had challenged him.

"You'll hear it at the memorial service. She was…" his voice trailed off, "…something else."

"I know you'll be great."

"So meanwhile, get that assistant of hers in here."

¤

AT THE START, LEO shared Rosa's pain, appreciated her loss, understood their mother-daughter relationship, assured her that her trip was fully paid for. And then, just when she was getting ready to leave, he had a few questions to ask.

"Rosa? I've known Carla Hutchinson for years. We go back to before you were born. So, close as you were, did you have any idea this was coming?"

"No, sir."

"She didn't talk about it? I guess I can see the appeal of ending it where she'd been so happy."

Rosa shrugged.

"She wasn't depressed?"

"She was looking forward to Cape Town. Some winery she liked in Stellenbosch. And the botanical gardens. Hilly botanical gardens. She warned me, I'd get a workout."

"Funny thing, Rosa. You mention all that pushing the wheelchair around. This whole voyage, I never saw her out of the wheelchair. I never saw her standing up. And you're telling me you wheeled her out to look at the waves and moonlight. And she wanted to have some time alone."

"Yes. Maybe she'd been getting me used to the idea of leaving her out there. Kind of training me, so it wouldn't seem odd…when the time came."

"How many, I hate to use the word…dry runs…were there?" Leo said, not able to suppress a smile at his unexpected cleverness. Dry run for a drowning, that was a keeper.

"I guess…three times…before last night."

"So somehow this invalid hoists herself out of the chair, grips the railing, and *vaults* herself overboard. You're a sharp lady. What's wrong with this picture?"

"She got to the bathroom okay at night," Rosa said. "For what that's worth."

"I can't help wondering if what you've told me is true," Leo said. "Bottom line, I think maybe you helped her out. For money. For love. Could be for both. They go together okay, don't they? I think you helped her out of the wheelchair. Over the railing. Into the water. I think you watched the splashdown. How long could you see her as the ship moved away? On a moonlit night? Was she struggling? Waving her hands, changing her mind, calling out to you?"

By now, Leo had expected tears. A confession. Something like what happened between a sinner and a priest. No punishment in this case. Forgiveness, maybe. It all depended. It all depended on him. A hug wasn't out of the question at the end. All this had worked, many times before.

"I left her on deck," Rosa Sanchez repeated. Deadpan. That thing about love and money must have backfired, like he'd been calling her a whore. "When I returned she was gone."

"All right," Leo said. "We're done. Just wondering, though. A hypothetical kind of question. If you had helped her out...would you tell me?"

"Never. You're the last person I'd tell."

"That's it?" asked Leo. "That's all?"

"Listen. That woman meant the world to me. Gave me work. Paid my tuition at a community college. Brought me on this voyage. We had a lot between us. Everything. We shared everything. And you..." She'd been downcast. Now their eyes met. "...I'm not sharing with."

"There'll be a memorial service," Leo said. "I'll be speaking. But if you wanted to say a few words..."

"No thanks," Rosa replied. "You're on your own."

"Well then," Leo said. "I'm thinking I don't impress you very much." He waited for a contradiction that didn't come. "So, just one thing," he continued. "Tell me how the loss of Carla Hutchinson impacted the students. She was lovely, she was likeable, she was wise, good in every way, all the way. So, did they grieve for her?"

"Not like you and me, that's for sure." Rosa Sanchez said. "Sure, it was an event. It went viral. A bit of excitement. Like seeing a whale or something. A creepy surprise. A little sadness, maybe. On a ship like this, it can't last."

She stopped. Leo sat there nodding. It was up to him to remember Carla Hutchinson. Him and maybe Rosa Sanchez.

"Okay?" she asked.

"Yes," Leo replied. "Okay."

Meghan heard it all. Leo left the door open. Even in confidential sessions he needed an audience. But he'd been badly off his game. The honeymooners, Bobby Rummel, Rosa Sanchez. He was having another off day. Off voyage, maybe. He was a true believer. Every voyage—at least, every voyage he was on—was transforming. But it wasn't turning out that way.

Leo left his door open on purpose, she realized. It was as though he wanted her to know what he was going through. Off day. Off voyage. He was a true believer. Every voyage he was on was guaranteed, even the ones that skirted disaster. On one voyage, a rogue wave slammed into the ship. That was something! Engines disabled, clogged toilets, no showers, no air con, kids sleeping out on deck at night. That was a voyage they would talk about forever. And this, now, this was kids taking pictures of themselves when they went shopping or got drunk. She slipped out without saying goodbye. Off-duty. She had promised to help Bobby Rummel pack his bags.

AFTER THE SHIP HAD gone as far back as decency required, Leo presided over a memorial service in the Union. His memories of Carla Hutchinson were touching and detailed. A half-dozen voyages they'd shared. He remembered an Atlantic storm, the two of them almost alone at breakfast, joking and laughing. An expedition to the old E & O Hotel in Penang for banana splits. A poetry reading group she'd coerced him into joining to contemplate T. S. Eliot's "The Waste Land." He wasn't much on poetry, he allowed, without adding that he was there because Carla Hutchinson was a great—i.e., a generous—supporter of the program. Yes, he said, the ending she chose had been inconvenient. But soon they'd be back on schedule. And he would miss his old shipmate. He didn't agree with what she'd done. He didn't condone it. But he'd remember her well. At the end, he wiped away some tears and he wasn't the only one who was crying. It was, Meghan granted, one of Leo's finest performances. But that evening, as they headed back to Africa, a huge sunset exploded in the west, a far finer sight than a floating body. A parting gift, Beckmann suggested, and Post agreed. Later, for the second consecutive night, Post found Rosa Sanchez at his door.

"I can't stay down there," Rosa said. "That cabin gives me the willies. The perfumes. The soap. Her books. Her shoes. Can I stay here?"

"Sure," Post said. And for a minute it was awkward. He didn't know what she wanted. "It's a little tight, sleeping in that bed. But I can take the couch."

"Who said anything," Rosa said, "about sleeping?"

LIKE AN AIRLINE SCREEN that shows a flight's supposed progress across time zones and datelines, a computer in the ship's library traced progress from port to port. As they approached Cape Town, the computer drew crowds. The screen looked like an Etch-a-Sketch gone crazy, zigzagging, spiking, crossing and recrossing. And outside, along the railing, now you saw Cape Town. Now you didn't. You could make out Table Mountain; trace the coastline that led down to the Cape of Good Hope where oceans met. But on the morning of their scheduled arrival, there were forty-to-fifty-knot waves in the harbor, so they couldn't dock. Morale quickly plunged. What about that five-day "safari experience," what about that trip to the game reserves or to Kruger National Park? People got cranky, worried about cancellations, and the program's policy on refunds wasn't clear. "It's not the weather," someone said. "It's that we haven't paid bribes." Students circulated a petition: to make up the Cape Town day they were losing, they wanted a day added at the end of their stay. Meghan announced a session of "meditation and prayer" that might serve as "a little collective for positive energy." How fragile the mood of the voyage was. How vulnerable. But then good news arrived: permission granted to dock in Cape Town.

¤

BECKMANN HAD LEARNED TO take his time going ashore. Immigration officials were more likely to interrogate the first people to come down the gangplank; later on they waved you through. Field trips debarked first, consigned to guides. He waited them out. Then came individual students, delighted to be at liberty in a new country. Beckmann and

Post stood at the railing, watching the slow emptying of the ship, taking in the harbor, the city, and above it the high plateau that had to be Table Mountain.

"Itching to leave the ship, our kids," Beckmann said. "And twice as eager to return to it. A constant state of itchiness. But what is that pack of students doing at the bottom of the gangplank? Waiting for what?"

"Fifth deck kids, most of them," Post remarked. "I heard something might be up."

Before Beckmann could press him, he saw the students, mostly females, form lines at the bottom of the gangplank as if to receive an honored guest. Then Bobby Rummel appeared at the top of the gangway, waving at the students who were waiting for him below, acknowledging others still on board, leaning over the railings. "We love you, Bobby!" they shouted, and "Hot, hot, hot!" and "Do it to me one more time!" Bobby bowed, waved, and, like a debutante descending a mansion staircase, made his way slowly down the steps. And when he got to the bottom, set foot on land, he bowed toward the ship that would sail on without him. Then he scanned the ship, waving a hand in their direction, pointing a finger there and there, an acknowledgement, maybe a benediction, that glided to where Beckmann was easy to see. Bobby waved at him. Then he homed in on the very front of the ship where Leo Underwood stood like a figurehead, arms folded and expressionless. Bobby Rummel blew him a kiss, turned and headed toward the immigration office, shouts of love following him.

"Could have been worse," Post remarked. "I figured he was going to give Leo the finger."

¤

"I'm feeling lazy," Harold Beckmann announced. "And I don't feel guilty about it."

He was with "the favela girls," Edith Stirling and Jody Phillips, in a winery garden in Stellenbosch. They'd left Cape Town after breakfast, stopping for a few hours' walk in the botanical gardens at Kirsternbosch. Out of Jody's earshot, Edith said that she wouldn't mind another "diversion" like they'd had in Ghana, where they'd napped under a palm tree, spent the night in a cottage where they did what students called a "snuggle." Well, they'd both lost partners. Mortality 101 was a course they were taking, required, not elective. And now she had a terrycloth bathrobe hanging in his closet, and today they sat in a garden at a winery that, it turned out, celebrated chocolate as well as wine. And made Irish coffee.

"I worked hard setting up South Africa," Beckmann said. "History. The Dutch, the British. Zulu War, Boer Wars. The Cape Colored people, mixed blood, complicated fates. First, they were caught between the blacks below and the whites above. Now there are blacks above? What has been achieved? Nationhood and liberation. What has not been achieved? Prosperity, equality, social justice. Big question: what defines us more, what matters more—race or class? Consider those townships we passed on the way to these gorgeous vineyards. Miles of shacks right along the highway. Are those people uplifted by the knowledge that their national leader is named Zuma, not Verwoerd?"

He smiled and lifted a glass of Pinotage, raised it toward two women he liked. Along with a sip of wine he'd never heard of, he took in the long tree-lined driveway that brought them here, the rolling fields. And felt a bit ashamed of feeling so comfortable.

"Perhaps I worry too much. Those students rush off to visit wildlife, explore beaches, climb Table Mountain. They don't want to impale themselves on issues they don't have time to investigate, let alone settle. But I hate to hear myself say that."

"Don't worry about it," Jody responded. "I didn't go on a safari. It wasn't that I objected on principle. It's just they were so expensive and, another thing, I can't travel in groups anymore, I just can't. Oh, there's a trip in India, one more SAS trip. But that's it. So, while studying Cape Town I figured something out. We're supposed to be students and we're expected to go ashore with questions—global studies stuff—about politics and economy, class and race. We're students and scholars."

How many times did it happen in a career? Half a dozen? How often was it that a student found her way to something a professor had been groping for? It was coming now, Beckmann sensed.

"I realize that you can't just show up in a place and take it on. You've got to be a tourist first. See the obvious sights, hear the stale jokes, walk the visitor's walk. What if a shipload of Semester at Sea kids showed up in Manhattan? Would you expect them to go straight up to Harlem and start interviewing landlords and tenants about rental policies? Could you do that before you knew Central Park and Greenwich Village? Come on. They're beginners. We're beginners."

Beckmann nodded and prepared a compliment. Great minds, operating independently, arriving at the same conclusion.

"So maybe it doesn't matter so much, what we do," she said. "It's a beginning. Awkward beginning. It reminds me of an elevator. Door opens on one floor after another and you get a peek…just that…so short it's comical. In a minute, the doors close. And that's it. I know, you can say it: 'been there, seen it, done it.' That's what they say, a lot of the kids, that's what they think. But some of us will be back. Again. For a lot longer. I'll be back. And it doesn't matter so much, what I did today, except one thing. This is where it began."

Beckmann and Edith were quiet when she finished. She must have wondered whether they were appalled.

"Did I say something wrong?"

"What you said…" Beckmann began and stopped, made her wait a little. "…is correct."

"Correct? I can't believe you agree. Of all the people on the ship, I figured you'd be the last to agree. Mr. Dignity, Mr. Rigor. And what I said, I'm not even sure it's a good thing. And you agree with me?"

"I do," he said. "There must be something wrong with me."

¤

THE CAPE TOWN HARBOR was a congenial place, a promenade with dozens of shops and restaurants. That afternoon after their trip to Stellenbosch, Beckmann repaired to the computer room where he played a favorite game: seeing if he could delete all incoming email while he held his breath. How little there was that mattered. He was an important professor: he'd put the college in his will, served on committees, made recommendations, offered opinions that—with increasing frequency—were respected and disregarded. And even if what he said turned out to be correct, even if his warnings and predictions were right on the mark, it was in the nature of colleges that they never remembered, never looked back, never acknowledged error, never said, *Hey, Professor, looks like you were right, we should have listened to you.* Never. How far away all those emails felt. Like weather reports from a place where he no longer lived.

Just when he logged out, Edith came up behind him.

"Oh, my God," she said. "You have to see something."

"What is it?" Beckmann asked. He couldn't help worrying about her. Whatever it was, it sounded bad.

"I'll tell you later," she said.

Beckmann had loved his wife, but "I'll tell you later" was an infallible sign of trouble, matched only by "never mind, you wouldn't understand." She held out her hand and led him down the corridor.

"Give me your key," she said. "And close your eyes."

She led him through the door, toward the back of the cabin and, just then, it didn't feel as though he were in trouble. He heard her slide open the glass doors that led to his deck. She guided him to the railing. What could it be?

"Okay," she said. "Open your eyes."

Table Mountain. He'd glanced at it when they sailed in. Well, yes, there it was, a high plateau hovering above and behind the city. And, to be sure, it might be called a table. So much for that. But now, an ordinary landmark had turned into a piece of late afternoon magic. A mass of white clouds had settled on top of the mountain and then—this is what took your breath away—the clouds slowly spilled over the edge of the mountain, like a waterfall, maybe, or an avalanche, only slower, more leisurely, like a falling gown or, yes, a tablecloth, white and turning pink as the evening arrived.

¤

IT WASN'T FAIR. ON a ship where seven out of ten passengers were female, Will Post had been celibate. High and dry. Any sex with a student, wildly consensual as it might be, felt troublesome. Bummer. Even Beckmann and Edith were a couple, though he couldn't tell whether their intimacy went past nightly Scrabble. Romance was rare, but pairings-off were rife. Still, Post had decided to play by the rules. But with so many people—not to dance around it—getting so much, he had felt the joke was on him. He felt like a loser. Hear the one about the guy who couldn't get laid on the love boat? And now Rosa Sanchez!

That changed things. Did it ever! He'd wondered about Meghan Shepard back in Nassau, where they'd spent a night together, a kind of bon voyage celebration, sampling rum on a hotel balcony and, later, in bed. On ship, her cabin was right across the hall from his. But she kept her distance. Maybe she was obsessed with Leo. Or resented Post's closeness to Beckmann. Anyway, friendship ripened into apathy and, in her case, free-floating anger.

Be careful what you wish for. They'd connected, just a little bit. And now he missed her despite—maybe because of—Rosa Sanchez. Rosa was a game changer. Now, when they walked to breakfast, her hair wet from a morning shower, students stared at them. "What's up with that?" Faculty and spouses, oldsters, staffers were surely wondering whether what they were doing could possibly be permitted.

One afternoon, he accompanied her up to the swimming pool on the seventh deck. She was wearing his terry cloth bathrobe over a bikini and, as they proceeded upstairs, a gaggle of students trailed along. Post had no intentions of swimming. The tiny pool, Rosa told him, was known as the "birdbath," home to "sorority sunbathers." One of them had told her, "I study better with a tan." He took a chair in the shade, well away from the pool, and watched Sanchez shed his bathrobe, turn slowly as if modeling, and hop into the pool. The Jamaican bartenders gasped, the Filipino hamburger cooks came out from behind the grill, the knuckle-dragger weight lifters stopped in mid-jerk and the women who'd been around the pool evaporated. No contest. Post remembered Bo Derek in *10*, Sophia Loren in *Boy on a Dolphin*. Not only was Rosa Sanchez spectacular, she was smart. And all his tales of the places he'd seen were new to her.

Rosa had left Cape Town to go on a safari Mrs. Hutchinson had paid for. Post missed his students. He had the fifth deck to himself and it wasn't the same. Beckmann had told him an empty campus—that's what this was—was wonderful, right after students left. But before long, it felt flat. You missed the kids. And deep down, every professor ached for the day they came back. Come back to school. Come back, all is forgiven. Make that: all will be forgiven. He couldn't imagine sailing without them.

He tackled the papers that came in from Ghana. He'd heard plenty already. Fifth deck talk. The students weren't inhibited by his presence; they included him, they saved stuff for him. He heard about a tour featuring Islam and Christianity which amounted to a bland lecture at a monastery and a drive past a mosque. A two-hour ride to a village that was visited for half an hour. The worst he'd heard about was about cops who stopped a taxi carrying one passenger too many. This resulted in a fine, paid by the taxi driver, the students, or both. But this was more than a shakedown. The cops proposed to separate the two female students and take them someplace. One of the guys promptly took a photo of the police car's license plate. The cops relented. Sometimes, just once in a while, you realized all the bad things that were waiting for a ship like this to dock. Now he wanted to see what his travel writers had produced. *Thank you, kids, thank you.* How many professors could say the same thing? Three hours later, he was still thankful. The papers were inconsistent. Some were dashed off. And even the good ones had problems. But they'd learned to avoid tourist clichés; they wrote more vividly. They were all sick of group travel but they were writing about it comically. One student had traveled from Takoradi to Accra:

> I look out the cracked windows of the rattling bus
> and take in the sights along the road. The random
> shacks are practically indistinguishable and it is
> hard for me to imagine large families in such small
> quarters. Women in brightly colored dresses walk

around with babies strapped to their backs and
some even have huge baskets balanced on their
heads, selling plantains or bags of water. The men
are mostly empty handed except for the occasional
machete and don't appear to be doing much work at
all. Next to me, Hannah's sitting, clutching her dark
green shoulder bag, and I silently pray that she isn't
stupid enough to pull out her $400 Nikon and start
snapping pictures like she usually does.

Not bad, Post thought. She offered a sense of place, noticed what
women did and men didn't, and ended with a sardonic swipe at a
photo-obsessed sidekick. Suppose she came up with three or four such
moments in each port? Paul Theroux and Pico Iyer wouldn't be out of
business. But these kids had snap, crackle, and pop. Could someone
on a conventional junior-year abroad program, one spending a
full semester immersed in a village in France or Chile, match up?
Measuring intimate knowledge of one small place with a tantalizing
glimpse of a dozen big places was, let's face it, a close call.

Accounts of movement in Ghana, on foot, in cabs, on buses,
worked to a point. Much more mixed were accounts of visits of two
or three days to Ghanaian villages and towns. The visit to Winneba,
Charlottesville's sister city, sounded like a botch, short on contact,
long on speeches, and great for travel writing. About a local dignitary:

He began a farewell to us, only to be interrupted by
his ringing cell phone which he answered. We sat
listening to him chat away for five minutes, thinking
about how rude he was being. Finally, he got off the
phone. Finally, he finished his pointless speech.

Some field trips worked. He came across an account of a visit to
missionaries caring for kids enslaved in the fishing industry—one had
watched his brother drown—and another about bringing art supplies

to a village school. Often, charity was met with cold-eyed calculation. It made you wince, reading about the awkwardness of homestays, smiles, strained conversation, playing with kids, and then, out of the blue, someone wants to be given the visitor's shoes or camera. One woman host asks: "What did you bring me?"

> We got to see how these people live and conquered
> the cultural differences for the eighteen hours we
> were there, but we all knew we would be waving
> goodbye in the morning.

That was from Darlene Tedrow, a.k.a. Amelia Bligh Jr. She knew that the trick was focus. Trade in vignettes. Capture a mood and thought. There was no way you could confirm or refute theories of global exploitation. Not in the time you had. Avoid that. Avoid big pictures. And premature wisdom:

> We have so much in America and in Ghana they had
> so little. I couldn't ask them how they felt about their
> life or how we looked to them. But when I held that
> baby in my arms, when I saw the light in the school
> kids' eyes and their smiles, I didn't miss America
> because I could see they were happy.

Grading this paper, Post thought, *was like kicking a puppy*. The writer was trying hard. But did this paper represent the beginning of serious thought? Or the end of it? What was it that Sanchez had said? He riffed through the papers. She'd turned in a sassy piece about students who were intimidated by Ghanaian taxi drivers. "They were so scared and weak, naïve and fragile, as if they could get through life by being sweet or something."

He wanted Rosa Sanchez back on board.

IV.

MAURITIUS

THE *MV EXPLORER* HAD docked at the far side of the harbor in a grassy wasteland with one terminal building and a dirt road leading to town. Beckmann and Post decided on a water taxi. As they set off, they saw Edith waving to them from the seventh deck.

"Boy's night out," she told them. "Or afternoon." The two men looked back at the boat from across the water. The voyage was about halfway over now, Beckmann realized. Time on the voyage was variable, as temperamental as the sea itself. Everybody had a copy of the ship's schedule, a calendar with rows of boxes, seven days in every row of boxes, fifteen rows in all, and on boring days it was easy to mark off the days, like convicts in a cell crossing off a fraction of the time they had to serve. But sometimes time flew, precious time, and to draw a line through a day was a process of subtraction, not addition. "It's odd," he remarked to Post. "You must have noticed the paradox: that a voyage around the world can dwindle so quickly. But if you go around the world by plane...as you must have done..."

Post nodded. "It takes forever. You've got that right, Professor."

From the harbor, Mauritius suggested Hawaii: a muscular, green volcanic island. They passed a long row of Chinese fishing boats, dozens of them, one next to the other. These were tired, rusty vessels, piping bilge water into the harbor, laundry hanging out to dry, crewmen eating and smoking and watching—as if from another world—as tourists passed, sometimes waving back at them, signaling no hard feelings about the way their lives had turned out.

"Three months at sea in a rust bucket, working their ass off for nothing," Post said. "What would they think if they saw our ship? Would they nod politely, admire everything? The spa, the swimming pool, the sunbathing, hair-flipping babes. Or would they run amok, rape, rob, pillage? I could understand that."

"I would like to see *their* ship," Beckmann said.

"What? You're kidding me. Not without a tetanus shot…"

"I mean it. That's how it's been lately. I can't pass a place without thinking if only I could stay here longer. In Dominica, even. At those waterfalls and hot springs. Who wouldn't want a day and a night and the following morning? Up the Amazon, on one of those boats across from where we anchored, headed God knows where. In Rio…"

"I'll give you Rio," Post interjected. "But…seriously…Takoradi? More time at the slave castles?"

"Those ramshackle villages along the road. Dogs and cows and kids. Little shops with Biblical names. I wanted to see how it looked to them, watching us pass through. I could get a haircut, maybe."

"You sound like a kid, Professor."

"I know," he said, still studying those Chinese fishing boats. Their names looked as if they'd been spray-painted onto the stern, and with the names came numbers, suggesting there were half a dozen more such ships at sea for every one in port. What was it like where they slept? How did they shower? Did fishermen eat fish? Were they working in shifts, night and day? If they weren't working, what did they do? Did they find women in a place like Mauritius? And the man who steered the ship. Did they call him Captain? Or Master? Did they even know his name? So many things to wonder about.

Of course it was Sunday. On shore about half the shops were shuttered. Post was annoyed. He'd asked Underwood about these Sunday arrivals. He didn't make the schedules, Underwood replied. Well, said Post, was it a vote of no confidence in the students? Are we counting on Sunday blue laws to keep our kids out of trouble? Make it difficult for our kids to screw up? Underwood threw him a smile that wasn't altogether friendly. "Difficult to screw up?" he repeated. "Difficult, yes. But never impossible."

"I was here on a junket," Post remarked as the water taxi slowed, moving in toward the dock. The passengers—mostly students— wrestled their backpacks over their shoulders. No matter what kind of transportation, nor how long or short the trip, there was that impulse to get off first. "Here's what I remember. There's no local population. What I mean is, no aboriginal tribes to feel guilty about. Or make handicrafts. It's the home of the dodo bird, now extinct, though you can find drawings, T-shirts, carvings everywhere. So everybody came from somewhere else, China, Malaysia, India, Europe…"

They approached a market and, Sunday notwithstanding, the place was jammed: bananas, pineapples, lychees, mangos, leafy vegetables, piles of coconuts and—in a rougher quarter—fish, poultry, beef, and goat, none of which they could carry back on ship. There were reasons for that, of course, but it felt as if you were infantilized, written off; you were not an adult consumer and the people in the market knew it, you were like kids who couldn't be trusted to carry a purse. The only person they could do business with was selling T-shirts. With dodo birds on them.

They walked out of the market and back to the waterfront, past currency exchanges where taxi drivers politely invited them to see the island. They really seemed to want to be guides, hosts. They found an Indian restaurant, nicer than expected.

"I call this place India-lite," Post said. "The people are here, the food, the style. But not the craziness. So tell me... Does this place call out to you like all the others? Or can't you tell yet?"

"Oh, I can tell all right. I can picture myself here. Going to the market, eating, walking. I suppose I'd need to be working on something."

"Could I say something, Professor? It sounds kind of lonely."

"There is that," Beckmann admitted. "On the topic of loneliness—"

"Hold it," Post interrupted. "It just got less lonely." He gestured at a half-dozen students at one table and the two deans, Underwood and Doris Stuart, Dean of the Faculty, at the other. Everybody waved and nodded and that was it.

"It's changed, hasn't it?" Post asked. "Back in Brazil and Ghana, if students met others on the street, they rushed toward each other, and it was where have you been, you've got to see, you won't believe, how much did you pay for... Now they almost go around the corner to avoid meeting..."

"I would say that's a good thing," Beckmann replied. After that, they drank beer, enjoyed lamb vindaloo, sag paneer, and grilled fish. The two professors studied their students—five straight females and one gay male—and found themselves wondering about their sex lives. They lived at close quarters yet they knew so little, they might have been Margaret Mead on her first day in Samoa. Was it what Post called a "gynocopia?" That was the reputation, after all. You noticed couples hand-holding, hugging all the time, and you couldn't miss that just-out-of-the-shower partnership at breakfast, the women wearing what Post termed "a just-slammed look." Yet there were others who seemed determined not to get entangled. Perhaps there was someone at home. Or maybe the voyage was what mattered. That would be good. Post recalled one paper—from that botched trip to Winneba, back in Ghana—where the author, a sharp woman, had been kept awake by a couple in an adjoining room; it went on for hours, and the walls were thin enough for the woman next door to be heard proclaiming, "I'm going to be so sore in the morning!"

The water taxi back to the ship was quiet, though that armada of fishing boats still intrigued Beckmann. Post could see it; he just smiled and nodded at his friend. Beckmann wondered about Edith. She was part of his voyage and—could he say it?—she'd gone from being companionable to indispensable. They'd connected. Certainly not quite to the point of Edith's saying "I'm going be so sore in the morning." But after just a half-day away from her, he was thinking about her. Fine. How would they leave things when the voyage was over? India, Singapore, Ho Chi Minh City, Hong Kong, Shanghai, Kobe, Yokohama, Hilo awaited them, and San Diego was halfway around the world. Yet he dreaded it. Did she? Was time on their side or not? The same question kept arising: was every passing day an addition or a subtraction?

¤

MEGHAN SHEPARD SAT IN her office reviewing the Semester at Sea offerings for Mauritius: a visit to a mosque with biryani lunch to follow, a city orientation tour (box lunch from ship), a sugar factory, a marine park with lunch buffet and local drinks provided, a tour of volcanoes, an adventure park and beach, a hike in the mountains and beach, catamaran and snorkeling (barbecue lunch), and a stop at villages for needy children. Not overwhelming, she decided, but not bad for less than a day. But many of the kids would go off on their own. Mauritius was a liberty port. She doubted they'd want to spend their time on a tour. By now, though, she was feeling lucky;

it was past lunchtime already and no one had called. Students were due back on board at six. Some kids had already returned, she could see them coming up the gangplank and the way they plodded up the steps said they weren't going out again to give Mauritius a second try. Been there, seen it, done it. Leo had pleaded with the kids and maybe they had listened. For the sake of the voyage, and future voyages, they should be on their best behavior. It reminded her of Girl Scout days: "leave the campsite cleaner than you found it."

She was the duty officer and every minute that passed reduced the chance of an emergency. And it gave her time to ponder global studies. Something had to be done. Odd. It was as though you had a restaurant in the best of locations—a view of the world!—and a lovely ambience and a reliable (captive) clientele. And the place was a must to avoid. What to do? The problem preoccupied her, it took on a life of its own, she thought about it while brushing her teeth, taking a shower. She'd done research at the start. She'd gone to class, taking notes. There were often problems with the microphone, an ear-piercing shriek at the start of every presentation. There were in-class quizzes, talk of quizzes to come, scheduling of research presentations. There were charts and color-coded maps, though it sometimes wasn't clear what the various colors represented. There were references to information that, though not covered in class, was available in this or that online folder. It was bewildering. One by one, the kids nodded off or chatted quietly among themselves, editing and sharing photos. She sat next to a student who reviewed photos of penguins all through class. But the problem went deeper.

The underlying mission was to convince young people of privilege to do good in the world and this meant recognizing the bad that had been done, by Europe and America, international agencies and banks. "What bullshit!" one student had snorted. *Maybe it was bullshit, maybe not,* Meghan thought, *but that wasn't the point.* What the students resented was that theoretical and ideological arguments were presented at the beginning of the voyage. They did not arise from experience—they were imposed upon it. It was time for someone to think about the program in a new way.

And then the phone rang. It was one of those rings—like a phone in the middle of the night—that you know means bad news. A living and learning coordinator was in a taxi, about half an hour from the ship, with a student who was in very bad shape. "What was the problem?" she asked. The doctor would want to know. She lost the connection. She called the infirmary, called the bridge, and headed down to the dock to see what was coming.

¤

IT WAS TIME FOR drinks: an hour before supper, also an hour before students were required to be back on board. So Beckmann and Edith were at the railing, watching them rush across the dock in time to beat the deadline. Lots of applause, cheering, and jeering from the people already on board.

And now there was a taxi on the dock and an ambulance and a student in a wheelchair. The ship's doctor was there, as well as Leo Underwood. What was it? Drugs? A fight in a bar? A climbing or a swimming accident? Meghan was down there too.

"I think…" said Edith, "the boy is foaming at the mouth."

The student was taken out of the wheelchair, put in an ambulance, and driven away. Meghan was the first person to come back aboard.

"Meghan, what's up?" Beckmann asked. She brushed by without a word. "Well…"

A moment later, Leo Underwood returned. Beckmann tried again. "What's up?" He was ignored. Leo's face was a fist.

"Knowledge is power," Beckmann said. "So people keep their mouths shut."

The *ding-dong* signal sounded. Meghan announced that Dean Underwood would be giving a talk after supper, another one of his "State of the Voyage" presentations. Will Post made his way up from the fifth deck. It took him ten minutes to discover that the student—a decent, quiet fellow, not a troublemaker—had done some climbing, something involving a cliff, whether clambering up it or rappelling down. All this on a hot day. He had a mighty thirst, joined some shipmates on a beach, and proceeded to drink a bottle of rum. And collapsed.

¤

"WE DID A GREAT job in Mauritius," Leo Underwood began. "I know it for sure. This voyage will be talked about for years. Your dedication to making a difference in the world. It shows up in your service projects, your donations. You make me proud. How about all those origami piece doves you've folded to take to Hiroshima? You make me proud! And those Valentine's Day cards you sent to the Hershey's Chocolate honcho! That makes me proud. But I'm proudest of your concern for each other! The way you help out a shipmate who needs it."

Will Post was glad that he'd gotten a deeper and more complicated sense of Underwood that went beyond the performer on stage tonight. But did he think more or less of him as a result? Hard call. In private he could be shrewd, troubled, self-deprecating, funny. No room for that tonight, though, as he turned a student screwup into a civics exam, passed with flying colors by the kids who'd found their friend in distress, the counselor who'd flagged a taxi and called the ship, the ship's medical staff who'd saved the kid's life, and the passenger—husband of one of the ship's doctors—who'd volunteered to stay behind with the hospitalized student while the *MV Explorer* sailed on to Chennai where everyone hoped the troubled student and his keeper would rejoin the ship.

That's it? Will Post wondered. *That can't be it. The kid screws up. Hospital bills, hotel bills, airplane tickets to India.* It was as if Underwood heard him.

"About the student," Underwood said. "Let's call him 'Bobby.' It hasn't been decided what we'll do. A key question is whether, after missing a number of classes this coming week, he'll be able to catch up. We'll look into that."

That's it? Will Post wondered, again.

What about discipline? Punishment? Apology? What about actions having consequences? Befuddled, he looked across at Meghan, who was sitting next to the seat from which Leo had arisen. His stare registered, she returned it. It wasn't a greeting. He put a puzzled look on his face, scratched his head. His meaning was clear. What's up with this guy? She continued looking his way. It was like a staring contest that no one was winning. Then she nodded a bit and returned his shrug. He sought out Beckmann. "Is it just me? Am I crazy? The kid causes us a world of hurt. And the crucial question is whether he can catch up in class? I don't get it. If a C student drinks himself to the edge of oblivion, creates embarrassment, disrupts another passenger's voyage and costs the program a bundle of money, he'll get kicked off. But if the kid is an A or B, by golly he's going back aboard."

"You have to trust them," Beckmann said. "And, if you don't, there's a line from T. S. Eliot: 'Teach me to care and not to care.'"

"I'm learning," Will Post said.

¤

THE CAPE TOWN PAPERS were a little disappointing, Post had to acknowledge. The writing that came out of Brazil and Ghana had been filled with incidents and accidents, all sorts of stories. First impressions combined with later reflections. South Africa pieces were flat, conventionally touristic. Will Post read half a dozen papers about climbing Table Mountain, many more about safaris to this or that game park. But there were some nice—if small—moments. From a climb up Table Mountain:

> The wind pushed us up the mountain. It would cool you off against the hot sun and press you against the mountain to keep you away from the dangerous edges.

Another fellow had a good moment in a Cape Town open market, remarking on:

> Vegetables that seemed to have the same level of steroid use as major league baseball.

The safari pieces were much alike: group travel by plane and bus, installation in a lodge, introduction to and conversations with the guide and then off in a jeep to keep a date with wildlife. You couldn't begrudge anyone the trip, but reading the papers felt like sitting through the same slide show a dozen times. Thank God for two women, who'd fallen for the same guide. That was the wildlife they wanted! He was their big game. They eyed him as he drove from leopard to lion, attended to his comments and character, shared his concern about poachers, attended to his reflections about life in the wild, its delicious solitude and occasional loneliness. Where one paper ended, wondering about what might have been, the other led to a teté-a-teté in the ranger's room, a bit of a make out and then an ending that made Will Post feel old and out of it. Imagine if, at the end of *Casablanca*, Bogart and Bergman had agreed to keep in touch via emails and Facebook!

"I need to talk to you," a student told him after class. This didn't sound like puzzlement about a paper.

"Why not now?"

She waited until the classroom emptied.

He liked her. One of the better writers. She didn't say much in class but she had an alertness, a sense that she wasn't going to do anything stupid. She wrote with anger, but it was controlled anger backed up by deadpan observations. Long rides, tedious welcomes, dumpy hotels. She was the one who'd heard students screwing all night. But there was more. In a paper of hers he'd just reviewed in class, a Ghanaian fellow—a twenty-nine-year-old student—came on to her, asks about scholarships, asked for her email address, and took it from there. But there was more.

> "You know," he continued, "us Ghanaians are really interested in white women." I laughed nervously and countered with, "Oh, is that so? I had no idea!" His eyes lit up and he said "Yes, to marry a white woman is very good for your career. I am personally very interested, but I don't want to jump into anything too quickly and get married right away," he warned. "Can I take you to have a shot later?"

She was rescued by a battery of welcoming speeches, followed by cultural dances which the Semester at Sea students cannot refuse to join.

It wasn't perfect; lots of tweaks were called for, but it had smarts and spunk. With all the talk about cultural sensitivity on board, this was a writer who believed that good manners were much the same everywhere and there was no reason to take shit because you were a foreigner. And now this bright woman stood in front of him, downcast but, to her credit, businesslike. She might have to leave the voyage, she told him. She had a blood condition they couldn't treat on board. That was that. Post felt as if he'd been stabbed. He hated that her voyage had ended halfway through.

¤

UNSCHEDULED STOP, MEGHAN ANNOUNCED. A couple of students were placed in medevac at Diego Garcia, an American base on a British territory in the Indian Ocean. No going ashore and absolutely no photography permitted. The collectors of places were over the moon. Diego Garcia, as hard to get to as any place on the planet, had dropped in their laps. What a bonus! And so, on a rainy morning, the MV Explorer approached a closely-guarded, un-visitable, maximum security military installation. Students were excited: it might as well have been an invitation to Dr. No's island, at least to see it and—they had to be kidding!—photograph it, too! It looked like a dozen other islands Post had visited: a beach, part rocks, part sand, fringed by brush and palms. If local people still lived here—they didn't—they'd be dreaming of hotels and casinos. Instead there were patrol boats manned by US Marines, returning waves from the girls who leaned over the railings. A submarine broke the surface, and on a hunch Post rushed down to the second deck where his student sat in a chair, packed and waiting. He watched her as she was helped into a boat that headed toward shore.

V.
CHENNAI, INDIA

"**I** FEEL SORRY FOR them," Beckmann remarked at morning coffee. These were quiet times, Edith drinking coffee thoughtfully, reviving with every swallow, and Will Post deleting emails on his laptop. They were at ease with each other. Silence was not a problem. It came as a surprise to them when Beckmann interrupted, and continued. "You've got to hand it to them, sometimes. It's an enormous enterprise when you consider all the things they have to worry about: inoculations, field trips, fuel, immigration, visas, student behavior, and…beyond that…a world that gets more dangerous all the time. At the end of the day there's something noble about it all."

"Noble?" Will Post asked. "I'm not sure that word ever has been used on board this ship. Or in reference to it."

"Noble. I use an old-fashioned word deliberately. A medical evacuation on Diego Garcia. My God, they're at the mercy of so many things. I'll bet it was different in the early days. The world was open. Who wouldn't welcome them? Now they're dodging bullets. I wonder how long it will last."

Beckmann wasn't alone. There was lots of talk about the future of the program. Leo Underwood insisted—in public—that the program's future was bright. Others had doubts. There was something quaint, goofy, vulnerable in it all. And noble. But lately they'd been talking almost every day over coffee in the morning, drinks at night. Fourteen trips around the world had left him with countless gorgeous yarns. Mechanical breakdowns, rogue waves, alcohol and drugs and stowaways, faculty breakdowns and uprisings, student deaths, famous visitors. It felt, more than ever, that he was in the market for a writer. But there was more—there were other moments when Post felt less like a potential writer and more like a priest in a confessional. Leo despaired about the future of the program. Insubordinate students, faculty arrogance. Everybody was jaded, everybody was linked, wired, and wised up.

What's more, he wanted this last voyage of his to be special. And so far it wasn't. It wasn't even average. And, even though Post pressed a bit, he remained coy about the threat that he'd been warned about, some kind of attack on the "student ship." That might enliven things. Whatever it was.

"Listen," he said. "Maybe they thought the chance of an attack would put me off. They got it wrong. They got me wrong. I was excited. I hoped it would come. I still do. When other people talk about nightmares? You know? For me those are the stuff of dreams. Just so you know."

¤

"HOW ABOUT DIEGO GARCIA?" Will Post asked him. "Did it pass the Beckmann test? Did you want to go ashore?"

"Good Lord, yes. Top of the list. An American Gibraltar that no one can visit. Oh, to walk that island, to sit in a mess hall, drink at an officers' club, watch the comings and goings, ships and planes and submarines! Two weeks, at least."

"You're really something," Edith said, her eyes shining. "I wish I'd met you years ago."

"Well…" Beckmann was awkward in moments like this. What to say? What to hope for? What to fear? "Thank you," he said. "Listen. We passed some islands yesterday. The Andamans and Nicobars. No one said a word, not a peep. No announcement. What an insult! They belong to India. Rough reputation. No trace of tourism. I doubt you could buy a postcard. But what an adventure it would be for us. All of us…"

"They'd have a stroke in Charlottesville," Will Post said. "No field trips, no excursions, no buses, no guides, no service projects! Sounds like a television show. *Gilligan's Island* meets *Survivor*."

"To me," said Beckmann, "it sounds like an adventure. It breaks my heart, the places we don't go, just brush past."

"I've got to ask you," Will Post said. "Were you always like this, Professor?"

"Maybe once," Beckmann replied. "That first book. After *Colonies and Empires*, things went in another direction. A certain kind of marriage. A college that I cared for. Students, watching them come and go. Professors and presidents, they came and went as well…" He paused and smiled. "Some other things. A garden…and a dog."

"My husband was always looking for that next big book… He never stopped waiting…" Edith said.

"Yes, I know. I changed. And listen to me now, going on about seeing the lights of Sri Lanka, and coming no closer."

¤

YOU COULD PULL RANK, make excuses, do damage control, but there was no way of avoiding at least one major field trip on shore. Beckmann was to lead a short tour in the French Concession of Shanghai. Post had signed up for the Cu Chi tunnels in Vietnam. But that wasn't enough. They had fewer courses than most faculty. People noticed things. They had to lead a major trip, Meghan told them. And not a walk around town, not a mere bus ride. A major trip.

"Whatever you need," Beckmann told her.

"Wherever Beckmann leads, I follow," Will Post added.

And now India. In the days before they landed, it was made clear that India was the voyage's main event. Advice and warnings proliferated. The pre-port session, with all its dos and don'ts, was opera-length. Anyone would have to wonder what a thoughtful well-turned-out Indian would think of Semester at Sea's preparation for his homeland. Take the training and weaponry of a WWII spy parachuted into occupied France with a map, a code, a list of contacts, a pistol, a first aid kit, and a vial of poison. Combine that with a slide show gallery of hovels, temples, dances, next slide, a few shots of Gandhi, next slide, growing middle class, next slide, overpopulation, next slide, beggars, sacred cows. Throw in medical cautions about meat, fruit, water, dogs, beggars, touts, and, somewhere in all this, by the way, three major religions, five thousand years of art and history, and, of course, the Taj Mahal.

The field trip catalog, which no one accused of candor, admitted that Beckmann and Post were assigned to a rough trip, crowded with travel by bus, plane, train, and rickshaw with late night arrivals and early morning departures. And, in addition to the usual strictures about signing people in and out and off of tours, carrying a phone and a medical kit, it turned out that no individual passenger was permitted to check luggage at airports because that might slow things down. Then again, the airline forbade liquids and gels in hand-carried luggage. What about shampoos and rinses and toothpaste and shaving cream? They were to be deposited and retrieved from oversize bags which the trip leaders were to check at one airport, pick up at the other, wrestle onto the bus, open in the lobby of the hotel, of all hotels, on the itinerary. Be flexible, the travel office kept repeating, be flexible.

"This," said Will Post, "is going to be—among other things—hell." They arrived at night at a Ramada Hotel in Delhi. Outside, the air was heavy and soiled like a pillowcase that had been slept, sweated, and drooled upon repeatedly. It was cooler in the evening, but the air didn't change: it would be waiting for them in the morning. After a few hours sleep, they were at a train station waiting for a train to Agra.

The train station fascinated Will Post in the way that the Manaus fish market had. There were passengers who waited to leave and there were people with no hope of leaving. They lived there, slept on platforms, on flattened cardboard boxes, under tattered blankets and burlap sacks, poor yet striking women, big-eyed children, wretched but beautiful, staring at the Americans. *Observe these Madonnas and their children,* Post wanted to tell the students. *Observe. Write.* Fat chance. Some snapped photos, others quickly turned away as if there were something here that they might catch. Don't get bit, hit, do it, etc., etc. A beggar whose atrophied legs angled off his torso like broken branches scooted among them on a wheeled pallet, holding out his hands. There were kids hawking water bottles, postcards, cigarettes, and matches.

In Agra, they breakfasted at the Gateway Hotel. Surely the students would have consented to relax poolside before it came time for the Taj. They wanted to have fun. Back at Chennai Airport, some of them had shouted "Spring break, Delhi!" Half a day at the hotel pool, half a day at the Taj sounded about right. But they'd been warned: there were two other visits and a bus to be boarded, headed—somewhere. Whatever. They entered and were counted. Soon they were sleeping. But this passage through India excited Beckmann: cows in the middle of a major highway, buses, lorries, trucks, bicycles, near accidents too numerous to count. Every time a faster vehicle passed slower ones, there was a near collision and someone's horn was always blowing: there weren't five seconds without a plea, a warning, a curse from the horn. Yet somehow, every bicycle or trishaw seemed to know exactly how far to move, and not an inch further, to get out of harm's way.

When the endless accidents-barely-avoided became routine, he noticed green fields, irrigation ditches, stands of trees interrupted by factories and small towns where—he would keep this to himself— he felt no impulse to linger. What did these people miss? If they went away, if they were working in Australia or studying in Canada, did they dream of this place? Did they long to be back here among these tiny-windowed concrete block houses, tin roofs, dirt paths? Could anyone from here feel homesick? And then he was reminded of how often he'd asked the same question in Ohio, passing drawn and quartered cornfields accommodating manufactured homes on postage-stamp lots.

Then he saw something that made him want to pull the cord next to his seat and, as bus leader, insist on an emergency stop so that he could share what he'd noticed with everyone. A teaching opportunity! Walk the students out to where people were digging at piles of manure, even as the cows responsible grazed nearby. The people were fussing with the manure, carefully shaping it into cow patties that were used for cooking fires and eating. Cow pies, yes, but handmade by artisans. Some were stacked like tiles, some nicely rounded like oversize chocolate chip cookies, and others, his favorites, braided and coiled like rope. This was magic, this was alchemy, shit transformed into usable art. Stop now! Get out! Welcome to India! Get your hands dirty. Observe work and art. No cameras please. Ah, but he could imagine the response. The eternal question, the shallowest and deepest: What are we doing here? Fatehpur Sikri was their first destination. He'd never heard of it. At first all he saw was what used to be buildings, lots of them, ruins on dry rocky ridges. He didn't look forward to walking up there. To his relief, his bus and Will Post's arrived simultaneously and the guide led them into smaller vans which went up to a sixteenth-century complex, part fort, part castle. A maze of paths, towers, battlements, mosques, tombs, verandahs, garnished with lawns, flowers, and a view of the world below and beyond. The Moslem emperor had spent less time in it than it took to build. An Indian King Ludwig II. The Taj Mahal, everyone knew, was a tomb. This felt like a summer place where summer never ended.

It was midday. The students were tired. If they'd had a vote—i.e., if this were a democracy, if they were treated like adults—they'd have bailed on the next stop, Agra Fort. Tumbling off the bus after an hour's ride, footing it over a bridge, through the walls, uphill on a cobblestone path, it all had the feeling of a forced march.

"How are we doing?" Beckmann asked.

"Fading, I would say," Post answered. "We're not yet half done. Too much of a good thing. Too much of a great thing."

"And the Taj is last."

"How have your students been on your bus?"

"The guide talks, the kids sleep. They haven't asked a single question. And the guide is good. It's quite sad. I'm the one answering questions. How long till we're there? Will there be toilets? An ATM? Shopping?"

"No mall?"

"No mall."

They came to the top of the fort and, once again, they were in the presence of something grand, broad gardens, royal chambers, offices, temples, halls, and a surrounding a wall that once had kept enemies out. Now it kept visitors in. After consulting with the guide, Post and Beckmann told the students they were at liberty for forty-five minutes. Then they needed to return, punctually, to this very place. Forty-five minutes seemed grotesque to Beckmann. No place so grand ought to be so brusquely treated. Some students wanted longer, others wanted to go back now, back to where there were stalls with souvenirs just outside the gate and a pair of air-conditioned buses. But this was group travel, he explained. They would have to be here, and be counted, in forty-five minutes. Check your watches, everyone.

"We try to do so much," Beckmann sighed. They'd found a shady spot where they could sit on a marble floor, their backs against a wall.

"We try," Post agreed. "There are other ways of traveling. They'll learn. They already have, some of them. Remember that kid who got kicked off after…was it Brazil? Some woman complained. You had that run-in with him."

"Bobby Rummel."

"You called the kid an 'asshole.' That's a quote. You're famous on the fifth deck. Gave you lots of street cred. One of the kids—you don't even know him—was in awe of you. It was like hearing Mr. Rogers say, 'Kiss my ass!' Anyway, that Rummel fellow is following the voyage. He'll be in Saigon. Is that loyalty or what?"

"Time's up," Beckmann sighed. Some students were already waiting where they were told to be. Others were coming, taking photos as they went. Beckmann had stopped his photography after his wife died. What was there to take a picture of? And who was there to share it with?

It was tricky counting students. Beckmann and Post did their best. The count that mattered would be in the bus, when they left. They marched down the hill, out the gates, past hawkers, onto the bus. When the last student finished haggling for postcards at the door of the bus, it was time for the final count, Post in one bus, Beckmann in the other.

One short.

Beckmann commanded the students to sit in their seats and stay in them. He started at the back of the bus, seat by seat, left and right, hoping all the time that a student, sweaty and apologetic, would come aboard.

One short. The driver had started the bus, the door was closed, everything was ready to roll. Post's bus was actually moving. Beckmann jumped out the door and waved it down.

"One short," he told him. It felt like the worst thing in the world. With Post, he returned to his bus.

"Okay," Post said. "You all sat next to someone when we started. And we asked you to learn the name of the person next to you."

"It's Melissa," said a young woman.

"Melissa…who?"

"I don't know. I think she's from Texas. Or Arizona. Wherever Tempe is."

"Okay," Post said to Beckmann. "Let's go back."

They headed into Agra Fort, against the traffic of exiting visitors. When they arrived at the gate, they stopped. They had no tickets to reenter. They waited, wondering how long they ought to stay before returning to the buses, calling the ship, and keeping their appointment with the Taj Mahal.

Then he saw her, walking toward them, crying.

"Let's go now," Beckmann said. "We'll decide what to do about this later." The student said nothing. She walked ahead of them, entered the bus, took a seat. On the way to the Taj, he glanced back and she was in lively conference with other students. No matter. He'd write a report. She'd get three hours of dock time, not more, three hours before she could get off the ship in the next port. Or nothing. It was hard to know. Or care.

They rode in silence toward the Taj Mahal. No presentation, no questions, no answers. Twenty minutes of panic had something to do with that but it was mostly about the Taj. It transcended guides and guidebooks. It was spectacular. It was also a tourist trap, and yet its beauty endured. Beckmann had visited once, years before. He was single then and he had vowed to return with the woman—he hadn't met her yet—he married. It never happened. Their travels turned toward Europe. They joked about it. They felt at home anywhere the Habsburgs had ruled. So India receded. It was only in Anna's last years that he regretted missing the Taj. He was sure he'd never return on his own. Yet here he was, tumbling off a bus, counting students, walking a gamut of tourist shops, standing in line to pass through a metal detector. Here, it was all in the visuals. Look first, talk later. Almost sexual. Post and Beckmann watched the students rush off to begin photographing things. This time, they'd been given an hour.

"Time enough for them to say 'been there, seen it, done it,'" Post said.

"They'd be two-thirds right," Beckmann responded. "I'll grant they're here. And they're seeing it, more or less. But as far as doing it goes...never..."

"Here you go again. You want to move in here?"

"No. But if I could be left behind, after they close the gates. If I had it to myself till sunrise, that would be a great gift."

"You're right," Post allowed. "A moonlit night, Jesus, it must be fine here." Now, no doubt about it, the place was jammed with as many Indians as tourists. What was it like to have something so fine in your backyard? You could visit on a whim, whenever you felt like it, as nonchalant as a walk in Central Park if you lived in Manhattan. Post and Beckmann took their time with the Taj, first exploring the gardens, then stepping up to the main building, then into the tomb itself. There were some things to deplore. The river that curved around the back, once a part of the building's elegant design, was a sewer, sluggish, weed-filled, loaded with plastic and Styrofoam. Add to that the souvenirs and security check at the entrance, and the epidemic of photography. Visitors aimed to capture the place yet it was just as likely that every click—how many thousands a day?—diminished it.

"If they check for bombs and guns as we come in," Post said, "they should check for cameras too. Leave them at the gate. The place deserves it. The purity, the elegance of it... Suppose they did it, and if they sold quality postcards and posters outside…would they still want to bring in cameras? Is it necessary to have a picture of yourself in front of the Taj?"

"People would complain," Post guessed. "They'd lose business. They'd have to search body crevices and cavities for pocket cameras."

"You're right, alas," Beckmann conceded. "But the quality of the experience would be enhanced… They'd be seeing things…with their eyes, their senses… How much stronger their memories would be. How much better to conjure a memory than search for a snapshot."

"You've got that right. Still…it's not bad is it? Right here. This minute?"

Close to the end of the designated time, they found a bench at the edge of the garden. It was, for some reason, out of the main flow of traffic and they had it to themselves. You felt you had the place to yourself and now, in the late afternoon, the white marble building was turning gold.

"The oldest cliché of travel writing," Post said, "is 'wish you were here.' Take your pick. Anyone, living or dead."

"You first…"

"My parents. Both dead. After that…there's a girl from high school I wonder about. Pathetic, huh? You?"

"Certainly, my wife," Beckmann said. "And Edith."

¤

THEY ARRIVED IN VARANASI in the late afternoon and, after a quick stop at a hotel, were immediately bundled off to the Ganges, Hinduism's holiest place. First they were on a bus, which parked near a lot filled with dozens of rickshaws. Two passengers in each, they turned into narrow streets, crowded places that assaulted every sense, the smell of smoke and exhaust, perfume and curry, music blaring, shouting, hawking, barking, beeping. Soon they lost any sense of balance, control, direction. They looked up at two- and three-story buildings, with a hopeless scramble of wires running from one to the other. How could someone attend to power here, or collect payment for it? At street level, pedestrians, cyclists, cars, and rickshaws clogged, elbowed, and cajoled their way down sidewalks where cows grazed in piles of garbage. Every life function—birth, death, getting and spending, eating and shitting—was compressed and entangled. You wondered about your students. Were they appalled? Scared? Fascinated? Or, like a kid in the backseat of a car, asking, again and again, "Are we there yet?"

They weren't there yet. Now they came to a place where the rickshaws could go no further. They crowded, pushed, and were pushed, down streets that had no room for them. The guide was far in front, the students in a long line, interrupted and delayed, that had Post and Beckmann at the end of it. No way could they take attendance here. What happened would happen. If someone got lost, so be it. Call it fatalism. Call it realism.

They were almost there. They could see darkness in the distance— the river perhaps, or its far shore. Movement slowed, three or four lines of visitors merged into one as they approached a security checkpoint, more guards, another metal detector. What a world! On the other side, they saw hundreds of worshippers and visitors sitting on steps leading down to the water, a kind of amphitheater. Behind them were buildings, with people looking down from rooftops, balconies, open windows. In front, just above the river, were priests chanting, singing, and praying. Like the Taj, it accommodated visitors who stayed for an hour—and others who might never leave. Out on the river, beyond the praying and incense, the water was a carpet of lights. They stepped into waiting boats which headed just offshore. Looking back, it felt like a landfall from another time, a sacred shore, with faith defining life and death. The lights in the water, it turned out, were little boats made of bark or dried leaves, fragile cup-size things that carried cargo of flower petals and candles. The boatmen sold them and the guide explained that these were blessings for the dead. They were all around, each one representing the life and death of someone who was loved. Right beside Beckmann, Jody Phillips was holding a little boat and sat there as if transfixed. The only movement was tears that ran down her face. No crying. Quiet tears. This from the most competent, grown-up woman on the ship.

"Are you all right?" he asked.

"No," she said. "Not right now." She lit the boat's candle and placed it in the water.

Something inside Beckmann sobbed. "I want one of those," he told the boatman. "No...two." He took them, one after the other, lit them, and gently placed them in the Ganges, watching while they flickered like fireflies on a summer night before the water and the darkness claimed them.

When it came time to go, the students were all there. The situation was so powerful, so intimidating, that no one would want to risk being left behind. Back to the rickshaws, back to the buses, back to the hotel. From a place of holiness to a place with a disco. Rise or fall?

"Anyway, we made it," Beckmann said when he and Post had counted the kids coming off the bus. "We guessed right. No one was misbehaving in a place like that."

"A miracle, no doubt about it," Post said. "I hope it stays that way. About twenty hours and back on the ship."

"We're not there yet," Beckmann said. Evening ceremonies on the Ganges were a kind of matinee. Sunrise on the river was the great event. That meant that, after a late dinner, the students would retire and set their alarms for a 4:00 a.m. return to the holy river. It was already 10:00 p.m., and, as they sat finishing their meals, emptying oversize bottles of beer, they noticed a pair of disc jockeys setting up at the end of the room, testing their equipment. Post asked them to turn it down. They obliged, grudgingly. The music was down but not out. The party would start, after they left.

¤

BECKMANN LAY IN BED waiting for sleep to find him. It kept on not showing up. But then, while he lay wide awake at 2:00 a.m., the phone rang.

"Hello, Professor. It's Tommy. I'm right down the hall in two-one-three/two-thirteen, Jody's room, and we've got a student here who's not in such good shape…"

"What's the matter?" He tried to remember Tommy. Was he the one who shared cigars with Will Post on the fifth deck?

"You just come and take a look."

He walked down the hall, rapped on Will Post's door, roused him, and proceeded down the hall to Tommy's room. By now, he'd seen every student on the ship, sorry as it was, and he knew this one, collapsed at the edge of a bathtub, alternately vomiting and comatose, was no exception. Darlene Tedrow, one of Post's favorites, utterly wrecked. What she'd been doing was drinking in the disco. Tommy had seen her there. When the disco closed, the group—which now included Semester at Sea students from another tour, staying at a nearby hotel—adjourned to drink in someone's room. Abandoned by other students as soon as she started to stagger and be sick, Darlene had evidently wandered around the hotel corridors, finally knocking and being admitted by Tommy, who'd been hanging out with Jody. They'd done what they could, patting, wiping, consoling, just waiting for her to come around. But she didn't. Now Post kneeled beside her. Talking, coaxing, lightly slapping her, "don't go to sleep," "talk to me."

"Could you go downstairs and see about getting a doctor here?" Beckmann asked Tommy. "Varanasi, India. Three in the morning. Should be a snap."

"I'll handle it," Tommy said. "It's only money." Heading out through the door, he passed Rosa Sanchez entering the room. "How's she doing?" she asked, glancing into the bathtub.

"She'll live."

"Oh. False alarm." Sanchez sounded disappointed and went back out, straight across to the room which she'd been sharing with Will Post.

Then, the mood had changed. Tommy and a doctor had taken Darlene to her room. Post had rejoined Rosa Sanchez across the hall and Professor Beckmann was alone with a woman he'd been wondering about.

"Crazy, isn't it?" she said to him.

"What do you mean?"

"That moment on the river. Launching those little boats in the water, remembering dead people."

"Yes."

"I'm glad we shared that, Professor."

"Thank you," he said. "I get it."

"And the same night, a drunk in a bathtub…"

Beckmann nodded, smiled, shrugged. "You and Tommy. I couldn't have guessed. Fine fellow. Not much of a SAS student."

"He's real smart, Professor. And, yeah, he's foolish. Still…" She gave him a certain look and he knew what was coming. She winked. "I have this feeling, Professor, that you're jealous of me and Tommy."

Beckmann was dumbfounded.

"Tell you what," she said. "I'm tired of this room. Let's sit outside." She took his hand, incredibly, and led him to a verandah with a bench that overlooked the hotel swimming pool where people sat drinking, late as it was. "About tonight," she said. "It was no accident I got into that boat with you. You lost your wife. I lost my mother." She described a tough-minded, entirely loving, totally untraveled chain-smoker, puffing away through the time she had left, talking about Jody's upcoming voyage, port to port, places she'd never seen or ever would see, not if she lived to one hundred. She wanted to accompany her daughter around the world, a wish her demise—three weeks before sailing—did not eliminate. Jody had dropped out of college to see her through her final year and when she saw those memory boats, when she'd lit and launched one, she'd whispered, "This is for you, Mom." And then she joined Beckmann in his memory of loss.

"I'm glad I could be there for you," Beckmann intoned. "And you for me."

"And besides," she said. "That Scrabble-playing buddy of yours notwithstanding, I've got this thing for you."

After a moment of silence, Jody leaned over and placed a finger on his lips as though to quiet or calm him. He felt her body against him, her hair brushing his neck, her lips on his, a deep kiss, mouths opening, tongues lingering. Then she arose and gave him a hug he'd remember.

¤

"YOU KNOW WHAT WE get paid for, what we do on a trip like this?" Will Post asked as they waited by the buses that would escort them to sunrise on the Ganges. "No, of course not. The handful of professors from Virginia make just what they'd be making back home. What's a semester's pay for them? Forty thousand? Fifty? More? The rest of us make ninety dollars a day. That's what I was making cradling an alcohol-poisoned girl in a hotel bathroom…"

"But you got the trip, Will. The cruise. And a discount on this field trip."

"Yeah. And I'll get to hear what a swell team we have on this swell voyage when I return. How the kids stand up for each other."

"There's Jody," Beckmann said. "I'd follow that girl into battle."

"Well, that would be better than coming up against her on the other side."

"There are others. Your writers. And those rascals on the smoking deck. That boy Tommy."

"Amen. Still, it was a rough night."

"Granted," Beckmann said.

"Remember, back in Ghana, Darlene said she wanted to be a travel writer? Like me? Like this Amelia Bligh character? Well, I felt she was pushing it a little. And I pushed back. I was tougher on her writing than I needed to be. Maybe I hurt her. I called on her in class, suggested she needed to get out, mix, mingle, take chances instead of sitting around being observant. That Emily Dickinson act won't work for her. So that's what happened last night. My fault."

"It may be a lesson."

"Maybe. But listen. Favor time. I don't want to write her up for drinking. Could we just say—I know I'm asking a favor here—that it was food poisoning?"

¤

AT 4:00 A.M. THEY watched groggy students climb aboard their buses. In a little while they would count them. Sleep deprived and exhausted, Beckmann was nonetheless exhilarated. When was the last time that he'd been out and about before dawn? How many years since he'd been up all night for any purpose? He'd have to go back to his undergraduate years, when he "pulled all-nighters" and, close to dawn, felt the way he felt now: light-headed, off-balance, oddly receptive and in a mood to welcome sunrise. Again and again, happiness found him, found the grieving widower, distracted him from—what was the phrase again?—ending his life on this voyage. That was impossible now. Out of the question. He couldn't inflict a second Williamson Turn on this voyage. That sweet, smart woman Carla Hutchinson had aced him out. She'd gotten to where she wanted to go, ahead of him.

They marched the same alleys as the night before. Less neon now, less music than before. They smelled bread frying, they passed sacred cows asleep on the sidewalks and vendors pouring tea into clay cups like tiny flower pots. No ceremonies now, none of the lights and color of the night before. They stepped into a small flotilla of boats and proceeded downstream. A gray morning, so far. Last night's magic was gone. Run-down modern buildings shared the riverbank with massive older palaces, some converted into flop houses for backpackers, others expensively restored. "That's where Goldie Hawn stays," the guide said, "and over there, George Harrison once visited." People were in the river, some bathing, soaping and scrubbing, some praying, some—women—pounding laundry on rocks. Upstream, piles of wood awaited cremations and burnt, ashy patches testified to previous ceremonies.

Post was still testy. When they went ashore to a place where dozens of people were practicing yoga, a student asked him if it was okay to piss in the Ganges. Post directed him to a nearby wall. Another kid asked about swimming in the Ganges. Post said no. Near the cremations, some students jeered and heckled, passing a bottle of vodka. Spring break!

"Listen, my friend," Beckmann said to Post. They were walking through back alleys, past beggars, touts, and a snake charmer. The people who approached them were hustlers. The ones who were not ignored them. "Listen," Beckmann repeated. "All you saw is real, all you say is true. But what a place! Isn't that a gift? These places where you come to die, to leave your body and ascend to the ultimate? The holy river is polluted. Does that make it less holy?"

"And your point?"

"Were you expecting the Garden of Eden here? Look, we all talk about going from the sublime to the ridiculous. Especially on this voyage. As if it's a paradox, a contradiction, a bit of a joke that life is playing on us. You know better. They're entangled, the ridiculous and sublime. A fouled, blessed river. Sacred cows rummaging among soiled diapers. Those aren't contradictions…"

"Okay, okay, Professor. You're a wise man."

"The wise man isn't quite finished. The students are part of the complexity. I wouldn't want to be here without them. I wouldn't want to be here by myself."

¤

AND NOW, THE LAST airport, the flight back to Chennai, the return to the ship. Beckmann heard a kid talk about getting photographed atop a camel *and* an elephant! At the same hotel! For once it wasn't necessary to count the students. They'd surrounded him as he handed out boarding passes and when his hands emptied, the counting was over. But one bit of business remained for the so-called wise man, a moment of grace and forgiveness. It was about the student who'd kept them waiting at Fort Agra. He'd avoided her and she, no doubt, had avoided him. He had some people to write up and so did Post: students drunk and hooting near the cremation site. Darlene's food poisoning took her to a hospital where the doctor proposed to keep her for three days. She'd miss the ship's departure from Chennai. That meant she'd have to fly to Singapore and someone would have to volunteer to stay with her in Varanasi and then accompany her back to Chennai. Then Tommy had a talk with the doctor and she was released. Compared to this, Melissa's infraction—tardiness returning to a bus on a field trip—seemed slight. He found her among a group of other students and called her off to one side.

"I've been thinking about what happened back at Fort Agra," he said. "And I wanted to tell you that I've decided not to write you up."

He'd expected a nod, a note of thanks. But, no, she flared up. She was angry. She'd been angry and she stayed that way.

"Write me up? For what?"

That was the end of it. He had forgiven her, but she had not forgiven him for abandoning her inside the fort. One short. He was still one student short.

VI.

TOWARD THE STRAITS

"COULD YOU PLEASE COME down to my office?" Leo Underwood asked. His call came to Meghan at 3:30 a.m. She headed down to the fifth deck corridor to Leo's office. The ship got spooky in the wee hours: long empty hallways and staircases, empty classrooms, and, outside, decks where you had the ocean to yourself. Whenever you met someone at that hour—and the ship was never entirely asleep—you felt startled and guilty. What was anyone doing up at four in the morning? Tonight, in the distance, she saw Beckmann at the railing. Deep in thought, she guessed. She let him be and headed to the fifth deck.

¤

LEO WAS SITTING BEHIND his desk in a bathrobe. Right across from him was Will Post.

"I had a dream," Leo said. "Or something."

Meghan glanced at Post. Why were they there? Both of them. She rolled her eyes. He shrugged. Leo didn't notice. He turned away, faced the deck outside of his cabin, the sea beyond. He wanted to be heard, not seen. Meghan fussed a bit at her desk.

"We'll be going into the Malacca Strait. And you know how it is, the students are all excited about pirates. They make a party of it, staying up all night, scaring each other. You notice the tension. Just the name of the place spooks people. Pirates? Hey, sometimes I wonder if we should have some locals come out and circle the ship, get sprayed with water, return home a little richer, a little wetter. Not a bad idea, not at all. Kids are on deck, it's like they're waiting for Santa Claus and his reindeer. You hate to disappoint them. Well, anyway, the ship's moving fast and the crew is on the alert. They've got high-powered fire hoses and searchlights. Well, I wake up before dawn because the ship's horn is blasting, the way it does on a river—you heard it on the Amazon—when some crappy little barge full of gravel doesn't make way for us. An angry motorist–type sound. But this time, it keeps coming. Like nobody's listening to our warning. I get up. It's dark. I head for the bridge, and before I get there, I notice that the engines have stopped. We're slowing down and in a few minutes we won't be moving at all. On the bridge, the captain just gestures at the monitor that shows the shape of the Strait—narrowing, like closing jaws— Malaysia on one side, Indonesia on the other… Indonesia, that's where trouble would come from. The monitor sees into the dark. And what I see on the monitor is dots, eight of them, four in front of us, two on the port side, two on the starboard. That's on the screen. I check out the window and all I see is points of light. Boats in front aren't moving, the ones on the side are edging closer.

"I ask the captain what he thinks. He doesn't know, but just then he orders all passengers into their cabins and behind closed doors. I wonder how many students are going to do as he says. If I were one of them, I've got to tell you, I wouldn't want to miss this, whatever it is.

'Who are they?' I ask. 'The captain doesn't know. Can't we just keep on moving?' I ask. 'Not until we know what we're dealing with,' he firmly tells me. 'They could be disabled ships, a medical emergency, a breakdown.' 'Eight emergencies,' I ask? 'Eight breakdowns?' I'm scared already. And now I'm scaring myself with what I say. 'Searchlights?' I ask. He agrees. I'm scaring myself, worrying about what I'll see, when we go poking into the darkness. So a pair of lights snap on and pan across the water, toward the boats in front and the ones that are close, real close to the side. They're not fishing boats, no nets and floats and rust and crud. They're not exactly alike, but they're all modern and they look fast. There's no one in sight. Where are they? Who are they? The wheelhouses are dark and the decks are empty. 'Let's get out of here,' I say. 'We can't run them down,' the captain answers. 'They're empty,' I argue. 'I don't think so,' he says. 'They're coming closer.' 'We could crush those ships." 'We'll wait," the captain says, in a way that tells me to back off, it's his ship. Now the eastern sky is going purple. And we wait, I wait, the captain and the crew and, forget the warning, there's passengers out on deck. Nobody wants to miss this. I hear another announcement, 'that this is not a drill.' No shit, Sherlock. Nobody goes back inside. What are we going to do? Give them three hours of dock time in Singapore?

"A pinkish-yellow sky now. And, all at once, there are people in the boats, four or five in each of them, dressed in T-shirts, shorts, and slacks, probably Indonesians and they're holding… What are they holding? 'Those are grenade launchers,' says one of the ship's officers who's from Croatia and therefore is in a position to know. 'One or two of them on each boat. I like their chance, I have to say, against our big high-powered hoses. Are the students moving away, inside, under cover? Hell no. They're zooming in, they're photographing. 'Get on the radio,' I tell the captain. 'I think we'll see about that,' he replies. He doesn't want the world rushing to his rescue, not on his watch, not yet.

"'Look there,' someone says, pointing at one of the boats that's close to the ship. We see someone standing in the bow. He's different. White slacks, white shirt and…oh yeah…white skin. Looks like one of our kids, some rich kid who'd missed sailing and hired someone to catch up with us and put him aboard. I wouldn't put it past some of our kids. Like that Bobby Rummel character we let off in Cape Town. A gangly, rumpled-looking fellow, leisurely and disheveled, like a movie drug dealer. He points to one of the lifeboats dangling off the fifth deck. It's clear he wants us to lower it, send it over, take him aboard. The captain takes a megaphone. 'You come alone,' he says. 'Unarmed.' The guy nods. And then he by God hoists a megaphone of his own. 'No radio transmissions,' he says. The captain nods. 'Agreed.' And he didn't even ask me. The captain asks me if I know the guy. I don't. Everyone watches the lowering of the lifeboat, its short voyage, the man in white nonchalantly jumping aboard, chatting up the boat driver, waving at the kids on board and, would you believe, getting a cheer back, even though at the moment more than a dozen grenade launchers are pointed in their direction! The two of us wait on the fifth deck as the lifeboat gets hoisted into view. Before it's secured, the guy jumps out.

"'Good morning, sir,' he says to the captain, not to me. 'You'll be on your way momentarily, captain, no worries. You look worried though…' They couldn't quite sink the ship, but they could wreck it without coming aboard, shell it, set it on fire. And if they came aboard…God knows. 'It speaks well of you that you're worried," he goes on. "But I promise you, in ten minutes, I'll be gone.' 'So what do you want?' asks the captain. 'Him.' He's looking at me. 'Him,' he repeats."

Leo's hands covered his face. Meghan had seen him on bad, brooding days, but never so undone. How different from the veteran of fourteen trips around the world, the man who walked the ship with the confidence that he could handle anything. "Just let me talk to the guy," he'd say, "just give me fifteen minutes." The guy could be a disgruntled senior passenger, an expelled student, a sluggish immigration official, angry hotelier, pompous consul, he could always find an angle. Not now.

Leo had a bad dream, Meghan thought. *Maybe someone wanted him to have it. And*—she thought—*maybe he was the one who wanted to have that dream.* She felt sorry for Leo, felt sympathy. And something else: suspicion. If only she had been called, she'd have allowed Leo's need to confess, to confide. But Will Post? That changed things. What happened in that office, was it a confession? Or a press conference?

Loud and late and rude, someone was pounding on the door to the executive dean's office.

"It's open!" Leo called out.

"What on earth is going on here?" asked the ship's captain, Jeffrey Holden. "Is this your idea of a joke, Underwood?"

"What joke?"

"This monologue…this nightmare about a fleet of pirates blocking us in the Malacca Straits!" He turned to Meghan. "Is that thing off now?"

Meghan flipped a switch. "Is now."

"Shit! Shit!" Formally presented by Leo at the start of the voyage, immaculately turned out in white uniform, Captain Holden was courteous and formal, approachable, but rarely approached. But now he ran amok.

"It was on the public address system, just now, the whole sick, self-serving thing and I guarantee that a rapt audience of passengers, several hundred of them, heard it all! Who turned it on? Who left it on?"

"Not me," Meghan said. "I made my evening announcements after dinner and turned it off. Absolutely."

"And it came to life on its own? My God! Go out there and you'll see every seat in the computer lab taken and dozens of people waiting in line. God knows about Skype and cell phones. They're excited, they're scared, you name it. How did it happen?"

"The cleaning crew?" Leo speculated.

"You ought to know better than that. Shame on you for blaming my crew. A good thing the microphone didn't pick *that* up or you'd be persona non grata. 'The butler did it!' Please. More important than who fiddled with the public address system, what happened…is *why* it happened. *Why* did this happen?"

No one replied.

"Turn the damn thing on again," he said to Meghan, who flipped the switch.

"This is the captain. You will not be surprised to hear from me. What you heard tonight was a deranged monologue, a bizarre and puzzling bedtime story from our executive dean. It was shared— possibly by accident—with all of you. What you heard was a fantasy. It is fictitious. It is false, false, false. Seven ships per minute pass through the Malacca Straits and tomorrow—as a dozen times before—we shall be among them, arriving on time in Singapore. Please advise whomever you messaged. Correct your earlier reports. And plan to attend an all-passengers meeting at eight o'clock tomorrow morning in which your dean will address you."

He nodded to Meghan to flip the switch, thanked her, and turned to Leo.

"You forgot yourself, my friend."

¤

WHEN HE ENTERED THE Union after breakfast, some of the kids cheered. Some of them always would, for Leo. But the response was weak. People were waiting for something they'd never expect to see from him. An apology. A moment of regret. At least, an explanation.

"We've got a lot of world in front of us," Leo began. "Singapore, Saigon, Hong Kong, Shanghai. But I've got to talk to you about Japan."

Post leaned toward Beckmann. "What's up with this? Another day at the office?"

"Wait," Beckmann said. Leo was describing the tsunami that had hit Japan, a devastated city, a leaking nuclear plant, poison water, radiated clouds.

"So a decision will be made about Japan. That's for Charlottesville, of course. But I'm asking all of you to choose where you want to go. I can't guarantee they'll do what you recommend. But I'll let them know. The choice is between Korea, the Philippines, and Taiwan. There will be a box down on the counter outside the field trip office on the fifth deck. Think about it, talk about it, cast your vote and I'll pass it on…"

"That means they've already decided," Post whispered. "Say 'sayonara' to Japan."

Then it was over, so quickly that Leo was almost gone before an audience that had been startled by his abrupt closure remembered to clap a little.

"It's getting weird," Post said.

"Meghan came up to me this morning suggesting we have an intervention. She thinks Leo is losing it."

"Well, I can see that."

"That monologue? At the end it's all about someone coming after him. He's still the star of the show. So what do you think about an intervention?"

"I think," Beckmann said, "that he won't listen."

"I agree."

¤

SINGAPORE WAS A ONE-DAY stop and Beckmann regretted that. He'd visited three or four times over the years. It had been about scholarship at the beginning. Singapore's history involved colonial, imperial, federated, and independent chapters. And, without entirely shedding its past, it became a world-class city. Beckmann savored the place and resented that his time there was limited to twelve hours. He'd sat through lethargic global studies sessions which reprised dated yarns of campaigns against graffiti, long hair, chewing gum. After a while, Edith Stirling had heard enough. Without consulting him, she approached the people in the field trip office who owed him a favor after what he'd dealt with in India. Now he sat in the auditorium, hearing himself introduced, in the laziest possible way, as a professor who needed no introduction.

"I am going to talk a little about a place I love," he began, "know and love. I have listened to accounts and descriptions of Singapore that have been offered to you and they..." He stopped. Choosing his words carefully and, at the same time, signaling that they were carefully chosen. "There's a bit more to the story." But tactfulness might not save him. No matter. He was in the sort of public dispute he'd avoided all his life and he sensed the audience perking up as if it sniffed controversy. He was surprised to find that he was enjoying himself. He gave the history of Singapore, the tale of a small island that had found itself abruptly evicted from its union with Malaya in the 1960s and, with little land, no off-shore resources, not even sufficient water, it had turned itself into a great city. It was not a western democracy. But its leadership, though authoritarian, had been smart and honest so far. And they had an advantage over the folks in Washington: the ability to plan long-term. He described the places he'd seen in the seventies, colonial buildings, playing fields, mansions mingling with seedy waterfronts, crowded Chinese and Indian neighborhoods. It appealed, he admitted, to the young man in him: it was quaint and dangerous and, like a certain kind of woman, it had a past.

He looked up and saw students glancing at each other, gesturing. *Who knew,* they seemed to ask, *that Beckmann was ever young?*

¤

EARLY ON POST HAD learned that all interviews came down to one question that, if asked and answered, obviated the need for any further interrogation: "What does it feel like to be you?" With Leo, Post didn't have to ask even that question. This morning Meghan joined them, for a reason it turned out. But her announcements came first. Six of them, including a rehearsal of *The Vagina Monologues.*

"Whatever happened to *Our Town*?" Post wondered. No one answered. Meghan changed the subject.

"There's something I don't get about what you said the other night," she offered.

"Please," Leo said, shaking his head, covering his ears. "I've been shagging phone calls all day. They're having a special board meeting in Charlottesville to consider my conduct."

"No, listen, this is different. Your story...at the end the man in charge of the attack wasn't a local pirate. He wasn't an obvious terrorist. He was a white man who came aboard and asked for you, by name. Like he had a score to settle, some kind of revenge. I hate to say this because they say it all the time but...it was all about you."

"Okay," Leo said. "It was. It is. You remember that kid I put off? Bobby Rummel?"

"Sure." She could have added more about Bobby and herself. But then the conversation would not have been about Leo.

"He wasn't the first. There's some people who don't remember me so fondly, good as I was about making fuckwits feel better about themselves. It scares me. It shouldn't, but it does. Listen to this. About twenty years ago—that's two ships back—on the Universe Explorer. There's a Bobby Rummel type, a rich kid, kind of smart-ass and not much of a student. None of those were hanging crimes, then or now."

"And then?"

"We had an interport lecturer join the ship in India. A student at the National University of Singapore, an Indian woman, and…well… she had it."

"You're losing me."

"It all came together. The figure, the hair, the eyes. Bollywood. Add to that, crisp British English. Class act. And this guy was a true smart-ass. Even later, when I kicked him off, he always had a smart remark. I told him he was gone and he asks, 'Is this what they call a Singapore Sling? On the house?'"

Leo paused and stared out to sea. There was land on both sides of them, Malaysian and Sumatran coasts, and a convoy of ships ahead and behind them.

"It was his word against hers," Leo resumed. "It happened in Singapore, in her apartment…a place the family gave her while she attended school. Kid came back to the ship drunk that night. And an hour or so later, she followed him."

"She didn't call the police?"

"She didn't want that. But she wanted him punished. I heard her out. I'm a good listener. I promised I'd take care of it. And she called me out. 'Thanks so much for the sympathy,' she says. But sympathy wasn't on the table. Wow, she was tough. And she was hot. I can still see her.

Extraordinary. I'm thinking, 'this girl is no kind of victim. She's going to be running the world.' Didn't go for my usual I'll-look-into-it-trust-me spiel. 'Justice must be done and it must be seen to be done,' she announces. 'Now.' Or she'll call the police. And that would only be the first of many calls. Have I mentioned this girl's family was important? Both parents were lawyers. Put that together with Singapore's tough reputation back then. Zero tolerance for juvenile delinquency."

"You're telling me you had no choice."

"That's right. I didn't. But that doesn't mean I wouldn't have made the same choice, anyway. Innocent or guilty, the kid is shit-out-of-luck in Singapore. And if I don't do something, it might be years before they let the ship back in. So I tell her that if she is at the gangplank at ten the next morning, she'll see her pal and his luggage coming ashore. And, like that, it was over. She'd gotten what she wanted. She nodded and walked away."

"And then?"

"Not so fast. About that girl… I don't know if she wanted the kid punished because of what had happened, or whether she wanted a second helping. Sorry if I sound like a heel. That's what I didn't know. Still don't. It wasn't his first screw-up. He didn't protest, he didn't press me. I was all ready to tell him I was doing him a favor. That's what I told myself. It didn't matter what went down with him and the girl, who curtsied, who bowed. He was finished on the ship and he was finished in Singapore. If the girl brought charges, he'd be in court a long time, and he wouldn't win."

"So off he went?"

"What a scene. Down he marches, a couple buddies helping him carry his stuff and all along the railing girls shouting 'we love you, we love you' and he's waving, blowing kisses and off he goes…Bobby Rummel stuff."

"I'm just curious. Was the complainant there?"

"There was a car parked near the fence. I saw her in it. It started up when Bobby walked that way. And…swear to God…I don't know…I can't see around corners, kiddo. Whether they walked past each other, glaring, hating. Or he hopped into the backseat and they started making out."

"You never heard of him after that?"

"Except at night. In my dreams."

"Well, I've got a question," Meghan said. "I didn't leave the mike open. That's the surest thing you know. And it certainly wasn't the crew member who cleans the room." She left it at that. Not an accusation. More like a chance for a confession, a shot of forgiveness.

"I didn't hear a question," he responded, studying her the way a father might regard a kid who just stopped loving him completely. "Accidents will happen," he said.

Later in the voyage, long afterward, Post wondered about what happened next in the office where he sat with Leo and Meghan. "Accidents will happen," Leo had said. A bit of a lie. An agreement not to take things any further, not to press. "Accidents will happen." Amiable closure. Leo found a bottle of cognac, poured three generous shots, and proposed a toast. "Here's to accidents," he said, a left-handed admission, Post thought, that what happened was not an accident. What came next should have arrived a month or at least a week later. That moment with the cognac was congenial. There was no trust in the room. That was gone. But there was congeniality, familiarity. They'd have settled, all three of them, for that. But then they heard an alarm blasting and the phone rang, bringing a curt summons to the bridge.

Accidents will happen, Post thought as he watched Leo jump out of his chair and rush out the door, unmistakably eager to confront his date with destiny.

"No, it's not your terrorists," the captain snapped. "No speedboats, no grenades, no white-clad villain like the one in your nocturnal emission. We're hours away from the Malacca Straits. Still...have a look."

Maybe it was a fishing boat without nets or a coastal freighter sans shipping containers. What they saw was packed with two dozen people, impossible to tell passengers from crew. The ship was dead in the water.

"It's half an hour from sinking," the captain said. "Maybe not that long. You may have noticed that with the decks awash, and there's smoke—can't you smell it?—coming from below."

"What are they going to do?" Leo asked.

"There's nothing they can do," the captain answered, "but drown or burn."

"Who are they?" Leo wondered.

"We haven't been introduced," the captain snapped. Post could tell Leo was pissing him off. The jolly giant hug-meister was stumbling. "We have no choice. We must take them aboard."

"We couldn't just...throw over some lifejackets..." Leo stopped. "Oh shit... Charlottesville is going to freak." He fell silent. In waters so full of ships, why had the *MV Explorer* been chosen? He knew why, though. None of those tankers bound for China would bother to stop. Shit...

"Hearing no objection," the captain said. "We'll take them aboard."

"But keep them in back, on the fourth deck," Leo stirred himself to say. "I don't want them wandering around the ship or mixing with our passengers."

By now, the word was out. Students and faculty lined the deck, cameras ready. No classes. The ship that gave its passengers the world was getting something back: company. They watched two of the ship's lifeboats getting lowered into the water. The ship's doctor—don't get bit, eat shit, do it, etc.—sat in the lifeboat, a nurse in the other. Both wore masks and gloves. So did the lifeboat crew. The visitors weren't fishermen: there were women and children among them. And there was something the matter with them: they lurched awkwardly, staggered around in soiled trousers. The crew struggled to hoist them into the lifeboat. And, even before the rescuers made it back to the *MV Explorer*, the ship without a name or a number, a flag or a radio antenna, rolled on its side like a moribund hospital patient seeking sleep or death and slipped beneath the waves.

With the nick-of-time rescue complete, a huge cheer arose. "We did it!" "God bless America!" Or—as at the Olympics—"USA! USA!" Everyone felt good about themselves.

¤

CAPTAIN HOLDEN, THE SHIP'S doctor, the dean of the faculty, the dean of students, and a single crewman who spoke Bahasa cowered in Leo's office. Will Post was there and no one seemed to mind. Meghan was there too and nobody noticed.

"So what did they say?" Leo asked a crew member who usually was seen behind the purser's desk, making sure the students turned in their passports when they returned to ship.

"They are saying they are from Thailand." Post heard something mechanical in the man's delivery, something that said he was merely conveying information, not evaluating it. "Sir, they are Muslims. Southern Thailand, plenty trouble for many years. Some Muslim people only wanting left alone. Others want more from Thai government. Others maybe want separate country. There is much fighting. Killing. With some children…" He made a chopping motion. "They cut off heads. The army is coming. And these people run away."

"Where were they headed?" Leo asked.

"Indonesia."

"A Muslim country," Leo exclaimed. "Bingo. If we get into the Straits we can drop them off…"

"Is that so?" said Captain Holden. "Save it." Now he turned to the doctor.

"These people are not well," the doctor said. "Vomit and blood and stool all over the place. It might be food poisoning. It might be something much worse. I recommend clean water and bland food. Antibiotics. But these are stopgaps."

"All right," the captain said. "Keep them on the fourth deck, in back. Access no further than the restroom. I want them watched. No contact—zero—with passengers, except for medical personnel. Run some hoses back there so they can wash. Give them blankets to sleep on. Umbrellas and tarps."

Then it changed. The dean of students noted that some of the kids wanted to be helpful. They felt this was what service was. That stuff they did onshore, cuddling orphans and weeding in gardens at public schools, was disappointing. And then the dean of the faculty glimpsed a learning opportunity. Perhaps some of the new shipmates could make an appearance in the global studies courses.

"Jesus Christ," Leo said. "They're a bunch of puking, bleeding refugees. Not a cultural troupe. They offer to sing and juggle, we'll let you know. Meanwhile…how long do we keep them? Where do we take them? They were headed to Indonesia. Tuck them in there and let them wade ashore to freedom. Throw in some T-shirts, boxed lunches, pills, whatever. And we'll be on our way to Singapore. Wham, bam, thank you, SAS."

"No," Captain Holden responded. *He was pulling rank,* Post thought. His anger at what he called Leo's "nocturnal emission" had changed things. "What you propose is an unauthorized and covert stop in a sovereign nation with consequences for this ship and for me."

"Who'll know?" Leo asked.

"*Who'll know?* I should think you can answer your own question, Dean Underwood. Your night chat is well-known. That was just a speech. This is a landing. Hundreds of cameras. The word 'viral' applies."

"It already does," Meghan said.

"What are you talking about?" asked Leo.

"Gone viral. Anna Cather called. It's crazy back there. They say there's Ebola on board. Anna says this could be the end of us. Not just this voyage, either."

"Doctor?"

"No word of Ebola in Malaysia. I checked before the voyage and I checked again. They have tested for it from time to time and those tests may have caused some confusion."

"Viral." Leo said. "Odd, the word for a mega-hit on the internet suggests a disease?" Next he took a deep breath. Then exhaled, like a prisoner hearing a verdict and accepting it. "Fine. Take them to Singapore. It's the right decision."

¤

THAT EVENING THE EXPLORER sailed undisturbed through the Straits of Malacca. Some students still hoped for pirates but the refugees had preempted their interest. Beckmann and Post were drinking in the faculty lounge. Suddenly they heard Leo on the public address system.

"Listen carefully everyone," he said. "The authorities in Singapore inform us that our ship will be placed in quarantine when we arrive. We'll be confined aboard until public health has evaluated our situation. That includes our guests and all passengers. When they clear us, we can go ashore. But our guests will not be admitted. They'll be with us awhile. We're working on our options. That's all."

"This is huge," Post said. "What are we supposed to do? Go back to Diego Garcia? Drop them off at Guantánamo?"

"They ought to be able to work something out," Beckmann responded.

"'Ought' doesn't come into it." Then they saw Darlene Tedrow tapping on the glass that separated her from the faculty lounge.

"I haven't seen you since India. I'm ashamed."

"I know what you're trying to do. Too bad about the food poisoning."

"The what?"

"That's what we reported. Not drinking."

"I thought I was in big trouble."

"One condition. You will be in trouble if you don't give me an account—and it better be terrific—of your adventure. Deal?"

She smiled at him. Lovely and rare. "Deal. Something else. A tip. Go up to the seventh deck. Now."

¤

WITH ITS SWIMMING POOL, bar, pizza-and-hamburger counter, and assortment of weights and mats, the seventh deck was a kind of student union. The two professors rarely visited. But tonight belonged to the refugees.

They were huddled down below. You could smell them. Urine, excrement, vomit. The world the voyagers had glimpsed on shore, the life of hunger and hovels, had come to visit. Some students waved, shouted, photographed. That's how it started. The people down below were unresponsive, though. They were kind of disappointing. And now the word was out. They were—so it was learned online— Thai Muslim, involved in conflict, and just recently some Christian children had been beheaded.

Now, the students divided. Some tossed towels, soap, T-shirts, or slippers down below, waving and gesturing kindly. Then there was food smuggled in from supper. Apples and bananas that were gently tossed and sometimes caught. But then another group of students turned against intruding jihadi murderers. "Feed the monkeys!" cried one of them, promptly slapped by Jody Phillips. But now food wasn't being gently tossed, it was being aimed and hurled in anger: chunks of pizza, fish, dinner rolls. A couple of guys assumed a front-of-urinal stance.

"Can't you two guys do something?" Jody Phillips demanded. Her anger included them. "Or are you just going to sit at the bar, finishing your drinks?"

Post slid off his stool, Beckmann at his side, both wondering what they would do when they got to the railing.

"Hold on!" someone shouted. It was Leo and a half dozen white-clad ships officers and some of the impeccably, impenetrably polite waiters—Jamaicans and Filipinos—who cleared tables and poured water three times a day.

"Get away from the railing!" Leo shouted. "You don't move now, you're going home from Singapore."

They didn't move. They consulted. That was easy to see. Taking their time, staying put.

"Did you not hear me?" Leo shouted. "Was it something I said?"

"You've already said a lot," one of the kids shouted. "Too much." Like the others at the railing, his back was turned to Leo. Hard to know who was speaking.

"The bar is closed," Leo said. "Seventh deck is closed."

"What is this shit?" someone asked. "We paid for this cruise."

"It's a voyage."

"It's a crock of shit." The kids stayed at the railing. Sullen, stupid, and a little bit brave. Post and Beckmann were astonished. It turned out that they were both thinking the same thing. It was a kind of mutiny. And God knows what went into it, what mix of boredom and hugging, anger and pride?

"Those people you were throwing garbage at and getting ready to piss on are poor and homeless and sick," Leo continued. "We don't know with what. But they tell me folks have been testing for Ebola in Malaysia. I'm not saying anybody has it. But I'd move away from that railing if I were you, and off this deck."

That did it. The troublemakers moved away from the railing, past the swimming pool, past the bar, out the door. The bar was closing and it would stay closed for a while but Leo told the bartender that two professors could stay.

"Jesus, Leo," Post said. "You know they're heading straight for their computers with this Ebola thing."

"It's already out. I've heard from Charlottesville."

"But why'd you do it?" Post persisted.

"You should know. I wanted to scare them."

"But you must know…there'll be a shit-storm."

"Not my first," Leo said. "I've always been a sucker for violent weather."

¤

Soon the place was empty. Holding beers, the two professors walked toward the railing. It was night, but a few light bulbs dangling from table umbrellas showed people sitting quietly. Some of them were sleeping. A baby cried. The deck was covered with the remnants of what might have been a campus food fight. An old man picked up a banana. Pizza remained untouched.

"Look at that," Post said, pointing to some white squares on the deck. "Hake. They didn't eat the hake."

VII.
SINGAPORE

T HE NEXT FEW DAYS were going to be strange. Beckmann stood on deck as the pilot met them miles offshore and guided them toward—but not all the way into—port. They could see the berth that was waiting for them. Meanwhile another boat brought out a dozen officials, doctors, and nurses. Declining breakfast as though it amounted to an attempted bribe, they proceeded directly to where the refugees were kept. With the seventh deck off limits, no one could see what they were doing. That was when an odd combination of anger and boredom kicked in. People who'd booked costly field trips from Saigon to Cambodia or from Hong Kong to the Great Wall worried about missing their flights, losing their money. Was their lateness an act of God? Or was Leo Underwood playing God?

You couldn't see much of Singapore from where the plague ship—as they now called it—was anchored off Sentosa Island. But he at least could picture—almost taste—the nearby city. What was worse, being so close to a city you were fond of or not getting to see it for the first time? He turned to Edith. They were sitting on the deck outside his cabin: at anchor, there was no wind to worry about.

"There's something to be learned from being in quarantine," he said.

"This had better be good," she said.

"It's a revenge. Or a reward. We picked up those boat people, gave them a bit of space. We confined them on deck four. So far and no further. Look but don't touch. Now we know what they felt like. We contemplate Singapore. A city we cannot enter. We feel what they felt: on the outside looking in."

"I don't see people learning much," Edith said. "But that doesn't mean you're wrong. Perhaps we deserve it. All of us."

¤

IN THE LATE AFTERNOON, the Singaporean health team departed. Their day was over. But the ship's ordeal continued. The schedule was filled by movies, an open mic comedy night, various venues for counseling and reflection. The computer center was jammed. Parents were getting into the act, outraged at Charlottesville. Outraged at Leo. The following morning, while the Singaporeans were surely testing the swabs, stool, and blood they'd harvested, the ship waited through the afternoon and into the evening. All this dead time. It was an opportunity to write, to make plans, to think. Beckmann confronted all sorts of decisions. Edith? Return to college? Retirement? And, oh yes, death? What better time and place to sort things out? Instead he played Scrabble. Reports of insubordination, vandalism, food fights found their way to Will Post, who passed them along. Then, even as they totaled their Scrabble points, a pair of naked students—both of them males—streaked through the lounge.

"Okay, everybody." It was Leo at last, on the public address system. "You've been cleared to enter Singapore as of eight a.m. tomorrow morning. Actually…you can leave the ship this evening right after we dock."

You could hear cheering from out on deck, from the bar in the faculty lounge. Beckmann wondered what kind of cheer arose on the fourth deck.

"Just remember to be back on ship at eight p.m. tomorrow," Leo continued. "Now, just one more thing. Our guests have been cleared to leave. They're not in perfect shape but they received advice and drugs, as a courtesy from the ship. No Ebola. But they have not and will not be admitted to Singapore."

Beckmann had foreseen this. What he hadn't expected was the sense that everyone on board was thinking the same thing, one cartoon cloud of great worry covering everyone: do we have to take them back to San Diego?

"Authorities on Batam, an Indonesian island just across from Singapore, have agreed to accept our guests. We'll leave tomorrow morning after breakfast and return here around three p.m. If any of you wish, you may make that trip over and take a chance to say goodbye. That's up to you."

Fat chance of that, Beckmann thought.

"One last thing," Leo said. "I realize that some of you have parents flying to Singapore. Maybe they're already there. Please remember that there was no Ebola. None. Semester at Sea has conveyed this to your parents but some of them have gotten attached to the idea of taking you off this ship. That would be a mistake."

¤

AT NOON ON THEIR one and only day in Singapore, Meghan sat in a patio at Raffles Hotel—"a venerable pile," Leo called it, reminiscing about the run-down, funky, charming place that Raffles used to be. Now it had been renovated, reincarnated, and embalmed, loaded with boutique-y shops. Still, Leo made a point of returning: you paid your respects, even if that meant paying more than twenty dollars for a Singapore Sling. Underwood ordered two of them and they sat in a quiet corner, as far as possible from a bar that was crowded with tourists and, alas, Semester at Sea students. They were easy to spot. And the flow of Singapore Slings, reddish and gaudy as Kool-Aid at Jonestown, just kept coming.

"Beckmann warned them," Meghan said, "about those drinks."

"A warning is like an invitation sometimes. Even from the esteemed Beckmann." Now he leaned forward. "Okay. I'm all ears. I owe you. I know you've worked hard. You've sat in on global studies. You've talked to faculty. And—shit—you can't miss hearing what students think. Meetings, petitions, there's a rebellion in the offing. So let's skip all the 'whereas' clauses and cut straight to the 'be it resolved.'"

"That's fine," she said. "Leo, I wanted to see if I could come up with something that's first-rate. Not just once-in-a-blue-moon okay, but great, reliably great. Something that would actually attract students—first-rate students—to this voyage, and end complaints."

"There you go," said Leo. "Complaints are easy."

"Especially when warranted." Then she laid it out. "Two first-rate professors in charge, captivating lecturers from different fields, economics and literature, say, history and geography, political science and religion. Not just different fields, but different attitudes. Think Siskel and Ebert, Carville and Matalin, or Buckley and Mailer. I want sparks to fly. Christopher Hitchens and Stephen Colbert. They'd argue. They'd teach the arguments. Instead of an opening dose of ideology and theory, a priori, they'd evaluate the voyage as it unfolded, react to it freshly, react to each other, a dramatic and highly-charged dialectic, thesis and antithesis. Surprise and excitement all the way... Now, the faculty. I'm proposing that everybody who applies to this voyage should—as part of their application—specify experience, knowledge, enthusiasm in at least two of the places we visit. Personal angles, on-the-ground tips. Residence and major research. I want to leave Wikipedia out of it."

"That'll reduce the pool of applicants," Leo said. As though it mattered to him.

"That'll improve the pool."

"You're probably right," he allowed. He was conceding to her, point by point, but it didn't feel as though he was with her. It was as though she were winning battles, one after the other, but not the war. But she owed it to herself to continue.

"Interport lecturers. You've had some good ones. Invite them, again and again. You and I know there are great people out there, not just academics. Especially not academics…"

"Amen to that," Leo interrupted. How he wanted to appear sympathetic!

"Journalists, businessmen, retired military. Expats of all kinds, people with great stories to tell. Enthusiasm. 'You've got to go…' 'You can't miss…' 'At all costs, avoid…'"

"So what are you doing with all this?" Leo asked. "I know you're looking for something after the voyage."

"Wait, Leo, please. Let's leave me out of it. This isn't about my employment. This is about a proposal. Up or down? Is it worth it? Does it make sense? Do you like it?" This was a crucial moment, a career maker, a life changer, Meghan knew. And yet she was bored. What had meant a lot was suddenly meaningless. Leo had gotten weird. So had the voyage. What was more, the life and death of the program no longer concerned her.

"It's impressive," he said. As if viewing a painting he wouldn't dream of hanging on his wall. Impressive. Like learning a foreign language, or losing weight.

"But…" she offered.

"But what? I said I liked it."

"There's a 'but' in the neighborhood. Let's hear it."

"I don't know if they'll buy it, or if it's worth it to them in Charlottesville. There have been suggestions before, but nothing so elaborate."

"Elaborate" was not a compliment. It suggested that she'd had too much time on her hands, had gotten carried away, lost her grip, gone too far. And—elaborate as it was, it would go the way of all the petitions and suggestions, all those heartfelt letters and hire-me thank-you notes that were like so much salt and soot, power washed off the ship's deck.

"You could write it up and send it," he added. "That kind of work could get you on board again. But if you push it—"

"Oh, hell. Forget it. I've got a question for you. A change of subject."

"Oh, hell, forgot it. Thanks for indulging me. There's something else that came in from Charlottesville. You wouldn't want to be there today."

"I never want to be in Charlottesville."

"Anna Cather called me. We talk from time to time."

"Yeah, I know."

"She's been asked…by the Trustees…to join the ship in Saigon."

"Did she say why?"

"No. She figured I'd guess what was coming. That you'd know, too."

"I do." After he said it, Leo sat quietly for a while. He glanced around Raffles, as if he wanted to take it in, to record where his control of the voyage ended. He wasn't angry, he wasn't hatching a counter-attack. This moment was about what he'd expected; it was about acceptance. It was, he probably thought, about time. "I've been thinking of Carla Hutchinson. She was about the only one who had my number. Just a few words if I hammered things up too much, went on too long, dropped a name too many. All it took was a look from her. And now I'm sorry I didn't have much time for her this trip. Just once that amounted to anything right after we'd gotten her…in her wheelchair…on board. Hoisted her up in a cargo net with a wooden flat bottom. That Sanchez woman came with her, looking like like a pro-wrestler, the nasty girl that gets pinned. 'This your last trip?' I asked. Expected her to say 'we'll see' or 'never say die' or quote that poem of Tennyson's."

"'Ulysses.'"

"Yeah. That's the one. 'Everybody leaves the ship eventually, Leo.' That's what she said. Later I wondered if she was talking about herself, going over the railing. Or was she talking about me? That's the way she was. Something she'd say would come to mind days or weeks later and you'd see a double meaning or a different meaning. *Everybody leaves the ship eventually.* And remember I took her to that restaurant in Takoradi? She talked about the voyage, about life in general, about enjoying it to the last drop like a glass of wine. Now I know that's not what she meant, at least not all. That last drop was over the railing. And she was smiling at me when she said it."

A waiter came along with more Singapore Slings, which they hadn't ordered. It was a gift—someone else was treating, the waiter said. "Who?" Leo asked, looking around.

"There's people from the ship all over the place," Meghan said. "And you're very popular these days. But look over there."

Meghan was pointing to the bar at the center of the patio. "See a former shipmate?"

"What… That's Bobby Rummel."

"Drinks are on him."

"Meghan. Damn it. What's going on? What are you doing with the likes of him?"

"Listen, Leo. He got thrown off the ship."

"You sat in on his hearing. You took notes."

"But that's not the whole story. The last few days on board, we talked a lot. Kind of connected. Know how it started? This'll interest you. After the hearing, late at night, Bobby knocks on my cabin door. I don't know what to do. Look up and down the hall hoping I'm not alone with this predator. He sees me panic. He pulls out his camera, clicks on something. It's a photo of me dressed up like a clown, like a fool. On your orders. Then he pushes delete. 'You're better than that,' he says. 'And I'm not so bad myself.' So I invite him in."

"What's he doing here?"

"Bobby's father is the principal of an international school in Jakarta. We've been going back and forth, email, Skype."

By now, Bobby Rummel was standing at the table. He made no move to sit down.

"Ready, lady?" he asked Meghan, who got out of her chair.

"See you back on the ship," she told Leo.

"Enjoy your Singapore Sling, old-timer," Bobby added.

¤

A MEMORABLE EVENING, WILL Post thought. Beckmann at his best in Singapore. Like a seventy-year-old veteran blasting a home run on old-timers' day. Edith had something to do with that. And now they sat at Samy's Curry House, wadding saffron rice into balls, dipping them into curry sauce, tearing naan and using it to pick up prawns and goat and lamb. Eating with their fingers. A patch of heaven, irrigated by Tiger Beer. After they finished they washed their hands at a sink, then dried them on a cloth towel that unreeled from a roller.

"Don't scrub too hard," Beckmann told Rosa Sanchez, holding his fingers against his nose. "If you're lucky the scent of the curry comes out from under your fingernails for a week or so." But, Post noticed, that didn't stop Rose from meticulously scrubbing every digit.

Twenty minutes later, they were back at the docks and in hell. Post had gone ahead with Sanchez; he wanted to do email before the system got congested. Beckmann and Edith lingered on the ground floor, investing in snacks for the next leg of the voyage: prosciutto, cheese, sardines, sausages. They had time to kill, they thought. This was Singapore, brisk and efficient; earlier, they'd breezed through immigration and customs. But now they encountered hundreds of passengers. Two or three other ships were in port at the same time, plus ferries to Indonesia and Malaysia. Total gridlock and mounting panic for the Semester at Sea kids. The fear of punishment, dock time, overcame them. If you were late coming off the ship, you could miss a tour you'd already paid for.

"If you guys aren't on the other side of customs and immigration in twenty minutes, you're getting dock time." This came from one of the living and learning coordinators, the same fellow who'd confronted Post about his deck chair and, later, threatened to write Beckmann up for calling an asshole an asshole. Farrington.

"What do you expect to accomplish with that announcement?" Beckmann shouted. He couldn't control himself. No, he could if he wanted to, of course he could, but he *didn't* want to. "Should we rush the metal detectors? Stamp our own passports? Jump the barriers?"

"I'm just saying what will happen."

"And I'm 'just saying' you accomplish nothing except to increase anxiety and aggrandize your own sense of power. You're the one who needs dock time." He turned to the students behind him, motioned for them to go ahead of him. He'd seen some of them at Samy's Curry House, had walked them to the food counter and pointed them to the wash-up sink. The whole evening was charmed until now.

"I'm not going to run," he told Edith once they passed through the passport check. Students were dashing by them.

"Of course not," she agreed. "We're grown-ups. We walk." She took his arm; if anything, their walk became more leisurely.

"That little squirt. They pal around with the students, then they bully them."

"It'll be over in a minute," she said. "And I'm feeling like a cognac."

When the two strolled out of the terminal, a cheer went up from hundreds of passengers on the railing. A faculty member and a life-long leaner, in line among truants! Not even running to save themselves. The dean of students was in charge of recording the latecomers; he nodded as they passed by.

¤

"PROFESSOR BECKMANN? HI." IT was the dean of students, a young woman from California, greeting him in the quiet hour before breakfast. He'd had no contact with her. She had a cheerful husband, a nice child, and a winning smile. That was it. "May I have a word with you?"

"Of course! Have a seat." Why was she being so polite? Why was he? Obviously, some shit was going to hit the fan.

"I wanted to give you this personally," she said, handing him an envelope. "And if you wanted to discuss it…"

"Read first, then discuss," Beckmann said. What he held in his hand, he saw, was notification that a Student Affairs Committee had found that, as a result of his tardiness in coming aboard in Singapore, he was in violation of ship policy and, as a result, he'd been assessed three hours of dock time on arrival in Ho Chi Minh City.

"Of course you can appeal it," the dean said. "It's there at the bottom. And I wanted you to know that your appeal will be upheld, no worries. You don't have to worry about dock time."

"Why?"

"Pardon me?"

"I am guilty."

"Yes. But we don't want…"

"Stop there, please. I don't want to be rude." He handed the letter back to her. "You ought to be ashamed of this. I will not accept and I will not appeal a judgment from a Student Affairs group. Sub-legal, para-legal, quasi-legal, illegal. A juvenile jury. I am a faculty member employed currently by the University of Virginia. This is a university-at-sea, not a kibbutz. If you have any complaints about my conduct, direct them to the dean of the faculty, Dr. Stuart."

"This is an embarrassing situation," the dean of students said. "I'm just trying to manage it, to minimize the damage."

"Fine. Here's what I want you to know. If this is not withdrawn, then I will withdraw. I will leave this voyage and contemplate legal action. It should make an interesting case, and story. A comic footnote to a troubled voyage."

She sat awhile, obviously disappointed. She was a people person. She dealt in rules, for students. She specialized in exceptions, too, the understanding conversation, the forgiving personal touch. And now she confronted someone who refused her help.

"I know you wanted to do me a favor," Beckmann said. "But this isn't about favors. It's about principles."

When she left, he stayed in his chair, studying the track of raindrops down the window. This morning's rain was something new, pounding the way only a tropical rain can pound. You thought it was the hardest possible rain and then, somehow, it rained even harder, and harder still, and there was no fancy zigzagging—the rain raced down the window as if nature itself had discovered that a straight line was the shortest distance between two points. He liked watching the rain.

¤

ANNA CATHER HAD A world of worries. She was boarding what might be the worst voyage ever. That's what the trustees were saying and they weren't saying it nicely. Still, when she checked out of the Grand Hotel, took a taxi that joined a convoy of trucks, vans, cars, bicycles, motorbikes, and pedestrians, then turned onto narrow streets where people were squatting, reading, or cooking in front of shops where they probably slept, past barbers, tailors, mechanics, and bakers—then, when she got waved through a gate and saw that ship, that magic, maddening ship, *that's* when she felt a surge of joy. Even now. Perhaps especially now. Part of her never left that ship. Wherever she was, she imagined it in this or that port, at the beginning and end of a voyage or somewhere in between. Leo felt the same way, she knew that. Always, anytime, that ship stayed with them.

"Welcome aboard, kiddo." He was waiting for her at the top of the gangplank, gave her a hug, walked her to the seventh deck cabin that was reserved for important visitors.

"This is my first time on the seventh deck," she said. "I was fourth deck on my first trip. A tiny, tiny place. Everybody else used a swipe card to enter their cabin. Mine had an old-fashioned key. It must have been a storage room."

"Well, you've come a long way. Is there anything I can do for you right now?"

"Not this minute. I just want to walk around. Every place is memory lane."

"I don't begrudge you that," Leo allowed. "But I reckon you have an agenda, what with everything that's gone down."

"It can wait. Let me just feel my way around. And Saigon's supposed to be terrific. Plus, I have to go back to the hotel, pick up some dry cleaning."

"Good. When you're ready to talk, I'll be ready."

¤

INDIA HAD BEEN TOO big for them and their time there was too short. That, Will Post decided, was his students' problem. He got a lot of vignettes involving rickshaw drivers, initially friendly and bargain-priced, who took students to malls where they were coerced into shopping and buying even as the price of the ride itself escalated. The worst experience, in an essay called "The Art of Getting Screwed Over," ended with four girls cornered by their new best friend and a gang of accomplices who coerced them into paying four times the agreed-upon price. The pieces were small and sloppy. As much as Post had connected with his students, some of them kept making the same mistakes, mis-punctuation around quotes, misspellings—peek for peak, meet for meat—misplaced adverbs, "hopefully, the weather would clear up." And, they got tired of having him point out such petty errors. And yet, there were nice things. A rickshaw driver stops at a store:

When we arrived at the first store, Aseem walked us to the door where we were greeted by a tiny, mid-sixty-year-old man. He seemed extremely overjoyed to see us. I was the last of my group to go into the store so I witnessed the handshake between the two men. There was something odd about the handshake. It seemed more like "nice doing business with you" than "hey, pal, it's great to see you."

One paper was worth the trip and it came from someone he thought he knew pretty well. Jody Phillips, she was smart and deep and—Beckmann had said it—soulful. "Easy on the eyes, tough on the guys," Post added. She wasn't enrolled in travel writing but, like some other students, wanted him to read something. Now it turned out that Jody was a year or two older than the other students. She'd dropped out of school for a while to take care of her ailing mother. The piece began with a feisty, chain-smoking, terminally ill woman talking about her wishes for her daughter. These, of course, involved travel. So the piece was potentially corny: i.e., seeing all the things my mom wanted me to see. But there came a moment on the Ganges when the daughter sees those little memento boats laden with flower petals and candles in memory of the dead. She contemplates them and says to herself, "This is going to be hard."

"All right then," Post said. They did what they could in the time that they had. That was the same thing he said about his own travel writing, a credo and an excuse. Get what you can and go with what you have. They had these lovely moments:

The morning mist still hung over the fields, making the scene outside the train seem dim and muting the colors of the grass and the rising sun. The train rattled by a stupa that rose behind a line of corrugated iron huts and was silhouetted against the lightening sky, its intricate peak perfectly outlined against the dawn. When the mist continued to hang over the fields, I realize it wasn't the picturesque morning fog but permanent smog-filled air that was a reminder of the pollution that is always present in India. There were still houses and trash piles along the side of the tracks. Power lines and smokestacks dotted the fields but somehow did not ruin the scene or make the countryside ugly.

Amazing how moods changed. When he was grading papers, irritation suddenly gave way to gratitude. That happened all the time on this ship. There was that piece of silliness involving dock time for Beckmann. Amateur night, bush-league stuff. But then they checked the rules and found out that Beckmann was right: his supervisor was indeed the dean of the faculty. And Beckmann, of all people, emerged as a faculty spokesman. When Japan got deleted from the schedule, he stood up in a faculty meeting and spoke eloquently about the Philippines. It was only fair, he said, that they go there and look at a place where America ruled. We'd been visiting, and judging, and sometimes moralizing about other peoples' colonies. Wouldn't we learn something by visiting a place which America had ruled for half a century? It was a nice moment, drawing applause and congratulations, and then the word came that, no, Taiwan would replace Japan. Leo Underwood made the place sound indispensable and—though the ship hadn't visited in ten years—the field trip office cobbled together a list of field trips that, at this late stage, wouldn't generate much business. But—talk about a change of moods—Saigon lay just ahead.

VIII.

SAIGON

I T WAS ODD, THE things, all sorts of things Beckmann noticed—the things that came to him, unbidden. The way a river port like Saigon differed from an ocean port like Cape Town or Chennai. Moving up a river felt much different than coming in off the sea. In ocean ports the movement was in and out. River ports involved penetration and constant movement, upstream, downstream, back and forth across the river, hydrofoils, barges, tankers, freighters, cruise ships, floating restaurants. The traffic was fascinating, sand and gravel overloaded into barges, scrap metal and bags of garbage (from the ship) and cords of lumber, but no matter what they carried, or how low in the water and close to being swamped they were, there were always some potted plants around the back of a vessel and some laundry hanging from a line. Those little touches pleased him. He leaned against the railing and studied the lily pads that were everywhere, floating up and down with the movement of the tides, and you came to know them, too, by the pieces of Styrofoam and plastic they carried. If he could photograph them, perhaps he could tell whether he was seeing the same lily pads with the same garbage, day after day. Did they ever make it out to sea?

Saigon was a place that mattered. America had happened here and things had happened to America. And there were little adventures that were unforgettable. Crossing the street was one of them. Saigon traffic was brutal, a beeping, belching onslaught of lorries, taxis, cars, and motorbikes that never stopped. Yet there were streets you had to cross. And the only way to get from one side to another would pass as a suicide attempt back home. You waited for a few locals headed in the same direction and, with them, you stepped out in the street, right into the path of incoming traffic which you did not even look at because you already knew that something, a bicycle or a cement mixer, was coming right at you, and you just kept walking at the same pace and if you continued in that way, the driver would see you and avoid you, but if you slowed down, sped up, or stopped you were dead. Miraculously, it worked every time. The first time, he stood on the far sidewalk, amazed, giggling like a kid who'd gotten away with something. What a huge test of faith it was, not faith in oneself but faith in all of them—dozens of drivers, possibly unlicensed, probably uninsured, and inevitably convinced, as he was not, in life after death. And he had to return by the same route. He looked forward to it. Next time, he would cross alone.

¤

THEY WERE AT THE Majestic Hotel, Edith and Beckmann, at the roof restaurant overlooking the Mekong and the open country across the river. From here, Graham Greene had watched American planes landing in the 1950s, studying flares and listening for mortars and small arms fire, right here where two Semester at Sea passengers had replaced him and ordered Irish coffees. A photographer approached them and offered to take a shot. He displayed some of his work:

western tourists at tables covered with beer bottles, flashing peace signs or v's for "victory," o's for "okay," and a middle finger for "up yours." To Beckmann, the photographer was as welcome as a strolling musician; he'd paid more than one of them to stay away. But Edith Stirling moved closer and signaled for the photographer to proceed.

"I always think of Joe DiMaggio and Marilyn Monroe when I see pictures taken in nightclubs," Beckmann said. "The photos that show up later with captions that say this is how they looked, in happier times."

"Well, this is a happy time," Edith said and the way she said it went so far and no further. Capturing the present, it seemed, and avoiding the future.

"Agreed," said Beckmann. "This is my favorite port, so far."

"I think I know why, but I'd be guessing."

"Well. Part of it is work-related. The layers of history… China, France, America all exerting themselves, coming and going. But I said all that in class. The other reason is Graham Greene. We've talked about him." They'd both read a lot of Greene. Left-wing ideology, Catholic faith, right-wing associations, free-ranging sexuality, Guinness-Book-of-World-Records anti-Americanism, conservative instincts, and lifelong conversation—or argument—with God. He wasn't on the list of writers, congenial spirits, they'd want to meet. But they raised their Irish coffees to his memory.

"He's still in the neighborhood," Edith said. "Something remains. For a while, at least. Never forever. But who wouldn't settle for 'a while?'"

"He's here…if we're here," Beckmann agreed, "though the sound of 'Bad, Bad Leroy Brown' coming from a band across the room wouldn't please him. But, really, he made a career out of being annoyed by Americans. That's our contribution. We gave him a target, played right into his hands. But you know what struck me when I walked around today? You can't miss it. It's as though America won the war.

His famous Rue Catinat—it's called Dong Khoi now—is German beer gardens, Italian pasta, tailors for tourists. They welcome Americans. Do you see any Russians around being hustled and cajoled? People are getting and spending, open for business. Let's make a deal. Who won the war? Why did we bother to fight at all, if it turned out like this? I wonder what Graham Greene would think. Or feel."

"I wonder what the students will make of Vietnam," Edith asked. "Vietnam is as far behind them as World War I was to us. A little bit of guilt, a glance at the Agent Orange babies in formaldehyde bottles at the war museum and then what…*Apocalypse Now*? That's the name of a bar they go to. You should have talked to them, pre-port. Someone should have." She gathered herself and got ready to leave. "I wonder if Will Post is back yet," she said. "I like hearing the stories he comes back with. Wonder what he'll ever do with them. Where did he go?"

"A day trip on a bus. He wasn't looking forward to it."

¤

IN *THE QUIET AMERICAN*, Graham Green's narrator, Thomas Fowler, and his American rival Alden Pyle meet at a temple in the city of Tay Ninh, ninety minutes out of Saigon these days. Back then, it was a longer and more dangerous trip. Tay Ninh was the headquarters of the Cao Dai, a modern faith that combined elements of other religions and included, in its pantheon of saintly figures, Sun Yat Sen and Victor Hugo. In the 1950s the Cao Dai had political and military power. That's why they attracted interest from Americans seeking a "third force" in Vietnam, non-Communist and untainted by contact with the French colonial government. *The Quiet American* was set more than sixty years ago and Will Post wasn't sure what he would find now, but he needed to lead a tour, just a painless day trip, and there he sat on a bus, first stop Cao Dai Temple, second stop Cu Chi Tunnels. He'd read Graham Greene, though not as thoroughly as Edith and Beckmann. And he'd seen both film versions of *The Quiet American*. More than that, he made a point of paying his respect to writers he liked. Better writers. That included graves: Ernest Hemingway's in Idaho; Willa Cather's in Jaffrey Center, Vermont; D. H. Lawrence's outside of Taos, New Mexico. The thing about graves, though, was that they didn't change. The world that a novel was set in was more vulnerable. No way of knowing what this trip would amount to. In Greene's day, the highway out of Saigon was disputed territory, controlled by the government by day, up for grabs at night. This morning, it took forever to leave Saigon behind. Yesterday's rice paddies and government watch towers had yielded to a blur of buildings that obliterated farmland yet never quite added up to a city, miles and miles of stuff: a bakery, a barbershop, a pile of tires, a medical clinic, a pig turning on a spit, a school, a pharmacy. The city went on forever. On the bus, the students numbed out. How they hated bus rides at this stage, how they regretted having signed up for them. Why, really, bother to go to a Cao Dai Temple? Did Graham Greene matter to them? Had they studied the war in Vietnam? Had one person on this bus read Stanley Karnow? Were they fascinated by syncretic religions?

Pretty soon, the only people awake would be the driver and the guide and—Post glanced over—probably not the guide. And then he saw something wonderful. At last, there were rice paddies and trees along the road and every few miles, you'd see a cluster of bicycles and motorbikes, trucks and trishaws, at the side of the road next to a place that was a coffee shop that had counters and tables and—there was genius at work along this highway—hammocks! A dozen hammocks under tarps or in a shaded grove, strung between poles and trees, and this was where people could stretch out and nap after—or before—coffee. What an idea! If only he could stop the bus, spend an idle half-hour in those hammocks, under those trees. Beckmann would love it. He'd never leave! But the bus rolled on.

After the war, the Cao Dai lost their army and saw their eccentric faith's headquarters become a tourist attraction. The politicians, agents, military officers and conspirators in *The Quiet American* were replaced by guides and people who came off of air-conditioned buses. Out they tumbled, cramped and not especially curious students filing into a temple with bubblegum-colored pillars decorated with dragons and eyes and a sky-blue ceiling sprinkled with stars that a high school decoration committee might have purchased for prom night. Down below, a service proceeded, men and women kneeling and chanting. Greene hadn't taken the Cao Dai seriously; a religion cooked up in the 1920s got no respect from an Anglo-Catholic. And it invited easy irony. *Paging Mr. Greene*, Will Post thought, again and again.

The Cao Dai were a tourist attraction. Greene couldn't have foreseen that. Or the Cu Chi Tunnels, a labyrinth of underground burrows, three levels of them, with Viet Minh—later Viet Cong—and armories, hospitals, barracks, kitchens from which guerillas emerged to harass Americans at a nearby airbase. Paging Mr. Greene! American kids watched a shaky, grainy newsreel—a vintage propaganda film—that attacked American imperialists and showed pictures of dead Americans. Then, the kids contended with those fatal tunnels. Or what was left of them. It must have been a spelunker's paradise just after the war, all the main tunnels, the laterals, the hidden exits and entrances. Now it came down to two tunnels, both barely underground. There were steps going down, steps coming out and the tunnels—one hundred feet long at the most—had been widened to accommodate Western bodies. It looked about as exciting as a highway culvert. Yet the kids entered—"there are bats down here!" one of them shouted. So here you had a Vietnamese redoubt, a secret stronghold, converted into an amusement park attraction. How long would it be before some dark-spirited entrepreneur got rich offering a concentration camp for tourists? Oh, the real ones were still daunting but inconveniently located and insufficiently interactive. It took more than an *Arbeit Macht Frei* sign to put the experience over. He pictured tourists arriving in a sealed cattle car. Getting herded toward a Mengele figure who'd decide their fate. Extermination or forced labor. Families separated. Some to ovens, some to barracks. No reunions this side of the visitors' parking lot. It made Post shudder, people paying for a touch of the ultimate evil. But he knew they would, they surely would. Casting themselves as guards, kapos, officers, gypsies, Jews, Communists, homosexuals, scientists, or executioners. Was there anything that couldn't be turned into shits and giggles?

¤

BACK ON THE SHIP, Post showered, mixed a drink, and reached for a stack of student papers. The funny thing about teaching travel writing on this trip turned out to be that your trip wasn't over until you'd read about everyone else's journey. Sure, they made every mistake a student back home would make, careless errors. The difference was that they were sailing around the world together. His class was a part of a larger voyage—that's what it came to. And the paper he picked up at random came from a student who was a fifth deck regular, a sharply-dressed Singaporean who was studying in New York. She was part of the crowd; she liked cigarettes and music, gossip and noise. But she held herself apart. There was more: he'd seen her in the mornings, before breakfast, sitting by herself, smoking, looking out to sea, and he wondered what she was thinking.

The piece she'd dropped off was called "Lip Service." That could mean talk, halfhearted agreement, insincere tribute. It could also mean oral sex, another insincere tribute. At a bar in Saigon, her narrator sees some Americans or Europeans on the prowl. *Burly blokes...ogres*, pot-bellied, T-shirted. They stare at her. She thinks they think she is a hooker. *At what stateside college would I be reading this kind of piece?* Post asked himself. Out late one night with an old friend, she encounters a child beggar selling chewing gum, a cute big-eyed kid who says thank you when she's given money. The narrator notices the child's lips. *Right now her lips were used to form and articulate words so simple and pure us foreigners fell for the adorableness and gave in... Would those lips be used for another purpose to keep her stomach from being empty?*

She's making this lips business work, Post thought. It could have been just an easy double-entendre. He liked her writing.

> In my years of living and returning to Vietnam, I've grown wise to the many times I'd been mistaken as a prostitute, be it the lecherous Taiwanese CEOs who came on business trips...or the Europeans and Americans that lurked around the Hyatt preying and praying to pick up a local girl...

The piece got angry. There was conflict. The narrator liked looking good, dressing sharp, attracting attention, yet hating the men who came after her. Fellow students come to her for advice on how to find a hooker. She notices that in Saigon classic formal wear, long white skirts and slacks, have yielded to miniskirts and high heels. "Saigon, *I said to myself, licking my dark, red-stained lips*, I am coming home to you, very very soon." If this piece were posted and blogged it would make people shudder.

Then it was time for a date with Rosa Sanchez. Some students had rented a hotel banquet room for a gala party that was going to be unforgettable. Something different, for sure. Student-faculty interactions on ship were confined to classroom and dining room. That was plenty close, more intimacy than the coziest liberal arts college offered. But proximity enforced a certain caution, a sense of territory. To really engage with students, you had to see them on shore. So Post agreed to accompany her and—shockingly—so did Beckmann when he heard that the chosen hotel was the Grand, where Graham had housed Alden Pyle in *The Quiet American*. They thought of it as a field trip. Edith declined.

The two professors shared a taxi to the hotel. They could have walked but there was something magic about passing down Saigon streets at night, the neon lights, the smell of food, the honk of cars, crowded sidewalks, getting and spending everywhere, appetites and temptation, pleasure and menace. The hotel lobby presented a version of Asia that appealed to tourists: expensive chairs, marble floors, stunning waitresses, overhead fans—despite the air-conditioning— and a sense of drinks and deals waiting to be made. Beckmann would have been content to sit a while but they were late, as it turned out, for the wedding.

"Two kids from the ship," Sanchez informed them. "Don't worry, you don't know them. But it's ten bucks a throw. My treat."

Around the room, they saw tables full of students already ravenously drunk, though the matrimony hadn't even begun. At the head table there were groomsmen and bridesmaids drinking wine out of boxes while their dates dueled with chopsticks. Beckmann pitied the poor waiters, stone-faced and impeccably polite, serving food, cleaning whatever had been dropped and spilled, even as guests pointed, gestured, shouted for more of this and that; they didn't know what things were called. The subtlest food on the planet was slurped and spilled, fingered, and sometimes thrown.

"My bad," Sanchez said. "But I wanted you to see this and if I told you it was a wedding, you wouldn't come."

"You got that right," Post said.

"Don't go," Sanchez pleaded. "At least, stick around for the ceremony."

"I'll stay," Beckmann said. "But if some revolutionaries, some ghosts of the past, Viet Minh, Viet Cong, came into this room, looked around, and lined us up against a wall, my last words would be 'guilty, guilty, guilty.' But I'll stay."

"Thanks, Professor," Sanchez said. "You're a stud."

"Well then…" Beckmann said, glancing at Post, who hadn't been complimented. Sanchez was interesting. It was hard to tell whether this evening was her idea of fun. As usual she was wide-eyed, tightly wrapped, and ready for trouble. But he knew that she was a biting writer. Maybe she was having it both ways: the experience and the story. Lots of writers had done the same thing. Not so many women, though, until lately.

The bride and groom made their way down the carpet that lay between the tables. The girl seemed nervous, unsure about what she was doing, what it meant. You could imagine her saying that it had seemed like a good idea at the time. Her groom was in an ill-fitting too-quickly-tailored suit, his white linen shirt already wine-spotted. A wedding was a great excuse for a party! His Mohawk would make him easy to identify on the ship.

At the end of the aisle, an official awaited them. When they arrived, he nodded and began to speak, and though his voice was inaudible, he seemed serious.

"He's a real monk," Sanchez said. "I mean, he has the authority to perform weddings. All this is completely legal." She was standing beside the two professors like a tour guide with a pair of tourists. And, especially to Post, she looked like she was anxious to ditch these older guys and get close to the action. So Post urged her to circulate while he'd look after the older professor. They sat together at a table that hadn't been ravaged and a waiter pleased to deal with adults brought them soup, noodles, fish. At a nearby table, the only student Beckmann recognized made a point of waving his way: Bobby Rummel, following the voyage he'd been expelled from. When he saw Beckmann he consulted with his buddies, then gave the professor a cheerful wave like a long-lost friend.

"Yo, Professor Beckmann," he called out. "Am I still an asshole?"

"Sure," Beckmann said. "But at least you're not alone." That cracked the boys up, thumbs-up and high fives and no hard feelings headed his way. He could hear what they were talking about. Dong were Vietnamese currency. So it was "give me your dong, show me your dong, I forget where I put my dong."

Up front the ceremony had ended. The official vanished and the wedding table turned into a drinking game. It was time to go, with no one to thank, no one to excuse them. A blown kiss from Bobby Rummel and, when she caught up with them at the door, an invitation from Rosa Sanchez for nightcaps at a marvelous bar called Apocalypse Now. Beckmann declined instantly. That was to be expected. Post's decision to end the evening came as a disappointment but not a surprise.

"Who are those kids?" a sharp-looking Chinese woman came to them in the lobby and asked. She wasn't a local, you could tell from the edge in her voice. "Are they Americans?"

"They sure are," Post replied. "It's a kind of wedding. Want to take a look?"

"This will do, I think." She was dressed in black slacks and what might have been a man's dress shirt, a pink and white oxford. Late twenties or early thirties, a marathoner with breasts. You could wait a long time to see one of those come across the finish line.

"What are they?" she asked. "It doesn't look like a family celebration."

"It's a kind of floating university, taking classes at sea and stopping in ports for…research."

Right then, there was a commotion, cheers and jeers, the start of a wet T-shirt contest that involved champagne.

"Is it Semester at Sea?"

"You got it. I'm Will Post. I teach travel writing. And Professor Harold Beckmann here does colonial and postcolonial history."

"Well then," Anna said. "I'm Anna Cather. I'm the head of the Institute for Shipboard Education which, I'm sure you know, runs Semester at Sea."

"Oh my God," Post said. "You wouldn't want to join the party?"

"No. I think I've seen enough."

"How about a drink at the bar?"

"Not here. Maybe on the ship. Let's share a taxi. I assume you're ready to leave."

As soon as they pulled away from the front of the hotel, Will Post heard himself saying things he couldn't believe. That's not the whole story back there, he said, we have some great kids, some terrific writers, take it from me, reacting thoughtfully to the world they find and even though a lot of them get no credit back at their home institutions they give it their best shot, which is kind of amazing when you think about it. And he was sure Professor Beckmann agreed.

"I certainly do," Beckmann said, turning to the side to look out at the street. He was laughing at Post, flacking for Semester at Sea. But Post couldn't stop carrying on about the discovery of new places, connections, confusion, and insight, all of it silly and serious, combining uncomfortably. He sounded like he was a PR man or, worse, a faculty member lobbying for another voyage.

"And you were at that party?" Anna asked. "Not as chaperones? As guests. You chose to attend? You thought it was appropriate?"

What a pair of clowns she thought they were, Post thought. When they got back on board she'd surely blow them off. If she kept a shit list, Post figured he was on it and Professor Harold Beckmann was not far behind. They'd blundered. Whether they said it or not, the entire faculty wanted to be hired again and again. Just now, Beckmann and Post sensed they wouldn't be getting invitations from Anna Cather.

"One thing you can tell me," she said at the bottom of the gangplank. She said it in a way that suggested that whatever they said would be taken seriously. "I gather some parents were waiting in Singapore to take their kids home. I haven't heard how that went. I could've asked Leo earlier today but I wasn't ready. Neither was he."

"I'll tell you everything," Post said. "But I'll need a drink. We all will."

They had the faculty lounge to themselves, but the bar was open. They ordered drinks, took a table at the far side of the room, and the time for fatuity was over.

"It happened in here. Meghan was with me. That's Leo's assistant…"

"We've met."

"About forty parents flew to Singapore and Leo emailed all of them asking them to a 'discussion and reflection' on the voyage. I guess he thought he could talk them out of it. He really believed that."

"And?"

"Six parents came. And it turned out they were just wanting something to do while their kids took their sweet time packing up and saying goodbye. It hurt, watching Leo walk in here and see so few people. Reminded me of a poetry reading at a bookshop."

"Sad," Anna said. "I can see him wince."

"So about a dozen parents. And me. And Meghan from Leo's office. But, I've got to say, Leo manned up. He let it all hang out. The dream of terrorists, which the captain called a 'nocturnal emission.' That burning, sinking ship out of Malaysia. That brutal scene on the seventh deck. The Ebola scare. Sending those troublemakers to help the refugees disembark in Indonesia. He took some blame. But look, he said, there were no pirates, no terrorists, and though he'd been accused of 'trawling for trouble,' those refugees were dead without us. There was no Ebola either. And there was no reason, now, to abandon the ship. And then he pulled out all the stops. I assume you know that Leo can be very impressive?"

"So I gather," she said, smiling.

"He talks about what this voyage meant, what it was like in the early years and what it was like now on his last voyage. The world had gotten dangerous. We used to be met at the dock by brass bands and school groups and dignitaries. Now it's trinket-sellers, touts, and guides. But we had to keep the magic going, that round-the-world magic, and what a loss it would be for the kids to miss out on it. 'The word unique is misused,' he said. 'But this voyage was unique. One of a kind.' And at the end he was crying. I swear he and Meghan were crying and so was I. You'd've shed a few tears yourself."

"Was that it? Anything from the parents?"

"We got two kids back. Lost thirty-eight."

"Any comments? Questions?"

"Questions about refunds. Comments about lawsuits."

¤

"I HAVE SOMETHING FOR you to read," Darlene Tedrow said. "And it's not about getting drunk in Varanasi."

She had a way of finding him, homing in whenever she wanted. This morning it was at the entrance to the faculty lounge.

"I thought we had a deal," Post said.

"Just read it. Soon."

"How about now?" He started on the first page. But she was standing there and it annoyed him. "I hate it when people hover over me while I'm reading. Back off a little, will you?"

She backed off. About six feet, turned away from him.

Her first paragraph was startling. A Thai Muslim returns from Bangkok on a visit to his home village, a prodigal son paying respects to his impoverished family, the dirt-poor farmers who watched him grow up. Then he tells them that they have an hour to pack before leaving the place forever. Angry troops are nearing the villages, seeking revenge for some murders nearby. Then: the packing, the departure, the last backward glance—nicely detailed and deeply felt but underscored by a mood of mounting panic—the flight to the coast, the coast, the ship, food poisoning, and seasickness.

"How did you get to them?"

"As a nurse's assistant," she said. She didn't turn around to face him. "The woman who took care of my food poisoning, dressed me up, gave me some food to carry."

"I understand the description…the smell, the dirt. And you get the mood. But the interviews."

"I wasn't interviewing," she corrected. "Just talking. You know? Conversation. The leader of the group, the guy who lives in Bangkok, took me around. Introduced me. That night of ugliness on the seventh deck? After I told you to go up and take a look? I rushed back out on the fourth deck. Huddled under a table, talking, while food rained down on me. And curses. And then those guys, unzipping…"

"And then you went across to Indonesia? To say goodbye?"

"I was the only one who took up the invitation. More talk. And I figured the story needed an ending. Sorry I missed Singapore, but I wasn't the only student."

"That's what amazed me. I thought you made it up."

"Nope."

"So you're telling me that Leo required the four students—the ones pissing on the refugees—to accompany them across to Indonesia? And carry their luggage for them when they stepped ashore?"

"Yes. Baskets, mats, bedrolls."

"And apologize?"

"Kind of. They nodded. Said 'sorry' as they walked back."

"Were they sorry?"

"Well, they were sorry they were there. And—this isn't in the story—so are their parents. One of the kids claims he was innocent. Oh, he was there all right, but he didn't quite urinate. Shy bladder, I guess. And his father's connected to SAS."

Darlene Tedrow stood waiting for a verdict on her piece and Will Post wondered what to say. Should he lowball it? Words like "decent," "competent"?

"This is terrific. The reporting and the writing. It couldn't be better." He almost added that it reminded him of what he used to do. "It's going to be published."

"Where?"

"On my website. We can't use your name, though. Not while you're on this ship."

"Understood."

"So pick a name."

"Amelia Bligh."

"That's taken." She just smiled at him. She was onto him, his other voice, his alter ego, dream girl, and better self. "How the hell did you find out?"

"Two words," Darlene Tedrow said. "Actually, one word two times. The word was 'humdinger.' It showed up in Tourist Traps, this odd piece about visiting cemeteries. Cemetery tourism. James Dean's grave in Fairmount, Indiana, is still drawing visitors after all these years. 'A humdinger of a tribute.' And then, a month later Amelia

Bligh on a beach dealing with some Jamaican guy who had 'home of the whopper' on his bathing suit. That was another 'humdinger.'"

"Busted by close reading," Post said. "Can you keep this a secret?"

"Sure," she said.

"So your name? Your *nom de plume*?"

"Up to you."

"How about 'Ladykiller'?"

"Works for me. For now."

IX.

HONG KONG

ONG KONG DAZZLED. No escaping it, no denying it, that matchless combination of land and sea, skyline and mountains. The glittering harbor, the Star ferries shuttling back and forth. Beckmann and Edith had taken the ferry as soon as they got off the ship, which had docked at Ocean Terminal. On the Hong Kong Island side, they took a taxi to the cable car that carried them up Victoria Peak. The world was spread out below them. And the memory of a movie, an old movie, didn't hurt.

"I wonder," said Edith, "if there's one student aboard who remembers *Love Is a Many Splendored Thing*? The novel, the movie, the song?"

"William Holden, Jennifer Jones. We could make a long list of the things that…slip away. Come here." They embraced right there, on a bench, with flowers and grass and, for the first time in the voyage, a sense of springtime. His garden would be missing him. It was a fine day—call it April in Hong Kong—and there was no rush. Chances were they wouldn't be back here. Ever. A few students passed by. When they saw two adults from the ship, they were startled, encountering a professor at liberty in the free world.

"I've been thinking about you, Harold. I was wondering what your plans were." She must have seen his surprise. "Not about me. Please. Or us. Please. The topic, at the moment, is you."

"All right then…plans. They've changed. I've been saying, these last few years, I'll just take life a semester at a time. Sooner or later, the old professor shuffles into the twilight…"

"That sounds like the way you looked when you came aboard, Mr. Chips. I wondered what it would take to provoke you, to penetrate those good manners. Could I set you off? Could anyone? But someone else beat me to it."

"Who?" He was alarmed. Was she thinking of the woman who'd gotten over the ship's railing ahead of him? Someone who acted while he dawdled?

"The kid you called an asshole. What I saw there was a new character emerging. You're lively in class. You challenge and contradict the powers that be. You almost got us both dock time in Singapore, you rascal! I've watched you react to the places we visit. The ones you know, it's like a reunion that you've been waiting for all your life. You can't believe it took you so long to get back in touch. Everywhere, almost, you want to stay longer. A roadside market in Ghana? You want to stay! Diego Garcia, for God's sake! The Andaman Islands! And…I'll be resting my case shortly…what are those tiny islands that four or five nations claim?"

"Oh, the Spratleys and the Paracels. It's not the islands themselves. It's the oil."

"But you're not there for the oil. You're all for the islands. Rocks, just barely above the water, with a shack and a flagpole on top. And, you said, it was just an aside, it would interest you to go there. Did you mean it?"

"Well, yes," Beckmann responded. He knew he was being ridiculous. But he'd meant what he said. "It's the reduction *ad absurdum* of all territorial claims…a cause of war, very possibly, over an island the size of a tool shed. Yes, I would like to go. I'm curious about what I'd feel…and think. Not for very long, though. A week would do it…"

"A week…doing what?"

"Well, I'd look out at the sea of course. The world of water. Would I feel the tides? Would the waves wash over the floor and send me up on the roof? And what would a heavy rain feel like in those circumstances? I'd think about all the islands, all the exiles, but none as extreme as this, not Elba, not St. Helena, not even close. And I would be sole occupant of a place five nations claim!"

"You'll go anywhere…and find a good reason for going."

"And stay awhile, yes. That is what I've found out about myself, this trip."

"What next?"

"Hong Kong, Shanghai, Keelung, Hilo."

"Keep going," she said.

"San Diego."

"Keep going."

"I can't…" He heard something in his voice. Confusion. Like a student who'd forgotten the last part of an answer, something that made the difference between complete and incomplete. "I can't say…" he repeated. Awkward as a kid. "I don't know."

"Then we'll talk again," she said, putting her hand in his as they walked toward the cable car station. But, back on the ship that night, his confusion lingered. Deepened. His thoughts of death—his wife's end and his own—returned. Was the voyage anything more than a reprieve? He'd studied the skyscrapers across the harbor, bright lights of a bright city, Epson, Panasonic, Samsung, Philips, San Miguel staking their claim. He couldn't imagine never seeing them again. Never, never, never, the very word made his heart ache. The most terrifying word in the language, his father had told him. Especially, he'd added, when you applied it to yourself.

¤

"Wᴏᴀᴛ ᴄᴀᴘᴘᴇᴏᴛ ᴀ ᴅᴀᴄᴀᴜ stays in Macau," Rosa Sanchez said. They were in a hydrofoil, coming over from Hong Kong, and Rosa's echo of Las Vegas' slogan got to Post. As a travel writer, he knew that places changed. It wasn't always a bad thing. Consider Singapore. But there were other places that were cheerfully, utterly destroyed. Post sensed they were headed for one of them.

"I want to say something," he announced. "Bear with me. I fell in love with Macau. Young love. Come to think of it, I was your age."

"You were *my* age?" When they went public, a forty-five-year-old writer and a twenty-three-year-old bombshell, he felt like quite a guy. But when the age jokes started coming from her and coming more frequently, he winced. "Okay, okay," she conceded. "I'm all ears."

"I saved up money from a lot of crappy summer jobs, bought a ticket. Got a passport, my first. First of many. It's amazing, the people who go through a life without a passport. I used to feel sorry for them. Lately…the more I travel, the more I write about it…the more I respect folks who just stay home. So, anyway, I'm twenty-three and I buy an around-the-world ticket and I come over here—from Hong Kong. Macau. The name alone got me going. I'd feel special, just being in Macau. Great place to set a story, to be a writer. There are names that turn me on that way. Surabaya, Koror, Zamboanga, Büyükada, Sidi Bou Said. So: Macau. And I wasn't let down. But coming back today…it kind of scares me."

His old hotel, the Bella Vista—a place with creaking wooden floors, overhead fans, and a view of a tree-shaded promenade curving along the shoreline right below—had been replaced by a resort hotel, part of a chain of five-star places. Sanchez didn't know what she was missing. Or care. She enjoyed the luxury.

The food rescued him from casino heaven, the Portuguese-style food that Will Post had never quite found on his first trip. Codfish cakes, clams with garlic and coriander, Portuguese sausage. Sanchez took charge and poured him a glass of wine. Post would have been happy to take a swim, laze around in terrycloth bathrobes. It wasn't laziness he was feeling. It was what he feared. He'd seen it when he came in off the sea, glimpsed more of it in a taxi on the way to the hotel, confirmed it while she showered after "a bit of a snack," one of her countless euphemisms for sex. He stood on a balcony and saw a forest of nondescript apartment towers and a slew of casinos, one after the other, a cluster of phallic creatures, pyramids, pillars, and towers that pointed up like syringes. The sea itself had been run out of town: everything was landfill. He wanted to stay in. Read a book. He missed Beckmann and Edith and Scrabble. Rosa Sanchez said no. Period. She wanted to get out and around, take the measure of the place, bright lights, big city. They dressed and stepped outside into dusk. Her acting like a hot young thing made him feel like an aging escort. Earlier those casinos down below had seemed as pretentious and out of scale: a pissing contest between gambling moguls. But at night they glittered. In Hong Kong, the neon lights were stationary: flags and emblems of global companies that had set up shop there. Here the lights were happening, they exploded, changed color, shifted, revolved, throbbed and pulsed in multiple neon orgasms. A disco city. And Sanchez liked the casino buzz; she measured herself against the people she met, croupier, sommelier, maître d'. She measured herself against the miniskirted Chinese hookers who loitered just outside the gambling halls. She didn't look at them in a hostile way, but it wasn't quite camaraderie either. It was about recognition. Appraisal. Gamesmanship. Luck. Finally he got her to leave far earlier than she wanted.

"One more stop," Will Post said. In the taxi he said "Sao Paulo" and the driver nodded. They drove uphill to the center of the old city, what was left of it, and stopped in front of a church. It was the skeleton of its former glory, a façade with intricate carvings, faded colors, fine lines, and nothing behind it. It was a wall, a silhouette, a remnant. And, if Beckmann ever got here, a metaphor.

"It's more than four hundred years old," Post continued. "The largest Catholic church in Asia. The kings and queens of Europe sent gifts. A typhoon and a fire turned it into what you see. A ruin where you pay your respects."

"That's what we're doing now?"

"Paying our respects. Dropping in on this scrap of spiritual life after cruising Babylon down below. Okay? And I wonder what we're up to, all of us. Ever notice how people on a plane say they're flying someplace when, let's face it, they're sitting on their ass watching a movie and waiting for someone to come down the aisle with pretzels? So who's flying? Really? Flapping wings? And look at us. We're not supposed to say 'cruise.' We're on a voyage, right? Better yet, we're sailing. See anybody climbing masts? Hoisting sails?"

"I've got to say something..." Then, she didn't say it. Her phone rang and she stepped away from him. After a brief back and forth which ended with an agreement, she returned to him.

"I've got to say something and this skeleton of a church is perfect. I came on this ship to have a good time and you're getting to be kind of a drag. I didn't notice at first. We had some fun. But maybe—I don't know—you spend too much time with old man Beckmann. You're always going on about how things aren't what they used to be or should be or might have been if American culture and tourists weren't wrecking the world. Maybe you're not wrong. But I'm tired of walking down memory lane holding a hankie. Okay? So I'm going back to a casino where some friends are waiting for me. I don't suppose you want to come."

"I don't suppose I do."

¤

SHANGHAI, LEO KNEW, WOULD work. But Keelung, Hilo, San Diego? Winding down? Winding up? Was there a difference, come to think of it? When you ended something, were you winding it up or winding it down? This was the time when Leo realized that there'd never been a voyage that he would have wanted to last even one extra day. That's why he was the first off the ship after the passengers. Like a pilot off an airplane. And then, after a few months, he'd start to wonder about another voyage. Not anymore, though.

"Hey there." Will Post was in the doorway. "I'm just checking up on you. How are you doing?"

"I could ask you the same thing," Leo said.

"Excuse me," Meghan Shepard said, entering without asking or greeting. "I have an email. It's important."

"Read it," Leo ordered. Things hadn't been the same since that meeting in Singapore. She didn't have his back anymore.

"Not such a good idea," she said. There was nothing subtle about it. Clearly, she didn't want Will Post to hear what was coming. "It's from Charlottesville."

"That means you've read it yourself, right?"

"Yes."

"Then read it aloud," Leo said. *You had to hand it to him*, Will Post thought. Always wanting an audience. Making a scene. Performing for an audience.

"It's from the trustees. Are you ready?"

"Well, then, this is what we call a learning opportunity. Get Anna Cather down here."

Meghan reached for the phone.

"Not that. Get her. Find her. Bring her here."

"I could page her."

"Get her. Find her. Bring her here." After Meghan marched out, Leo turned to Post. "This reminds me of the next to last scene in one of those TV shows where everybody is in a room and Peter Falk or Angela Lansbury explains everything and someone in the room is dead meat. In this case, probably me." Then he broke into an unexpected grin. "I'm happy you could be here."

"I'm not in trouble, am I?"

"Not yet."

Now Meghan returned with Anna Cather, who apologized for the delay. "I was having a massage," she said.

"Did you finish it?" asked Leo.

"Half an hour to go," she replied. "I believe I'll start again from scratch. We all need something to look forward to, right?"

"'We are disturbed by the direction of the current voyage, which has gone from eccentric to dangerous,'" Leo began reading. "'The Board of Trustees will meet tomorrow to determine a course of action that is in the best interests of the program. You deserve to know our specific concerns. Your broadcast—whether by accident or design—of your nightmare about the Malacca Straits generated a wave of worry from students' parents. Your lighthearted, gratuitously cynical suggestion that we might hire people to mimic pirates and attack the ship failed to amuse. And now, with your acceptance of refugees on board and the loss of several days, we will be required to burn excessive fuel to get back on schedule, which will likely put the entire voyage in the red. Last, I hope, is your humiliating treatment of four male students involved in an incident with your refugees. Worst by far—and this has been all over the Internet—is your use of the fear of Ebola to control unruly students. That has resulted in withdrawals from this, your LAST voyage, as well as future trips. Add to this, requests for refunds, pending lawsuits, and the worst publicity this program has ever encountered. You may, if you wish, remain on board, but, as of your receipt of this note, Anna Cather shall replace you as executive dean. More in sorrow than in anger, Hugh Twombley, Chair.'"

They sat there. No one said a thing. *Odd about moments like this,* Post thought, *that things which surprise you at the time in retrospect turn out to have been inevitable.*

"Well kiss my ass," Leo said. "'More in sorrow than in anger.' What a wuss. Didn't have the guts to kick me off. You know what I'm going to do? I'll leave the ship in Shanghai, I'll go down the gangplank and stand there on the dock, watching it leave, and I'll know—everyone will know—that it wasn't me leaving the ship, it was the ship leaving me."

"You'll get an audience, Leo," Anna Cather said. "You've always loved an audience."

"What's that supposed to mean?"

"Look around. You got that message and promptly gathered us around you for the reading of it."

"And your point?"

"You had to have an audience and give a performance. I can't even picture you sitting by yourself and reading that message. I can't imagine it and neither can you. But I have another audience in mind for you."

Leo said nothing.

"I heard about your session with the angry parents. Talking about what the voyage means. Pleading with them. Crying."

"Don't remind me. It was pathetic."

"That's not what I hear, Leo. It's been described to me as your finest hour." With that, she nodded at Meghan. Leo turned to her.

"You really thought that?"

"Yes."

"Now listen," Anna said. "We've been swamped by inquiries from the press, TV networks, bloggers. You have no idea. They've been feasting on us. Rough sailing for the love boat. Tons of schadenfreude. I think you can turn that around, Leo. I know you can. In Shanghai.

We'll invite the media on board, cameras, tape recorders, microphones. Everybody. Al Jazeera has already called. It's our only chance."

You could see Leo change. He reminded Post of one of those inflated goblins or Santas people put on their doorsteps during the holidays that had a way of deflating overnight, sagging and distorted in the morning. Now they could see Leo, pumped up to bursting.

"I'll do it," he said.

¤

"GOOD MORNING, EVERYONE," LEO began. "Thanks for coming. And thanks, as well, to our special guests from Shanghai, reporters and photographers, I'm grateful to all of you."

No doubt about it, Beckmann saw it as soon as he walked into the auditorium: Leo had a perfect audience. The students—wised up and all too familiar with his act—were mostly off on field trips. The handful present were outnumbered by senior citizens, life-long leaners who could never get enough of Leo. And then—the magic touch, tonic and elixir to a vast and wounded ego—were the journalists who'd been roaming the ship since breakfast, exploring dining rooms, classrooms, the faculty lounge, and the now historic seventh deck. Around the back of the stage sat the captain and his officers, decked out in crisp white uniforms, supporting the program as did the dining room waiters and the kitchen crew. Maybe they knew that their jobs were on the line.

"This is perfect for him," Beckmann told Post. They were sitting in the front row next to Anna and Meghan.

"He has a shot," Post agreed. "He's in the zone. All his stories are new."

"One thing before I say what I need to say," Leo continued. "This is being taped and streamed and photographed and people will be looking at it. Some of the reporters and cameramen may want a bit of your time, a few words, after I've finished. Say what you want, which is no more or less than what I'm going to do. I'm going to talk about this program, this ship, and…" a timely pause, a tremor in Leo's voice, "…our country."

"Buckle your seat belts," Beckmann whispered to Post.

"Bear with me," Leo continued, "I know you've got questions. But do me a favor first. Hear me out. And then you can fire away."

At first, there was nothing that they had not heard before: the story of the program from its beginning, funded by a Chinese entrepreneur on behalf of youth, learning, and international goodwill. The movement from ship to ship. Leo recounted visiting the burned wreck of the Queen Elizabeth in Hong Kong harbor. He covered the program's shift from school to school, all the controversy and skepticism that the so-called love boat had endured. And—his tour de force—accidents and surprises at sea, engine problems, storms, waves, stowaways. And predicaments on shore, port officials with hands out for gifts, local cops, devious tour guides, angry barkeepers, drugs, drunkenness, unauthorized car rentals, shameless shopping, out-of-control parties, he held nothing back. And when Leo presented them, his stories sounded new or at least like new, all full of pain, humor, and surprise. And then he went somewhere he'd never been before. He offered a necrology. A recounting of deaths on the voyage, surfers in Sri Lanka, a swimmer in the Caribbean, climbers attempting a sunrise photograph at the top of the Great Pyramids, a kid who'd wandered into traffic in Hong Kong, another who'd ventured into Taiwan's Taroko Gorge and was never seen again, and a half-dozen kids killed in a van in India. "The list goes on," he said. "It's not complete. You get the idea?" And then he came to Carla Hutchinson. When he was done, the voyage wasn't about rich kids sailing around the world for the fun of it. Now the program felt audacious, brave and—as it made its way around an ever more dangerous world—rewarding. Errors and accidents abided. He could swear to that. His hallucination about pirates, terrorists, the refugees—"we couldn't not pick them up"—the Ebola scare. A loss of passengers, which was regrettable. But the loss of the program would be unforgivable.

He could have stopped, Post thought, *and answered a few questions*. But he had more.

"I was offered another voyage even though, a few years ago, I was told that my style wasn't in fashion. Well, I'd had fourteen voyages and a lot to be grateful for. And maybe a little bit to be angry about. I didn't know why they'd come back to me. Part of me—I'm not kidding—wanted to tell them to go to hell. Another part of me—a better part—said yes. I guess I'll always say yes."

Another round of applause. People were standing. The Filipino waiters were crying. Once again, it could have ended. Post felt he was in one of those movies—Spielberg's *Lincoln* came to mind—a film that cruised past three or four fine endings before it at last consented to stop.

"Do you believe in this voyage? Because people take shots at us all the time. They don't see the magic of American students on a ship, trying to make sense of the world we live in, making it a better place, becoming global citizens. So...do you believe in this trip of discovery?"

He saw the cameras turn from speaker to audience, time to catch the reaction. Now it came. The audience rose, old-timers in front, students in the aisle, offering cheers, waves, applause. Tears, too. Beckmann and Post had to stand as well; otherwise they'd be the only ones remaining in their seats. Edith had said she'd just as soon watch the show on the television in her cabin.

"Then I heard—don't ask me how—of a threat to this ship in the Malacca Straits. It wasn't a government warning. More like one of those Code Orange things you hear at the airport on the way to the gate. That's number one. Here's number two: you worry. Anytime you hear something like that, you have to worry. I worried every day, every night. The nights were the worst. I could imagine terrible things; my imagination ran wild. But I had to ask myself, do we cancel a voyage, or reroute it—God knows how—because somebody runs their mouth on the Internet? If that were the case, trust me, we'd never sail again. And I couldn't bear the thought of that. I didn't come aboard this ship to preside over its final voyage. I want this thing to go on forever. Do you?

"Look, I'm going to finish now. Maybe I slipped up, talking about the Straits of Malacca on—so it turns out—the ship's public address system. And there are folks who think I was wrong in rescuing people who would have drowned, and getting us delayed and quarantined in Singapore. What's more, I've asked some people to leave the ship and I've disciplined some others. And just now I've shared a secret about a terrorist threat to this ship that I insisted should *not* lead to the cancellation of this program. I wanted to share all this because knowing is better than not knowing. I believe in a program—and a country—that stays on course. So thanks for listening. Your applause didn't hurt either. Especially from you hardened reporters. But I think I've said enough. And now that I've been replaced as dean, I'm just another passenger, after all. If you have any questions please address them to my successor, Anna Cather."

She'd been distraught. But now Anna Cather's hands left her face and one shot up in a wave. Everyone in the room was looking at her and it was easy to see that Anna Cather knew it. She realized that she was the bitch bureaucrat who replaced a legend she could never hope to equal. She raised her hand to acknowledge the introduction. But Leo wasn't quite done. A damnably faint bit of praise came next.

"I'll leave this to her," Leo concluded. "I have every confidence in her ability to bring us all home to San Diego."

Post looked around. Some of the Filipino waiters were crying again. So, for that matter, was Anna Cather. And then the applause began as Leo left the podium. People followed Leo through the door, hell, they'd have followed him if he walked off the ship, if he *jumped* off of it. Then, with Leo no longer there, the room slowly emptied: the cameramen and reporters chose the deck, the pool, the railing for their interviews. Before long, Post and Beckmann had the auditorium to themselves. It felt ordinary, then. It was the place where global studies met.

X.

SHANGHAI

A SPRING DAY IN Shanghai, green lawns and blossoming shrubs right across from where the *MV Explorer* was berthed. That nip in the air awakened cells that had gone dormant in southern latitudes; it had that bracing slap that said *get moving, walk, run, you can't build your day around reading and napping.*

Edith had remained on board. She'd be Beckmann's, tonight and tomorrow, she promised, but today she had business in the computer room sending and receiving. That was something he admired. She didn't depend on him to devise a daily program—she had work of her own to do. And so, today, did he.

A good thing about growing older, the professor had discovered, was you saw how things turned out, landscapes and lives, what rode out time and what perished. He felt that way about his home campus where students' lives were formed, where faculty and administrators flourished or flopped, where buildings were razed or renovated or sometimes left alone even as new glittering glass and stone edifices sprang up. Time would judge them all. History had a way of judging. And Shanghai! Oh, what a place, what layers of time and money and power. His students, had they not rushed on field trips to The Forbidden City or The Great Wall, could learn a lot here.

He stood on the dock and looked across the river to Pudong. When he'd been here many years ago, it was a scraggly expanse of fields, dumps, factories, and warehouses that reminded him of the marshland—the so-called Jersey Meadows—between Newark Airport and the Lincoln Tunnel. A wet place, a vacancy, a dumping ground. But now, beyond a carefully gardened harbor side promenade, there stood a wall of high-rises, one of which had—briefly—been the tallest in the world. It impressed from a distance, but those shaded high-rise alleys did not invite exploration. Maybe it was his age: he avoided campus buildings back home that were constructed after his arrival. Or maybe it wasn't age: who'd want to walk in those shaded urban canyons?

The Bund was different, older, better: an elevated walkway along the river, in front of a line of buildings dated before World War II, ambassadors from past to present, survivors of invasion, revolution, colonialism, capitalism, communism, and whatever people decided to call the current state of affairs in China. None of the buildings was as high as those Pudong cloud-busters across the way. What they lacked in height—thank God—they made up for in depth and, if such a thing could be, experience. At the north end, he strolled past the old British Consulate, a luxuriant low-rise place whose gardens and benches drew him in. Part of the property had been absorbed by the Peninsula Hotel. What remained was a government dining club.

Interesting, the fate of colonial buildings, the use that was made of them. Sometimes, in revolutionary situations, the character of the place was utterly changed: a palace became a hospital or a prison. Just as often, though, the new regime found—once ensconced—that they liked rooms with dark wood and meticulous service, they liked gardens and golf courses and expensive bars. And he sensed another lecture coming on—for every newly-liberated colony that cast out its hated occupiers, razed their buildings, forgot their language, there were two others where you could revisit parks, opera houses, and hotels much as they were and food—oh those baguettes in Saigon!—that the colonists (barbarians) had brought. It went further, though, the connection between colonist and colonized. What about all those Algerians in France and the French in Saigon, Hanoi, and Luang Prabang in search of their vanished *Indochine*?

At first, he walked along the river, a pleasant enough stroll: Pudong on the left, the Bund on the right, future and past confronting each other. He enjoyed the morning sun, the breeze off the river. The idea of sitting on a park bench—a different one, every twenty minutes or so—was hard to resist. Chinese cities were the best when it came to people-watching. There were kids in school uniforms, young couples posing for pictures together, and best of all the old people, groups of them, sitting and talking. It felt like they belonged, they were in the scene, in the daily game. You didn't see them that much back home.

At last he crossed over to the old buildings, all part of the British Concession under foreign control and law, an ignoble assault on Chinese sovereignty, yes, and despite its being a high watermark of imperial power, somehow the communized government had kept these buildings, replacing foreign banks with Chinese banks and agencies. The buildings endured. Old names: Banque de Indochine, Jardine-Matheson. Bank of China, Sassoon House, Russo-Chinese Bank. He passed wrought iron fences, gleaming revolving doors, poked around in art deco interiors, walls full of nymphs, murals, and mosaics. Temples of capitalism. Marble floors, vaulting ceilings. At the Sassoon Hotel—long since renamed the Peace Hotel—he took a cappuccino and tilted back in his chair, taking in a circular lobby, marble floor, and wood paneling leading up to a dome of paneled yellow glass. He missed Edith just then. He was all right alone, he assured himself, but it would be fine to have her here. To take a room—$800!—would be a frivolous expense, considering his seventh-deck cabin on the Explorer. But still...

He walked south, a connoisseur of gates and lobbies. He wished he had an office, even a desk in one of those buildings, a reason to come to work there. "Beckmann's Syndrome," Will Post called it now, defined as the ache for a new life everywhere one went. So why not succumb? At last, he reached a place he knew of. The old Shanghai Club, at the far end of the Bund, now part of the Shanghai Waldorf-Astoria, but he couldn't just walk by the place without popping in for a drink. Once again, he missed Edith. After Anna died, he'd learned to live alone. Then Edith came into his life, and now he wondered whether another lesson in loneliness awaited him, a loneliness from which he might not return. So, he thought, he'd make a quiet toast to Edith. But as soon as he entered he saw this wasn't going to happen.

"Professor, come on over here!" Post shouted. He, Ms. Sanchez, and four students had gotten there first.

"Just one drink," he said. "I'm scouting the French Concession. I'm taking a busload of people there tomorrow."

"A good argument for *more* than one drink," Sanchez said.

"Well…one at a time."

"And no Singapore Slings here," Will Post said.

"I suppose it's time for an Irish coffee."

"Professor Beckmann is sampling Irish coffee around the world," Post explained to the students. "That's what I call scholarship."

"It's not so easy," Beckmann said. "Takoradi? Chennai!?"

"But someone's got to do it, right?" Sanchez asked. Beckmann nodded and suddenly relaxed. He was extra careful about drinking with students, even if they were of age. It didn't take long, no more than a second drink, before a kid might say something that crossed the line, sort of by accident, sort of on purpose. But Post was there and the students were from the fifth deck, which was closed today because the ship was taking on fuel.

"I decided to take these characters on a field trip," Post said.

"You've been here before?"

"This is my first time at this particular tourist trap! Of the highest order!" He turned to his tour group: Sanchez and two other girls, both striking, and a couple of young men. Post had a way of attracting people who were probably somebody else's dropouts. Would Beckmann have collected a group like this? Probably not. But he liked this bunch. And, unusually for him, he decided to take a chance.

He told them all to look around because he was sure that they'd never been in a place like this. Oh, no doubt they'd seen their share of bars. But did they know what was special about this place? They glanced at the floors and pillars, the dark wood, leather chairs, ceiling fan.

"Consider," he began, "the bar. The Long Bar." He watched them study it. "No cameras, please." A needless comment. No one had touched a camera. Their hands were on their drinks. It was a close call, but at this point in the voyage he preferred students with drinks to students with cameras.

"You have to know this club is about a hundred and fifty years old. It was an exclusive club, all male. A colonial hangout. A matter of imperialists thinking globally and acting locally. And it was famous for a long bar, such as you see over there. The closer you got to the end—with a view of the Huangpu River—the higher your status. I don't think you could sit there without thinking that your day or night—or your life—had turned out pretty well. Powerful people came here. This area was an international settlement, so you had diplomats, businessmen, military types. Also, in those days, spies, hustlers, gangsters. Rick's Place in *Casablanca*, if you've seen that movie. What you see over there is thirty feet long. The original was thirty yards long. Noel Coward put his head on the bar, looked from one end to the other, and said that he could detect the curvature of the earth."

The kids laughed. This was a faculty practicum they could go for. He hoped the French Concession went as well, the next day.

"Hold it," Will Post said, facing the kids. "Who's Noel Coward?" Silence. "Anybody know? No?"

"Okay," one of the kids said, in a way that students had, the way that implied, we'll go along with this silly game of yours. "Who's Noel Coward?"

"Too late," Post responded. "Today, you pay for your own drinks. Tomorrow, I'll be here. You come here and give me an impressive account of Noel Coward's career, I'll pay you back."

This doesn't happen anywhere else, this connection with kids, Beckmann reflected. And it might never happen to him anymore. But, just then, he liked it.

"Continue, Professor," Post said.

"So what happened to the original bar, you may—you ought to—wonder? I'll answer that with another question. Easy. KFC. Do you follow?"

"Kentucky Fried Chicken?" a couple of them asked. The kind of shaky response that had a question mark at the end of it. KFC? Might it stand for something else? Kids for Communism? Kill Foreign Companies?

"You're right. You've gotten one out of two questions. Hall of Fame in baseball, going one-for-two. Less so, I would say, in surgery or on tests of any kind. After nineteen forty-nine, the place ran down. The old bar was destroyed in nineteen ninety when this place was turned in to China's first…"

"KFC!" the kids responded, laughing, high-fiving. "Kentucky Fried Chicken."

"That's right. But that's not the end of the story. Of the *history*. The Colonel's franchises have moved elsewhere and this is an elite hotel. So the place had gone from elegant club, to postwar dump, to franchise food place, to five-star hotel. You can find similar stories— histories—in Singapore and Saigon and Hong Kong. But you have to do some homework. You have to be curious. You have to care when you travel, when you enter a bar. *Especially* when you enter a bar."

That might have been the end of it and it was high time that Beckmann bundled off to the French Concession, which he hadn't seen in twenty years. When you revisited a place after so long, you always worried whether it was still worth revisiting, especially with a busload of Semester at Sea people. The Bund had survived and prospered yet the Chinese could be remorseless when razing the past. He started to stir, but Will Post delayed him.

"Hold on a minute," he said. Then he turned to one of the students, a pleasant Chinese-American kid who was one of his fifth deck commandoes. He was Tommy, Jody Phillip's pal, who'd gone looking for and found a doctor at 3:00 a.m. in Varanasi. And more. This fellow had confronted Beckmann outside his class, asked if he might sit in. No, he didn't want to enroll, didn't want or—evidently— need credit. Just a chair to sit in. Beckmann had beckoned him to enter, wondering how it would turn out. Usually auditors, as they were called, or pass-fail students were a waste of space. But, in this fellow's case, the reverse might be true: his disinterest in grades gave his presence a kind of value.

"Tommy," Post said. "You've been in a few bars lately. More than I have. Talk to me about them. Start with a list, from the beginning."

"What?"

"Listen, you're among friends here. No living-and-learning whatchamacallits. No alcohol counselor. Start with a list and we'll take it from there."

"Okay," he said.

"Nassau?"

"Senior Frog's."

"Dominica?"

"That was a tough one. We arrived on a Sunday. It felt like a pop quiz in class. Or maybe an outward-bound adventure. Can you find a bar? We did, though. Crazy Coconuts. They opened for us. Hope they made out okay. The place got trashed."

"Manaus…"

"The bar at the dock, outside the terminal. They had these glass columns of beer at the middle of the table. Kind of a reservoir you had to empty. It was okay, sitting there, watching the action out on the river. All those little boats going God knows where."

"Ghana."

"Oh, God. Do I have to? I got into a fight there. Got dock time. Makes sense, the bar was on the dock, outside the Duty-Free. Bunch of kids getting drunk and Ghanaians trying to work an angle on some European guys off the oil rigs. They were the ones who threw those bottles out on the street. Honest. Not us. Not me, anyway."

"Okay."

"Worst bathroom I saw, anywhere," Rosa Sanchez offered.

"Cape Town."

"Quay Four. Right near where you catch the ferry to Mandela's prison. Robben Island. It was okay. You go out to Robben, see his cell and then knock back at Quay Four, like it's the nineteenth hole at some golf course. Kind of strange. Like going to a kosher deli outside a concentration camp. Something definitely wrong."

"Chennai?"

"Hard Rock Café. I wasn't impressed."

"By the place? Why not?

"By myself. It was like…so ordinary. Like going around the world and eating at a KFC. Sitting there, I gave myself a C-minus, no lie."

"Well then…Singapore was next."

"Hold on, Professor. Have a little faith, here. It gets better in India. Also, it gets worse. In New Delhi, I went to the Ice Bar."

"Ice. Like drugs? Or Ben and Jerry's?"

"Ice, as in frozen water. Thirty-plus tons of Canadian ice. Everything in the place is made out of ice, the walls, the bars, the couch, the glasses, the flower vase. A world of ice. They keep it at ten degrees below centigrade. In New Delhi! They give you a parka and gloves and a cap before you go in… In friggin' Delhi. What do you think of that?"

"I think…" Will Post glanced at Beckmann, almost as though answering for permission. "I think you're the Vasco de Gama of world bars. But I wonder what you think…what you make of it…"

"I think it's insane," Tommy said. "You go from one extreme to the other. Money is all it takes. You escape from a hot, polluted crowded city to its…polar opposite."

"Money can do that," Post agreed.

"Listen, you know I've bagged global studies. But if going around the world on a ship means anything, it's about the distances you travel and the differences you discover, real differences in the world. And I think if a bunch of Indians with deep pockets want to get cold…it shouldn't be so easy. Matter of fact, it shouldn't be so easy for us."

"Duly noted," Will Post said. "Singapore."

"What'd we have? Eight hours and the threat of a spanking?" He raised his glass, saluted Beckmann. "Nice job, Professor. I hear you beat the rap."

"No secrets on our ship!" Beckmann said. "One small step for Beckmann is one giant step…etcetera, etcetera."

"So like every other no-hoper on board we went to Raffles Hotel and paid too much for a Singapore Sling. All those tables with glasses of pink stuff. Isn't it funny, how those old places find out that people consider them quaint and charming, rich in history and atmosphere? And the MBAs arrive. Twenty bucks a throw."

"Saigon?"

"Now you're talking. There was a Hard Rock. So what? *Apocalypse Now*. A bar named after a movie that's about American defeat and craziness, am I right? And there we are with beer and babes and just what are we celebrating? Did we win something? The war? Oh, then there was the Lush Bar and here's a new trick, no hookers as far as I could see. Maybe I missed them."

"Sounds like a good stop for a drinking man."

"Better than you know. Also, there were hotels. That wedding at the Grand Hotel. What a clusterfuck. I saw you guys and I thought maybe I should hide. Then I say to myself, 'Hey, they're not hiding.' Doing research, maybe. Scholarship. So I told myself I was doing the same thing. God, it was gross. So I got a suite at the Rex Hotel along with some friends I won't name, some of them are sitting here, and the Rex is an old US military place, it's where they had those press conferences where nobody believed the official line about the war. 'Five O'clock Follies,' right? We took a suite and got blasted on vodka..."

"Hong Kong?"

"Not much. I went to the Wall. I'd been working too hard in bars."

"And now...this."

"This and more. Nice as it is, and thanks for the history, really, I appreciate it..."

What Beckmann felt, listening to Tommy, was gratitude. This was someone who attended school on his own terms: B, B-, C+, incomplete, whatever. But he wasn't stupid. After graduating, it would be pedal to the floor. While A students wrestled with graduate school, the Tommys of the world took over. You might even hear from someone like Tommy years later asking for the titles of some books worth reading. That would be after he'd made a fortune.

"My work's not done," Tommy continued. "There's another field trip. Anybody wants to come, it's on me. Drinks and snacks, maybe a cigar."

"Where?" asked Post. The cigar got his attention.

"Cloud Nine. It's over on Pudong, on the eighty-seventh floor of the Grand Hyatt. The highest bar in the world, folks. And I'm buying. Meghan'll be there. And the flying Dutchman."

"Who's that?"

"Better known as an asshole. He'd love to see you. Bobby Rummel."

"Thanks, no," Beckmann said. "Give him my regards. But I have a question. What have you learned in all this?"

"Can't you tell? I've seen high places and low. Rich and poor. Hot and cold. Retro and cutting edge. Authentic and fake. Global and local. That's something, isn't it?"

Beckmann nodded at Post as if to say, *watch out for this guy. He's something.*

"There's more. I've had this bunch of friends I met on the ship. I've seen their ups and downs. Gross stuff. I've had some moments myself. And I'm figuring who I'll want to see again. And the ones I don't care that much about. That's something else I've learned."

"Okay, Tommy," Post said. "Better than okay."

¤

THE FIELD TRIP GROUP to the French Concession, thank God, was small, with more faculty spouses and life-long leaners than students, but some of the students were among the best, like Darlene Tedrow, Jody Phillips, and Tommy. All that was fine. And Edith was there.

"Sorry I had to rush you out before breakfast," he announced on the bus. "But when I reconnoitered yesterday, I realized that some things can only be seen in the morning. And we'll start to see them in about twenty minutes."

He sat next to Edith. He reached over, took her hand, and watched Shanghai pass by. Hotels, highway overpasses, malls, and markets: he wondered how long it would take to master a place like this, not the whole city, just a single neighborhood. Chinese cities were intimidating. Beyond the harborside fringe of hotels, restaurants, and malls that were global, international, and visitor-friendly was a world of crowded streets and alleys where people baked bread, sewed, butchered, repaired tires, ate porridge, sat out at night drinking tea, slept (when they slept) in back of their shops. A visitor might never get there, never get past the boutiques and coffee shops and Indian touts who wanted to sell you tailored suits. The city went on forever, and knowing it took more time than you had.

"You're coming now to a piece of the past," Beckmann announced when they were five minutes from their destination. He listed the pieces of China that foreign powers had wrested from a fading empire. Germany, Portugal, Britain, Russia, Italy, Belgium, England, and France had presided over enclaves that were under their flags, their laws, their police. At first, you might compare them to embassies, bits of foreign-ruled territory. But embassies were based on reciprocity. These concessions were not—they were colonial and imperial. Hong Kong and Macau had been the last of them. Most of the others perished long before, some after World War I, more after World War II. Not a moment too soon.

"And yet...I quote William Faulkner... 'The past isn't dead. It's not even past.' And now I confess something for which I must ask to be forgiven. If I played the old game, 'where and when would you live?' and if you could go back to any time and any place, the French Concession between the two world wars would be my choice. Almost a hundred years ago. And yet, visiting for a few hours, I hope to demonstrate that Faulkner wasn't wrong."

By now, they'd reached Fuxing Park, and without a word Beckmann led them into a European place inherited by Chinese, a zone of sidewalks, hedges, beds of flowers, squares of grass and, along the sides of the park, plane trees and benches you might find in Paris or Vienna. A little bit of Europe left behind, including—he pointed out—the two statues that they were approaching: Karl Marx and Friedrich Engels.

"Well then," Beckmann said. "The lingering past. Exhibit A: two Europeans, founders of communism, presiding over a still-elegant colonial park. But now I must explain why I obliged you to hurry your shipboard breakfasts. You could visit these fellows anytime. But now, turn around and consider what you see…"

It was wonderful. A badminton match, right in front of the German philosophers. Older people deep into tai chi, lifting a leg, extending an arm, accompanied by slow, nasal music. Farther away, kids flying kites and roller-skating and couples dancing to ballroom music, Arthur Murray style. Old people. Beyond them, at a half-dozen tables in front of a concession stand, men were playing dominos.

"If we came here, later on, you would miss this," Beckmann said. "It's a morning kind of place. A Chinese place. A mix of life, French and Chinese, young and old. I wanted you to see this, to enjoy it, to think about it. Come along now. There are more exhibits."

Two official stops came next and here, Beckmann let the guide have his say. First was the residence of Mao's long-time foreign minister, Chou En Lai; after that, quite near, was the home of the Chinese Republic's first president, Sun Yat Sen. Inside, furnishings were sparse compared to, say, Monticello. No gimmicks or gadgets or personal touches. These were homes converted into museum shrines and attention was duly paid to photographs, writing desks, and a few scraps of period clothing. But the houses were what mattered: European villas where residents could sit out on porches, stroll in gardens, all this in what, at that time, was a mixed neighborhood (to put it mildly), foreign officials, businessmen, diplomats, prostitutes, writers, and a plethora of gangsters who escaped prosecution for crimes committed elsewhere when they came home to the French Concession. When they finished the tour of Sun Yat Sen's place, Beckmann asked the guide for permission to chat a bit more with his students and friends. The guide shrugged and joined their bus driver for a cigarette.

"I'd like to add a bit to what you've been told," he said. "Not to contradict. That's not my style. I never *contradict*. I *complicate*. Consider Chou En Lai, who is presented as the important figure he was. Mao's number two. I need to tell you that he was a charming, adroit, sophisticated Mandarin. A cosmopolitan. He met and liked Charlie Chaplin. They had lunch together. And Ernest Hemingway. He knew his way around Paris. Yet in the nineteen fifties, in Geneva, the US secretary of state, John Foster Dulles, refused to shake his hand. And, despite his long service to Mao, he eventually fell out of favor during the Cultural Revolution. His adopted daughter, a playwright, was killed. When he died, he was excoriated. No public mourning was permitted. Today, he is revered, properly so. But his life was more difficult, more complicated than you've been told. Until now."

Beckmann glanced outside, where his guide had lit another cigarette. Tobacco. An addiction. And a protection.

"Sun Yat Sen. Does it tell you something that both Chinas, mainland and Taiwan, claim him? More complications. Did you know that Sun Yat Sen was a Christian? That he was educated in Hawaii… and yet was praised by Vladimir Lenin, whom he praised in return? Praised by both sides. Complicated, no? So. 'The past is never dead. It's not even past.' Exhibits B and C."

When he stopped he heard a round of applause; not a Leo Underwood room-levitating sound of thousands of clapping hands, for this was a small audience. But he wondered how many field trip leaders ever were applauded unless, on the spur of the moment, they decided to delete a museum visit and add a stop at a mall.

"Now the fun…" he said. "This bus will return you to the ship ninety minutes from now. You will find it where it is now parked. What I invite—but do not require—you to do is join me on a walk, a repeat of a stroll that I took yesterday. A slow stroll. If you come along, fine. If you wish to go elsewhere, have fun. If you wish to stay longer and take a taxi back, just leave a signature on the sheet that you'll find in the front seat of the bus. My name is already on it. I'm signing out as well. All right?"

He took a few steps to see who had followed. They all did, all sixteen of them. He led them down the street that he'd discovered the day before. If a European city ever fell into Chinese hands, it would look like this, old art deco apartment buildings, colonial mansions, some pristine, walls painted, floors varnished, gardens weeded. Those were the lucky ones in turnkey condition: you could picture your life there. Others had been chopped up, subdivided, neglected. Dust-covered cars sat in unkempt yards, a one-time goldfish pond was filled with charcoal or rubbish, clotheslines ran off balconies. The buildings all had stories to tell. So did the streets themselves, narrow, tree-lined, graceful shaded alleys, and when you turned a corner onto a busier street, there were wine shops and bakeries and small, chic restaurants: French, Thai, Chinese.

Beckmann walked with Edith arm in arm, but on the other side, almost as close, was Tommy—the Marco Polo of bars—with whom he'd shared the Long Bar yesterday. He'd come along and that pleased him. He didn't say much, but he listened carefully, and Beckmann spoke a little louder so Tommy could hear.

"Being here," he said, "makes me wish that I had—this sounds corny—more time to live. That I could have a Shanghai chapter in my life. A year or, at the very least, a season. A springtime in Shanghai. And that I could share it with you." And now he acknowledged Tommy. "And you could come to visit also."

"No need to put me up, Professor," Tommy replied. "I've got family here. Matter of fact, they'd put you up. In this neighborhood, even."

"Well, thank you. I'll remember that."

"Another thing. Remember…back at the Long Bar…I said that on this voyage, I divided the people I met into one group that I was okay with never seeing again. And others who were keepers?"

"Yes…I heard you."

"Well, you're a keeper," Tommy finished.

Another lesson, Beckmann acknowledged. What an interesting kid. Again, his indifference to the program's requirements and its academic credits was impressive. It was a little like coming on board without a camera. Admirable, even. He'd been planning a talk with Edith and tell her some things he wanted to say. But Tommy was good company. He talked about a winery he'd seen in South Africa he was thinking of investing in. Hadn't made up his mind about it. And he wasn't boasting; it was just the way he was.

"All right, everyone," Beckmann called out. "I walked this street and it spoke to me. It's clear these buildings come from another time, but somebody owns them now. Bureaucrats, businessmen, swindlers? Today's China might be more like the French Concession than it admits. I wish that every house had a plaque outside, a list of owners from first to last. And then, yesterday I found it. My street. And my house. And as the realtors say, 'do not curb appraise' and 'needs tender loving care.'"

Was it a legal dispute, something about ownership? A family fallen on hard times or bickering over a will? Or waiting to put up a condo? Anyway, this house was the one for Beckmann, a pleasing mix of decrepitude and promise. A chain with a padlock prevented entry, but you could look through a rusted, wrought iron fence at what was left of the place, the driveway, the garden. The house was closed, that was clear, windows shuttered; no one lived there, no one looked over what had once been a formal garden where a round outdoor table remained, too heavy to move. Waiting, it seemed, to learn its fate. How long since someone had sat there, taken coffee, read a newspaper, smoked a cigar while an amah watched the children and was that person a blood-stained general, a Chinese patriot, or a mobster? And how pleasing it was to see that long after the trees weren't pruned, the weeding and watering had ended, all the puttering, yet some flowers, some vines, some trees remained and prospered on their own. No one could fail to enjoy a street like this as it was right now, a mix of tastes and pleasures. And its history was what gave it depth and made you wonder about what lasted and what didn't. Oh, granted, nothing lasted forever. Nothing. But things stuck around awhile, odd things, and they were worth knowing.

"That's my house," Beckmann declared. "If anyone comes back this way before I do..." He met Tommy's eyes. "...Let me know how this place is doing. Whether it gets the care it deserves." Tommy nodded. Pulled out a notepad. Wrote down the address. And came out with something he needed to say.

"There's something I couldn't tell you on the bus or at that bar. Maybe I've got it wrong but I'm thinking that this *MV Explorer* is a little—not so little—America. We've got our dean who broods and bullshits his way around the world. We've got foreign workers in the kitchen and the engine room. And refugees climbing onto the fourth deck. Meanwhile we go around the world to places we hardly know, kissing orphans, painting schools, making friends, getting ripped off, getting drunk, buying souvenirs and taking photos of this whistle-stop adventure campaign. And so on. So I'm wondering. Can this go on much longer?"

"These voyages...or that country?"

"Both."

"I wonder," Beckmann said. "But I don't know."

¤

They decided on a late lunch in a bakery café. Some of the group had taken the bus back to the Explorer. Others had decided to rummage around the French Concession on their own. In some cases they went off by themselves, thus disregarding the standing warning never to go anyplace alone.

"My last tour," Beckmann said. He and Edith and Tommy had ordered soup, bread, cheese, charcuterie, and a carafe of wine. "How'd you think it went?"

"You're fishing for a compliment," Edith declared. "A lovely walk. But I'm sorry it was such a small group."

"I'm not," Tommy said. "I like walks. Not parades." Their food came and they settled into a comfortable silence. A French-Chinese scene outside, crates of eggs, piles of vegetables, fresh noodles on a cobblestoned street. They'd declined an outside table but they were right at the window and it felt like they'd become figures in a painting, a street scene that would hold them forever. Beckmann and Edith wondered about dessert but Tommy had to excuse himself, repeating his invitation to an Irish coffee that evening at the world's highest bar.

"I have something I've been waiting to say to you," Beckmann announced as soon as Tommy was gone. *An awkward, ponderous opening,* he thought. The male equivalent of a woman's "we've got to talk."

"I've been saving something, too," Edith replied. "Ladies first."

"I thought that applied to going into lifeboats."

"Just listen. Cards on the table. I saw and knew your name on the faculty list. I remembered you, not fondly. But my husband thought the world of you. So I wondered. What I saw at first was an old professor not worth disliking." She stopped, whether to catch her breath or gather her thoughts, he wasn't sure. "And what I want to tell you is that you're not a goner, not in any way. There are professors here that students 'like.' And professors they 'respect.' Not many who are liked *and* respected."

"The respect comes first," Beckmann said. "Then the liking. Some try the other way around, but it doesn't work. And shouldn't."

"And now this walk through the French Concession. Do you think I could have a little something with the coffee? A cognac?"

"Fine." He ordered two. "I feel a nap coming on. Meanwhile…"

"Apple tart for me."

"The Linzer tart for me."

"Now I come to my conclusion, Professor. Conclusion, coffee, cognac, dessert, then nap. Does that appeal?"

Beckmann nodded. He loved their afternoons together, their "snoozes."

"You've responded to every place we've been. The French Concession most of all. And I say to myself, this is not the man who left what sounded like a suicide note on a table back home."

"You know about that? Where did you hear about that?"

"Never mind."

"Meghan?"

"Stop it!" By then the tarts and coffee and cognac arrived. Oh, that nap, how it beckoned. More inviting than the conversation they were having, which she'd taken over altogether. The conversation that mattered kept getting postponed.

"I think you meant it, no matter what you told Leo Underwood. Your wife's death. The prospect of one or two or four more years doing the same thing in the same place didn't appeal. But you were in for a surprise. Your life's not over. Nor is your work."

¤

THE BUND WAS THE first to go, stately and elegant, slipping away. And then—it took much longer, Pudong, as in your face as any place Leo Underwood had ever seen, a fireworks display that never ended—even Pudong slipped away after a while, a blossom of light that darkness swallowed.

And now, what? he wondered. Anna Cather would have her work cut out for her. This was the rough part, these next weeks—this was when complaints and disputes that had been postponed and suppressed, like shrapnel, worked their way to the surface. Global studies rebellion, coming right up. Irony from faculty members, grouchiness from passengers, complaints about the food which—he had to admit—had a way of going downhill around now. Little annoyances. The puddles of water you had to walk through after the crew hosed down the deck, the endless announcements, the travel department, drumming up field trips in Taiwan like someone gave a shit.

That morning, he'd found Meghan cracking up a group of life-long leaners at breakfast, out on the deck behind the sixth floor dining room. They were laughing the way kids laughed, convulsing, rolling on the floor, holding their stomachs, the way you don't laugh anymore after you grow up. When they saw him, they urged Meghan to let him in on the joke, as if they wouldn't mind hearing it a second time themselves.

"Okay, okay," Meghan said, trying to collect herself. But she broke out into another fit of giggles. Unlike her recent self, edgy and downbeat. It had been a while since he'd seen her laugh.

"So there's a field trip I took in Taiwan," she began. "They advertise a village where all the groups—tribes—minorities are represented. It was as if we had, you know, Seminoles, and Mohawks, Sioux and Apaches and Cherokees living in the same place, with hogans or tepees or pueblos, cooking alligator or buffalo or whatever, making moccasins which are handicraft and baskets which are handicraft and weapons which are handicraft. Well, we arrive early, right at opening time. And you can tell they weren't expecting us. So we make our first stop and they stumble out in native garb—this was a fishing tribe, I guess—and they show us food and handicraft and, thank you very much, all of the luck in the world, sure hope you survive, and we're on to the next village, on this trail, and then we look down below and there's another trail running parallel, kind of a service road, and they're running along it, and while they're running, they're changing clothes, getting suited up to be a mountain tribe and…duh…the light goes on… They're gonna be in costume for us every place we go…"

Meghan was laughing and so were her friends and Leo, good sport, chuckled appreciatively, moving to breakfast at an inside table in a seat with a view of his sea and his back to the students.

Too damn bad about losing Japan, Leo thought. Manila was out because of a State Department travel warning. What a crock! There was always an embassy guy who didn't want to get out of his chair. Manila would have been fun. Maybe that was the real reason they said no. South Korea would have been his second choice. Great food. Long history with America. Neither Manila or Seoul matched up with Japan. But Taiwan! And Hilo! That last leg, that was when you talked about the meaning of it all, the voyage was great, they'd been great, the world would be a better place with them in it and, by the way, 100 percent participation in the alumni fund campaign would be appreciated. He'd said all that. He always had. But now he was just another passenger.

"WHAT HAPPENS IN SHANGHAI, stays in Shanghai," Will Post and Rosa Sanchez agreed. That was their slogan, having great sex while sailing around the world. Beckmann would never know that he and Rosa Sanchez had made good use of a room far above the Long Bar. No need for him to know that Sanchez felt that she'd never quite checked into a hotel room before she had sex in it. The way some guests promptly tore the hygienic paper seal off the toilet or threw some complimentary soap and shampoo into their luggage, Sanchez indulged her "nesting instinct" which involved sex in a shower, on the bed, or, circumstances permitting, a balcony. She was something. God, she was smart, instinctively smart, quick on the uptake. What brains. What a body. Sure, she had a lot to learn from him. He was a wordman, he'd been around. The other day he told her he was taking a chance, hoping that he could risk ticking her off. She nodded. She might be thinking he was getting jealous, about to ask whether she'd connected with anyone else on board. To judge by the way she dressed—tight shorts, tightly-packed halters—you'd be safe betting that sex was always in the neighborhood. But maybe not; some of the best lookers on board turned out to be careful, thoughtful people. Maybe they had serious boyfriends back home. Maybe their idea of a shipboard fling seemed like a waste of time. Maybe they liked the idea of an uncomplicated voyage, clear-eyed and undistracted.

"I just remembered," Will Post continued, "that one of our girls was walking around Dominica that Sunday we arrived and was dressed in…I don't know…something flimsy. Bathing suit and towel? And an older woman coming back from church told her she should be ashamed of herself…"

"And your point?"

"Was that you?"

"If it was…what's your point?" She was bristling, in a way that left no doubt, this conversation was a mistake.

"Okay, let's just leave it at that," Will Post said. It was a conversation he wasn't entitled to have. He'd presumed too much.

"If you stop there," she said. "You're toast."

"Okay. Since you asked…"

"Wrong. Since you started…finish."

"Listen. I think you're terrific. You have a way of seeing things. Of creating scenes. You live them and then you write them. And you write them well. But I wish you didn't dress like you wanted everyone to know you're the hottest dish on the menu. You could let people discover that, over time. You don't have to advertise it before you say hello…"

She stayed quiet. She might still be deciding never to talk to him again. But she wasn't angry.

"No one ever told me that before," she said. And left it at that. Later Will Post wondered about that conversation. The benefit to her. The cost to him.

¤

PROFESSOR HAROLD BECKMANN HAD something he wanted to say. He told Edith, who told Will Post, and it went on from there. The two professors combined their classes, the word got to the fifth deck, the life-long leaners passed the word, and now he stood at the podium and noticed that Leo Underwood was in the audience. What was meant to be a small audience had gotten larger.

"Some thoughts that have come to me in the course of this voyage that I wish to share," he said. "Some of this has to do with what I've been teaching about the subtle tangle of past and present that we encounter as we sail from place to place, colonies and empires yielding to global cities, postcapitalist, postcommunist, post-ideology. Some has to do with Professor Will Post's writing class, where the question is how to report on what you've seen and discovered and—beyond that—whether the word 'discovery' can even be applied to places that have been so visited, so photographed, so blogged and tweeted, where we spend a handful of days, not more."

As he spoke, Beckmann found it remarkable that anyone had showed up. If he'd announced this sort of speech at home, would anybody come? Students? Not unless he threatened to take attendance. What about his colleagues? They'd assume that, after all these years, Beckmann could have nothing new to say. They already knew him as much as they wanted to. He had no surprises left in him and, if anyone appeared, it would be people watching for signs of his decline and retirement. Here, he surprised people. He surprised himself.

"Nobody stays at home forever. Oh, granted there may be individuals who don't stray far from where they were born. I would like to think of them as happy. But I'm not sure. But few nations stay at home. They go out into the world for all sorts of reasons, high-minded and low, selfless and self-serving, acknowledged or suppressed. People travel to foreign countries. Period. And you have joined this company of travelers, the latest of a long line. Your visits are brief. Perfunctory. And yet you can't shake—I can't either—the idea that this trip is a great gift. So it's a mixed bag. You are innocents abroad, and innocence is always accompanied by ignorance. And yet, innocent as you are, you are guilty of wealth, arrogance, indifference. What a situation!"

I am glad I am here, Beckmann thought, *looking out from the podium. I am here for them and they are here for me.* It couldn't happen on land. It couldn't happen anywhere else.

"No one sails around the world unscathed. Let's consider your experience with animals, of which you were told to be wary. Some of you have been bitten by monkeys and mosquitoes and—so I hear—piranhas. Anything else? Dogs? Oh, also bats: I remember the precautionary rabies shots in Brazil. Let's not even go into germs, microbes, and other critters that may be cruising—or voyaging—in your systems, digestive and reproductive. And the ocean, let's not forget the ocean. Calm most of the way, but there have been nausea-inducing moments. And that is as it should be. On shore, you have been overcharged repeatedly, almost routinely, you have been conned, laughed at, misled, misinformed, herded and hustled. The places that you came to, blithe and curious, targets of your interest, your charity, targeted you in return. That too, is as it should be. I would not have it otherwise.

"Whether you talk about missionaries, businessmen, soldiers, anybody coming ashore, whether to meet host-country students, tour guides, shopkeepers, families, everyone is a kind of predator and a kind of prey. Sometimes you come out ahead. Sometimes you are disappointed. There are winners and losers on both sides. Have we not had our casualties? Two students—that I know of—hospitalized for alcohol poisoning. Two more put ashore in Diego Garcia. Two injured in a very serious fall off the Great Wall of China. Those are cases we know about. Surely there are more. Bottom line: good things and bad things await us as we travel around the world. We think we sail in as winners. Consider us! Consider where we're from, our youth, our wealth! And—please—consider our ship, which bespeaks our good fortune. Much good awaits on shore. But there is also something that is contrary and hostile. You know this now. I wish your parents knew it, as well."

"Amen to that!" someone shouted. It was meant to be heard, and it came from Leo Underwood, who tossed Beckmann a mock salute. "You've got that right!"

"Thank you, Dean Underwood. You've brought me to my conclusion. I want to share something personal…" He stopped and anyone watching might think he was working up to a hard disclosure. It wasn't that at all. He saw Edith Stirling, wondering—maybe worrying—about what came next. Was she afraid he would propose to her, in public?

"Shortly after our voyage began, Dean Underwood called me into his office and asked, in the nicest possible way, if I intended to commit suicide while aboard the MV Explorer. He then produced a note that I'd left at home on my kitchen table. A list of instructions— drain those pipes, water those plants, pay these bills, etcetera, etcetera for a relative of mine who takes an interest in me. At the end of my list was a phrase, a bit of a closing: 'I may end my life on this voyage.' And some words on the location of my will, the name of my lawyer. My niece panicked when she read that morbid line. She contacted Charlottesville. And Dean Underwood contacted me.

"I told him that I wasn't suicidal. That I only meant to acknowledge what was obvious. A man of a certain age goes away for four months— who knows? I regretted that my note was ambiguously phrased. So we had a laugh or two and that was that. Thanks, Dean Underwood. For your understanding." He nodded at Leo, who responded with a wave.

"Now, Dean Underwood, I have to say it… I lied. That note was more than ambiguous, more than suggestive. I came aboard thinking that I would jump to my death. That's what I planned."

The room froze. A good-natured and apprehensive audience was frightened. This wasn't what they'd come to hear.

"Jump," he repeated. "And I don't mean jump the ship, that is, disappear into this or that port. I lost my wife…after months of watching cancer…devour her…and me as well. I was alone, living half a life. My home, my career, my garden, all my pleasures and satisfactions seemed oddly dispensable. And I asked myself, who would be with me when my time came? Who'd watch over me? Could I confront, by myself, what my wife and I went through together?

Could I die…again…that way, that slow, hopeless, medicated way? When I could end it in minutes?

"Now I come to the part where I have to say what you hear after watching some stunt on television: 'Kids, don't try this at home.' I went out on deck and thought about it. The argument for a fast exit was irrefutable. Not the seventh deck. That—I know it sounds absurd— was a bit too much. I'm not a diver. So, the fifth deck, the notorious fifth deck. Only if Will Post and his irreverent cohorts had gone to bed. So, late at night, it would have to be. And, please, a calm night. Dying is one thing. Getting knocked around like a beach ball, spun and buffeted, no thank you. In the wee hours, yes, a calm sea, and it would be nice, when you thought about it, to have a moon in the sky, looking down at me as I looked up at it, before I got tired and slipped beneath the waves. Yes!"

The mood of the audience had changed. The life-long leaners had been on the edge of tears earlier. When he described what was waiting for all of them, soon, the tears were still there, but they were smiling, they were entertained by his increasingly fussy preparations for suicide. They were smiling at him. Somewhere along the way he had gone from tragic to comic.

"And then someone else, someone better and braver, went over the ship's railing first. A memorable lady, Carla Hutchinson. To follow her was out of the question. A copycat professor, that's what I would be. A plagiarist. No Williamson Turn for me. No suicide. No jump. It has to do with this ship, with our life together, with the oceans and the ports along the way. I felt alive. Looking forward to classes, looking forward—would you believe?—to the meals, not for the food but for the good company. My life was enriched. Saved. Renewed. Why didn't I jump? I didn't want to miss my classes. I couldn't picture it, them showing up in a classroom and me not there. I had to finish my course. And finish the voyage. Thank you for that."

He panned the room the way he often did near the end of a class. It would be all right if he stopped here.

"I mentioned the Williamson Turn that finds its way back to find someone lost at sea. When I came on board I was lost, I was in the water, I was on my way to drowning. And this ship, from the first moment, was a kind of Williamson Turn for me."

That was the ending he wanted. "I'll be seeing you."

XI.

KEELUNG, TAIWAN

KEELUNG WAS A FILL-IN, an afterthought; it was like one of those sad substitute teachers who shows up in high school classrooms when the regular instructor phones in sick, and then the class can't seem to remember what they'd been doing the day before, what lesson they were in the middle of, what page they were on. Will Post didn't expect much. Nobody did.

As for teaching, the voyage was about finished. Just two weeks remained, a mere handful of class meetings. Now silly stuff prevailed. Activities, reflection, reentry, packing, and convocation. It was over. The papers about China confirmed it. Too much travel time to tourist destinations, marching through the Forbidden City, hiking the Great Wall. Not much time for reflection. So there were guide-and-shopping yarns, tales of vendors who trailed visitors for miles along the Great Wall in hopes of selling a bottle of water or some postcards. Irritation and pity mingled in the students' reactions, as if the trinket seller had subtracted from their experience. Would they please go away, these pesky Chinese, and leave them alone with the Wall? Whether it was the Taj, Angkor Wat, the Roman Coliseum, all these ancient fine places—throw in the Parthenon—where you went to connect with the past, with princes, gladiators, priests, artists, the locals were always around, ruining the moment, blocking the view, trying to sell you something plastic. Pain in the ass! And yet, against all odds, his kids always came up with something. One of them described the Great Wall going up and over and down rocky mounts and he was reminded of a Mohawk haircut. That got to Will Post. He'd been to the Great Wall, once. Once was plenty. But if he'd gone there again and again, he wouldn't have come up with a line like that.

He sat back on his cabin sofa and admitted that the travel writing courses had exceeded his expectations. And he'd gotten close to a bunch of kids he liked.

Tommy—his cigar man—turned in a story even though he wasn't enrolled in the class. He was in the neighborhood when two SAS students who were camping on the Great Wall arose to pee, stepped out onto an unrestored zone, and tumbled into a precipice, falling and rolling thirty feet. One student needed forty stitches on her knee. The other student was unconscious. Tommy and his pals—"every one of them a C student," he later boasted—improvised a stretcher and carried the kid to one hospital which refused admission. The local guides they'd hired faded away. Tommy got to another clinic where money talked. Not great writing, but it was something he wanted to keep and share. Something about how the world turns dangerous. They'd written their way around the world on a schedule that was tight and cluttered and came back with some good stuff. Now he'd ask them to revise a couple of their best pieces and submit them to him in lieu of a final exam. But there was a final assignment. He couldn't wait to see how they'd do. And after that, after the last papers, the last class, the final grades, what then? The life he'd left was waiting for him. But—what was the student lingo?—he wasn't feeling it.

¤

MORNING HAD ALWAYS BEEN Leo Underwood's favorite time at sea. Waking up and confirming where he was pleased him, every day. He loved the feeling of a harbor, the tugs and barges, the lure of the shoreline, but the ocean, by itself, out of sight of land, was better still. And morning meant breakfast in his cabin, which he now shared with Anna Cather. Or she with him. Never mind. He arrived early and stayed as long as he liked. No need for either of them to be proprietary: neither one of them would need this office again.

This morning they were in Keelung. Keelung in the rain. You had to laugh. No postcard here. No photo ops. No one expected much. Last night's pre-port session had been random and odd. That's what the whole operation was like at this stage. The day before when a professor remarked that someone—a staffer—had taken the last orange off a fruit tray, she turned and threw it at him. The kitchen was just going through the motions, emptying out the freezer, chunks of fish, cubed beef, thin-sliced pork, and no more chocolate croissants in the morning. Students started wandering into the hitherto off-limits faculty lounge and no one quite had the energy to kick them out. All the ship's rooms had names spelled out in letters that were attached to walls near the entrance. Bit by bit, they were peeled off—the Hudson Computer Center became HUD PUT ENTER. Kids were testing limits like a bunch of high school seniors already admitted to the college of their choice, suddenly indifferent to discipline or detention. Time, which had passed so quickly, now slowed: as the days dwindled, the voyage got longer.

"Look at that," Leo said to Anna Cather, gesturing at a table full of breakfast food, fresh-squeezed orange juice, bagels, smoked salmon, and the chocolate croissants that had vanished from the cafeteria line. "Supper, they ask me what I want. Like a condemned man, getting his last meal, again and again."

"I'm glad you stayed on board," Anna said. "I expected that, after they purged you, you would want to leave in style. Something—can I say it?—theatrical."

"Theatrical? Damn straight. I pictured it, like I could taste it. Like Johnny Carson's last show or Ted Williams' last home run. Oh boy…"

"You changed your mind?"

"Your buddy, Beckmann, he couldn't take the idea of leaving his class unfinished. That's how I feel. How do you feel, lady? That's what I've been wondering. I'm wondering what your home life is like these days."

"Oh, please. You could care less about my home life. You're curious about my sex life." This was how they used to talk, not when she was a student—Leo was careful that way—but later on. He admitted wondering about her, half Chinese, half Irish-American ("That's what I called a hybrid," he once cracked), a Mandarin-speaker, a computer whiz, and a Springsteen fan. She told him about her early boyfriends. He accused her of using men like Kleenex.

"Remember that guy you brought along to my place to see the leaves? Nice fellow. Some kind of graduate student. Justin, right? I called him 'Justin Time.'"

"Well, that visit was the end of poor Justin."

"Was it my fault?"

"Our fault," Anna said. "There we were going on for hours about our voyages. Nonstop. We fed off each other. And Justin went from amused and attentive to bored and angry. And gone. But finding guys is easy."

"I guess so," Leo said. She had that alert, handsome face, eyes and cheekbones from the Chinese side of things and hair which, when she let it down, fell below the belt line.

"So what's the word from headquarters? What'd they think of our press conference? I know we got a ton of coverage. But nothing from Virginia."

"Mixed reviews. 'A dazzling performance!' says one trustee. 'Ship him straight to *The Jerry Springer Show*,' goes another. On the whole it was very impressive. Whether it brings in new customers or keeps the ones we already have, it's too early to tell. But you gave it your best shot. That's for sure." She stood up, wiping croissant flakes off her shirt. "I've got to talk to the field trip people."

"You should talk to Will Post sometime."

"I will," she said, stopping at the door. "Stay as long as you like."

"Just a second. A question. There I was, giving my grand finale about sailing in the shadow of a terrorist warning…"

"That was our secret," she said. "I wish you hadn't."

"Looked like you were sitting there crying."

"The trustees think you invented it."

"We know better, don't we?"

"We do," she said. "I invented it."

"What?"

"I'm sorry. You were ready to say no to my offer. I couldn't blame you. I needed something else. Now you're out there, taking shots, and I'm going to front-and-center on this one. I'm going to fight for you."

"The hell you are," Leo said. "No need for both of us to ride off into the sunset."

"I thought I was doing you a favor," she said. On the edge of tears, maybe. *You could never tell about tears*, Leo thought. Sometimes they happened, sometimes they were summoned. "I thought I was doing you a favor," she said.

"You did."

Not more than a minute after Anna had gone, Will Post popped into his office. "I thought she'd never go. High-level conference?"

"Friendly chat," Leo said.

"I'm wondering—can't help it—what you think went wrong. This American ship goes out into the world and—shit happens."

"You know, I just pictured you coming in here, just like you have, and asking that very question. And the simple answer is that I made a mistake. But not the mistake you think I made. Hey, but first, make yourself a sandwich, will you? That smoked salmon…that fish died for you."

Will Post assembled the bagel, the cream cheese, the lox. So far, the food in port had interrupted a cafeteria that had gotten predictable. But pretty soon they'd be on what Beckmann called the Yamomoto Run, the long haul to Hawaii, when the kitchen's offerings went south. So he took advantage of the dean's buffet. He sat and Leo began talking.

"A ways back…was it Shanghai?… I was up late and I found myself in your enclave, the fifth deck," he said. "Late at night and it was mostly empty, but not quite. Just this one woman sitting on the deck in front of a laptop and it takes a while but I figure out that she's talking to her mother back home, and one by one they're reviewing pictures she took. This is some kind of temple, here's the Forbidden City, and this square is where it was tanks against protestors, and here's something I almost bought, but some other kid beat me to it. A mother-and-daughter confab that went on and on, as if she was back at home already, like she'd never left home completely. Eventually she sees me, smiles, waves, and goes back to Mom. And here's the mistake I made and I'm kind of proud of it."

I like this guy, I have to admit it, Will Post thought. *Huge ego. Four months, everybody and everything orbits around Leo. But I like him. Because he's taken all those voyages. Because there are tectonic plates grinding away inside of him, ego and anger and vulnerability. Because he's toast. That clinches it.*

"No, it's not that I didn't know about our brand-new interconnected world, kids never out of reach of Mom and Dad," Leo continued. "I didn't want to acknowledge it. Be governed by it. It would have cramped my style, I couldn't let that happen. By the way, have you noticed there've been parents in almost every port we visited after Ghana?"

"I noticed," Post replied, "and I wondered about it." He'd seen parents shopping, dining, joining field trips, parents on ship, parents at a reception in the faculty lounge, rich parents, potential donors being courted. And he'd sensed that something was lost, something was missing, and what had changed is what did Leo Underwood in. A voyage around the world in a ship—that famous slow boat to China— had once been all about departure, separation, adventure. From dozens of films and newsreels, he recalled those scenes that had a ship slipping away from a dock, all the people who'd come to say goodbye standing down below and the passengers at the railings waving at the folks they were leaving behind, and crepe streamers unfurling as they were tossed off the ship and then you had the first movement away, the first inches of a great voyage. Distance and perspective, gone now.

"It's changed," Leo said. "It's not what it used to be. I know, that's what all the old farts say. That doesn't mean they're wrong. That kid on deck, God love her, looking over snapshots with her mom. The voyage isn't even over and they're scrapbooking. So yes, I kind of blew it. Those kids think they're ahead of the game. I think they're out of it. But I'm not."

"Beg your pardon?"

"If it had to end, it couldn't have ended better." At breakfast, students filled every seat at his table, Leo told him. Whenever he walked, there were greetings, even in the faculty lounge which he had previously avoided. Plenty of free drinks. And, as he'd suspected, his last speech was out there on the Internet. His emails were endless piles of "give 'em hell" messages from former voyagers. Then there were notes from strangers who wanted to friend him, link him, share his space. That gave him the willies. There were offers to speak at seminars and conferences, at commencements and faculty retreats. And—at last!—an inquiry from a literary agent.

"He thinks I've got a book in me," he told Will Post.

"After the publicity you got," Post said, "I'd say it's a slam dunk. The early voyages, all those stories, all those voyages. And a hell of an ending, too."

"I want my name on that book," Leo said. "It's my story. And I want it there alone."

"Of course."

"Thing of it is, I'm not a writer. I'm a talker. You're a writer. You've been on a voyage. That gives you an edge. It's yours if you want it."

"As a ghost, a pure ghost," Post mused. It didn't bother him. His name had appeared so many times already, in so many places, it was time to give it a rest. "Actually, if I did that kind of work—big if—that's the way I'd want it to be. Better for you, better for the book. Look, when you get a contract, let me read it."

"That's just what I was going to ask," Leo said. "Only the guy said there were people he knew who did this kind of thing."

"I'm sure he has a list of names. And two commissions are better than one."

"Are those agents all wise-asses? He goes on and on with all the reasons the book can't miss. And then, you know what he said?"

"I think I do."

"What?"

"He said it was too bad the pirates didn't show up."

"Bingo."

"Well, let me look over what the agent says when it comes."

Leo handed him some papers. "It's here. A honey of a deal."

Post gave what Leo handed him a manila folder filled with emails. A half-dozen publishers were ready to bid on Leo's book. It couldn't have been better if Leo had planned it that way. And, Post realized, he probably had. From the beginning of the voyage, from before the voyage, back in New Hampshire when Anna Cather came to him with a welcome offer and an exciting warning.

"So we're in business,"

"I guess we are. And you'll have to tell me all your stories all over again."

¤

THIS LATE IN THE voyage, everyone avoided field trips. Still, some life-long leaners wanted to see the art treasures that Chiang Kai Shek had hidden from the Japanese, then shipped across the Straits to Taiwan when the Civil War went Mao Tse Tung's way. That meant a final bus trip to the National Palace Museum in Taipei. Some students were at loose ends on a rainy day, in Keelung, so they came, too. As Edith and Beckmann settled onto the bus—surely their last—a dispute arose between the faculty member who was leading the trip and the local tour guide. The guide insisted that admission to the museum was not included in the price of a tour; the faculty member disputed this, showing the tour description in the Semester at Sea catalog. The guide was unimpressed and so it all went badly before it began, the passengers forced to fork up the price of admission to the National Palace Museum. Some senior passengers paid for the kids.

"What a mess," Edith said. "These things happen more than they should, don't they?" Beckmann nodded. He was glad to be just a passenger, his hand in Edith's, headed to the museum, like a pair of seniors on an outing from a retirement home.

"What's Will up to today?" Edith asked.

"He wasn't interested in the museum. He likes small museums. Monticello, Mozart's Vienna apartment, Mencken's home in Baltimore. Anything bigger than that, he numbs out. He said he wanted to 'just walk' and, he added, 'in the rain.' As if the rain were an added attraction. It sounded like he wanted to be by himself…"

"And with that Sanchez girl?"

"I don't know. Something tells me…no."

¤

IT WAS A GREAT museum, an endless museum, and they were good for two hours. They'd have to be selective. They avoided jades, which seemed to draw hordes of Chinese families. They strolled slowly past works in bronze—cooking pots, mostly—that were sturdy and shapely and sometimes there was an added personal touch, a quirky monkey added to the handle of a pot lid, a bit of a joke from some unknown someone who had been dead for at least four thousand years. Almost forever. That appealed to them, it moved them, talent spanning time, good nature and humor riding through millennia. The paintings were what mattered most, paintings from a long time ago, and it felt as if they'd been waiting for the elderly American couple to come along. "A Branch and a Blossoming Vine," "Wishes for an Early Spring," "Slender Bamboo and an Elegant Lady." And most of all, the one that caught and held them, that they walked away from and returned to: "Waiting for a Ferry on an Autumn River." In the background were rounded mountains, in front a winding river headed nowhere fast, and then meadows and trees and—dwarfed to insignificance—two figures waiting to cross from one side to the other. That painting— that title—felt right to Beckmann. Almost too right.

"It has something to do with our voyage," Edith offered. "Something to do with us. Is that us standing on the riverbank?"

"Our voyage…" Beckmann repeated. He didn't answer her. He was taken by "our voyage." Three months and well across the world, they'd met on the steps of a favela. They'd stretched out on the grass beneath a palm in Ghana. And now here.

"Our voyage is ending soon," he said. That was intended as an opening sentence. He had more to say.

"Yes, that's right," she answered, as if he'd just glanced at his watch and told her what time it was. She suggested a snack in the museum coffee shop before they boarded the bus back to Keelung.

"How'd you like the museum?" a student asked, sitting down beside them. Everybody in the same boat, everybody a shipmate. But this was the worst time.

"We were dazzled," Edith responded. "Did you see that one painting that a woman did—a vine that goes on for yards, panel after panel?"

"I concentrated on the jade."

"Well then…"

"The museum didn't do it for me," she said.

Beckmann held his tongue while Edith chatted up the student, giving her the attention she thought she was entitled to. Then the girl went out to have a cigarette before boarding the bus.

"I have an idea," Edith said. "Just hear me out and—this is the hard part—when I've finished, don't respond. I want you to think about it."

It's coming, Beckmann thought. *It might be what I want. Or dread. A life together, for as long as we have. Or something else, much sooner, much shorter, much less.*

"I have a book in mind for you," she announced.

"Well, fine. By whom?"

"To write. No further questions please." As if to enforce that warning she took a bite of Sacher torte, followed by a sip of coffee. "I've reread that first book. Your one and only book, really. That first book—my husband was right about it. It's fine. And it stays in memory. But he had a theory about writers, especially Americans, mostly about novelists but that, more or less, is what you were in *Colonies and Empires*. He said the first book had energy. It was an act of creation, liberation, all that. After that, diminishing returns. He looked forward to hearing from you, of course. But those other things you wrote, you didn't even offer him."

Another bite of cake. Another sip of coffee. She enjoyed them profoundly, Beckmann could tell. She enjoyed still being able to taste things.

"I know, I know, you're not a novelist. You don't write fiction. Still, there was a writer present back then. I'm wondering, Henry, if he's still around or in the neighborhood. I think you have another book in you."

"A sequel to *Colonies and Empires*?"

"Not quite."

"Specific countries? The world is lousy with specialists. It would take years, lifetimes."

"Relax. You're not competing with Jonathan Spence. I have another empire in mind. It is an empire, though no one admits it, with a past, present, and future. Brutality, romance, idealism, exploitation, all those complicated things you told the students to watch out for. It'll bring out the best in you, anger, humor, nostalgia, the works. You'll make them laugh and cry, my dear… You'll make them angry, too."

"Enough!"

"The American empire. Think of it, the places we claim or control beyond the United States. Puerto Rico, the Virgin Islands, American Samoa. Also Guam, the Commonwealth of the Northern Marianas, the Republics of Palau and the Marshall Islands, the Federated States of Micronesia. Scraps of atolls and islands…Palmyra! Christmas! And Guantánamo! And the places we used to rule, Panama, the Philippines. When the flag is lowered, as you well know, that's not the end of the story. And Vietnam. I picture you on China Beach, around Da Nang. All the bases, the colonies, the client states and outposts... the little Americas."

"My God!" he said. "I must say—"

"Nothing!" she interrupted. "Remember your promise? Just think about it. It can start with magazine articles, that'll get the project rolling, and you can expand them into chapters later on. They can get you a contract if you haven't already got one. I think you can get one well before that, though."

"With a publisher?"

"Well, yes, Henry, a publisher. As a matter of fact, *your* publisher. *Colonies and Empires* has never gone out of print. You're still their writer. There's a woman there. My husband's last secretary..."

"Beverly? Would it be Beverly?"

"Yes."

"I remember her. Always reading. Thrilled to death talking to a writer. I suppose she's gotten past that kind of enthusiasm."

"Way past. There are stories that people like to tell. One is about my husband. The caring, meticulous editor, the career-long mentor. The other is the brainy secretary who digs a best seller out of the slush pile. Beverly is both of those. She found her best seller. Now she's a senior editor."

"Give her my best."

"You give her *your* best. She's waiting for your call when you get back. She wants to work with you. At first, she was surprised. 'It's like Amelia Earhart radioing for a landing spot at O'Hare,' she said. But she likes the project." Edith took a pen and jotted a phone number on a napkin.

Then, as it happened, it was time to get back on the bus to Keelung. A few students were browsing in the gift shop but most passengers surrounded their guide, waiting for the bus and debating, the way they always did, whether the trip was worth it. Edith slept all the way back to the ship. Beckmann's hand rested on Edith's and, even when he moved it, she did not stir. Was she faking sleep?

You think too much, Professor. That's what he told himself. How do you know it's too much? It's when your thoughts run in circles, circles that aren't even concentric, no—it's the same circle, same radius, diameter, circumference, over and over again. *That's me,* he thought. He closed his eyes, but not to sleep. He pictured that painting—"Waiting for a Ferry on an Autumn River." He closed in on it, he almost entered it. Five hundred years old, ink on paper that had turned brown. Had it been brown at the beginning? Either way, it suited the mood of the piece, the color of leaves that were about to fall. The smell of time turning, the smell of childhood, those burning leaves. Lost now. Also gone, the raking of leaves; now it was leaf blowers. Could the decline of America be connected to the invention of the leaf blower? Oh, that painting. Go there now. Go into it. Close your eyes. That might make the bus driver the last person on the bus who wasn't sleeping. And even he looked tired. Never mind. Into the painting, those distant mountains, rounded peaks, worn down over the centuries. How many centuries had the artist been dead? Five? What was left of anybody after five hundred years? Out of reach of DNA, surely. But the painting? A river ran through it, lined with reeds or maybe cattails that he'd attempted to smoke when he was a boy. Geese flew overhead. And—but you had to look hard—there were figures in the landscape, a scholar—so he'd read at the museum—a scholar waiting for the ferry to carry him across. What was left of that scene, reeds and trees, the river itself, or even the mountains, after so long? But nothing was more perishable than these people waiting for a ferry in autumn, two of them, one a scholar, the other the scholar's companion. He saw himself on an autumn river with Edith, both waiting to board that ferry. Would his companion, the one who was sleeping next to him, their hands touching, be setting foot with him onto the far bank? Watching from one side of the river? Or waiting on the other?

¤

SANCHEZ WAS A GAME woman. In some ways she reminded Will Post of a type that he generally disliked, the kind who said, "I'll try anything once." But Sanchez was way better than that: streetwise, tough, adventurous. But not indiscriminate. There were some things she wouldn't try and some that, having tried, she would not repeat. Will Post put himself in that second category. "Brains are sexy," she told him. She hadn't been outside the United States, and even then just barely outside of Texas. He was the world traveler and she must have known he'd be good to hang out with. She'd learned a lot: she asked questions all the time. But she was the one who decided what was worth learning. After that, after him, she'd find new instructors. And Keelung, Post realized, might be the start of that—Keelung was where their connection went from indispensable to optional. She was going to stay at Taipei's Grand Hotel, a famous place in its time. There were clubs in Taipei, there were places to shop, and a street—Snake Alley— where you could drink shot glasses of blood from freshly-beheaded snakes. A lot of fifth-deck kids were going to Taipei, she said. Post demurred. He said he'd prefer to hang around Keelung. That baffled her. There's nothing here, she said, everyone was getting out of town. He said he thought of it as a kind of experiment, staying in a place that had nothing to offer. If it didn't appeal to her, he could understand that. She said she'd seen plenty of places that had nothing to offer, her hometown included. So nothing personal, she said, but she'd head to

Taipei, see him in a couple of days, and they could compare notes. Fine, Post said. And that was that.

All right then, Keelung was not a tourist town. Fine. Most of the other places they'd visited were waiting for them. In Ghana and India, up and down the Amazon, at the Great Wall, everywhere they went, people were on the lookout for them. Keelung was different. No postcards, no photo ops, nothing close to an international hotel. The shops sold cheap, mass-produced goods, no handicrafts and souvenirs to speak of. T-shirts galore but none of them bragged about Keelung. And the Taiwanese he passed went about their lives without much attending to a passing American. He felt it most in the night market, several blocks of hanging lights and crowded alleys a five-minute walk from the ship. It was just what he was looking for, and it was so easy, pointing at and choosing from bubbling pots of stews, soups, noodles, pork, and fish on grills. Barbecued ducks and ribs, fresh-squeezed fruit juices, the name and price of everything clearly posted, no difference between visitors and locals, and it went on that way, inside and outside, upstairs and downstairs, block after block. That first night, he had a skewer of quail eggs, sautéed greens with pork, an oyster omelet, and a tall can of local beer. And for once on this trip around the world he was no one's target. Some people spoke English, had relatives in the States and seemed pleased that he was there. Would Sanchez get this place, he wondered? Maybe so. Once. She'd get it, or at least think she'd gotten it and want to move on. She wouldn't want to hunker down.

Meghan would get it, he decided. At the night market over noodle soup and barbecued fish, they avoided—by mutual consent—all talk of the voyage, which they'd soon leave behind them. Sometimes, that felt like a good thing. She asked about Indonesia. Something might be happening for her there, he gathered. Jakarta was an impossible city, he warned her. But then what a list of places an hour's flight away, places people flew halfway around the world to visit, places with magic names: Bali, Sumatra, Komodo, Surabaya, Bandung! He'd been there three times on short visits. He envied her visiting for the first time and staying for a while. He might show up, he said. "I'd like that," Meghan said. He might not leave for a while, he added. "Okay by me," she said.

As they came back to the ship, Meghan glanced at a long line of students waiting to be checked for sobriety and contraband before going up the gangplank and remembered she needed to pick up some shampoo. Then, as he approached the end of the line, Post realized she'd seen something that he had missed. Rosa Sanchez was standing at the very end of the line.

He tapped her shoulder and got a hug. She hadn't been so impressed by Taipei, she admitted. She'd gone to a Mongolian barbecue place with a group of other students who'd fled when they saw a rat scurry down the wall of the dining room. They got pizza someplace. How had he made out in Keelung, she asked. Fine, he said. She didn't follow up. Back on ship he read in his room, waiting alone for the ship to make its first moves toward home.

XII.

HILO

*T*HEY MISSED JAPAN, POST thought. If you considered the ports remaining, the voyage was ending with a whimper. A glance at Honolulu. A peek at Hilo. And San Diego. From major to minor, from foreign to domestic, from exotic to familiar. And more bad news. Just lately Greg Mortenson had fallen: a TV exposé charged the author of *Three Cups of Tea* with fabrication, short cuts, self-promotion, and shoddy bookkeeping. "Three Cups of Bullshit," someone called the book that all students and teachers had been required to read and be inspired by. Still, there were things to like. Post wished someone would announce that they were crossing the Pacific, the biggest thing on Earth. Have all the students spend a day contemplating the Pacific and write a thoughtful three-page essay and let that serve as a final exam. The endless Pacific. It made the Atlantic feel like a lake. Hour after hour, no sight of a ship, no birds, only flying fish for company. No land as well. Until Beckmann called him—on the ship's phone—the second day out of Keelung.

"Please come to my cabin right now," he said, hanging up before Post could reply. He rushed upstairs, fearing something awful, a loss of sight, garbled speech, blood in the toilet. Beckmann opened the door and led him to where Edith was standing by the railing.

"Do you see?" he asked.

Post saw a bank of clouds on the horizon, like the clouds that he'd studied since he was a kid. Then it happened. Beneath that pile of clouds, there were islands, three or four of them. New islands, new to him. The ship didn't notice them.

"Why, oh why, can't they point them out as we pass?" Beckmann asked. "Acknowledge them? Give us their names? Some are fairly large. I see steep pinnacles, I see no place to land. On others, there's some shoreline. Does anyone live there? Do they have water? Can you see anything green? I'm not sure…"

"I know, Henry," Will Post said. "You want to go and stay awhile."

"Could we not come a little closer for a better look? Is that asking too much?"

Post looked over at Edith, smiling at Beckmann. You had to love the guy.

"They're getting smaller now," he said. "And I don't know their names. We haven't even…been introduced."

He sat down to watch the islands slide away, like a chapter unread, a remarkable person unmet. Before long, they might as well have been clouds.

Post got up to go. "Can I just say, Professor, that you've meant a lot to me?" With that, he left. Beckmann sat down across a table from Edith. Something about the islands had made him speak—that, and the fact that Post had already offered a kind of goodbye.

"Now I have you," he announced. "Will you listen to a few words from me?"

"I'll listen," she said. "It's time."

"High time. We've come to know each other on this voyage…" God, he reproached himself, he sounded like a character out of another century. "And I want us to have a future."

"A future?" It sounded like the concept hadn't occurred to her. Was she already at that stage? That zone of last things? "We're both getting up there. But you've renewed my life. My ambitions. I was talking to Will Post about Laos. There's a place there, he tells me, along the highway from Vientiane to Luang Prabang. Vang Vieng. A lovely place along the Mekong. Dramatic, jagged limestone karsts. Something like we saw in our painting."

"'Waiting for a Ferry on an Autumn River,'" she said, as if she were quoting a line from an old song.

"Now it's all about hippies and backpackers. Once it was a secret airport, in the war years. Hundreds of pilots and mechanics. A long runway in the middle of nowhere..."

"Perhaps you can get him to go back there with you."

"That's not the company I want. Listen, the time you and I have left, I want us to share."

"No, you don't. You think you do, and it's lovely, but...you don't."

"Please. You lost your husband. I lost my wife. The loves of our lives. He died in his chair, you said..."

"Reading a book. Jonathan Franzen."

"Anna's death was much worse. You heard me talk about it. Cruel, painful, demeaning. But if that's what happens, I am telling you—and I know what I am talking about—I would go through it again, with you. For you. Whatever, whenever. This isn't what I expected when I came aboard. I was thinking about myself, picturing a way out. But life surprises us."

"Oh, Henry," she said, putting her hands over her face, moving it from side to side. "Thank you. May I think about it...just for a little while? I'll let you know by Hawaii," she said. She seemed to brighten, then. He pulled her out of the chair and held her, the kind of embrace that could fit as a greeting or a farewell. Like the sun at the edges of the day, impossible to distinguish between dawn or dusk, until you saw which way it was moving. It all depended on the time of day.

¤

ANNA CATHER ASKED POST to stop by her office. He felt sorry for her. It was one thing for her to sit in Virginia, supervising things. It was another to join the ship where a lot of people detested her for what happened to Leo. Was she a sucker for punishment? Almost anyone could have managed the voyage from Keelung to Hawaii to San Diego. He agreed to chat with her but he knocked on the door fifteen minutes before he had a travel writing class. A closed-ended meeting.

"Have a seat," Anna Cather said when Post knocked on the door of the office where he'd sat with Leo a dozen times.

"I've spent a lot of time here," Post admitted. Cards on the table from the start. "Talking to Leo."

"Leo and I go back forever." Anna answered. "Saved my ass once. I was riding in a car we weren't supposed to rent in Thailand. We brushed a kid on a bicycle. Just a scratch. But they put me in jail. They liked having me there on the day the ship was due to sail. I was dying there. Then I heard that booming voice, down the hall…"

"I'm just wondering… How is it with you and Leo?"

"It's coming along," she said. He waited for more but nothing came. Then he decided to take a chance.

"You want to learn about this voyage?" Post asked. "Come to my class. Travel writing."

¤

"WE HAVE A SPECIAL guest today," Post said. A needless announcement. The kids bristled when they saw Anna Cather invading their space. Beauty and bitch, that's what they thought. "She's my guest," Post added, putting his hand on his chest the way he'd seen athletes do after an error or a foul. "My bad." They laughed at that. Was it already out of date, he wondered? He looked at Sanchez for help and got none. "Ms. Cather is this program's boss. Ever wonder how much the boss knows about what really goes on? Ever wonder about how much she gets, how much she misses? Well that's why she's here today. You didn't know she'd be here. Neither did she. I just asked her. So would everybody please relax?"

He reviewed, mostly for Anna's benefit, the assignment that was due today. He'd asked everybody to prepare a list of their best and worst moments during the past three plus months. That's what they'd be reading aloud, that's what they'd be hearing for the next eighty minutes.

"You can leave now, if you want," he told Anna.

"I think I'll stay."

And so it began. He decided he'd go through the good moments first, then the bad. He scanned the room, found one of his good students.

"This lady," he said, gesturing at Jody Phillips, "came up with one of the best lines of all. It was from Ghana." Jody nodded, pleased that he remembered. She knew what was coming. "She wrote about a fairly half-assed service visit to a village, she wrote…" Post stopped, as if he were an English professor channeling the opening of *The Canterbury Tales*, just pulling the lines out of the air. "She wrote: 'It's going to be hard to leave because we haven't been here long enough to make it hard to leave.' Ouch. That's good. Okay, lady. Got any good stuff to share?"

"I think so," she said. "Brazilian village homestay, piranhas, betel nuts… Ghanaian market… Being dragged around by rickshaws… Safari…"

Pretty ordinary stuff, Post thought, *and too bad because the girl was sharp*. It was harder to be a booster than a knocker. It was harder for everyone. He missed the "senior list" she'd given him a few days before, things students wanted to do before leaving. Smuggle drinks into the dining room; have sex in the faculty lounge, the computer lab, a lifeboat, the gym, and behind the smokestack on the top deck. Was it her list? he asked. This was prying. She had it all—looks, brains, soul—and she knew it. "Mostly my list," she said. "I missed the sex in the faculty lounge." They laughed at that. "Still time, I guess," she added.

He moved quickly to the next writer.

"Kayaking in Brazil… Food courts under malls in Singapore… Ha Long Bay in Vietnam… Star Ferry…"

He'd hoped for more, Post said. But the list hadn't ended.

"Breaking my need to control every aspect of my environment, allowing myself to accept what comes…"

That was okay. He listened to more lists of good things. Too much food, sightseeing, shopping. The exercise was starting to drag.

"Okay," he said. "I know your time on land was short. 'Not long enough to make it hard to leave,' as the lady said. But what if the rest of you look over your list and eliminate everything to do with food, transportation, or shopping? That should speed things up."

"Jumped off a cliff in Dominica," the next student offered. "Going to a mosque dressed in Muslim garb… Walking around on my own in Singapore… Going to Taiwan with no plans."

"I like what I hear," Post said. "Keep it coming."

"Seeing sunrise on the Ganges," the next student said. You could see him skipping items on his list, finding the next good comment. "Seeing the Shanghai skyline at night… Standing on the deck watching the ocean… Ditching my group on the first day in Taiwan… Falling in love with Asia… The names of businesses in Ghana… The fresh air off the ocean and combating a stressful moment by having the ocean to look at… Not having a phone or Facebook, trying to stay disconnected… Sudden islands I notice…"

"What do you think?" Post asked when they finished the good list.

"I can't wait for the rest of the story," Anna responded. She sounded okay. Maybe it was the first good moment she'd had on board.

"Okay," Post said. "The bad moments. Same rules as before. Go easy on shopping, food, and such. No seasickness or diarrhea. Hangovers? I'm okay with hangovers. Hangovers are self-inflicted moral punishments. I'll start with a personal favorite. It's too long to memorize but I brought it along. One of my favorites." He rummaged in his manila folder and found what he needed. He turned to Anna. "This was from a fishing village in Ghana where kids were dragooned into forced labor, dangerous and sometimes fatal work. So the Semester at Sea students visit a charity that's trying to help the kids. They help serve them lunch someplace, hard-boiled eggs and crackers, and then they're back on the bus and here's the conversation the author of this piece reports:

> "When I get back I am going to eat five burritos from Chipotle," one student says.
>
> "My mom's homemade lasagna, yum," another chimes in.
>
> "I want a Dunkin' Donuts, right now, oh my God, I want real food from home," a final student chimes in.

"I would say that is a legitimately bad moment," Post said. "Got any more where that came from?" He stared at Darlene Tedrow.

She was ready. "Disappointing classes, not enough time in countries, not enough time between countries... Not being able to get away from people on the ship when you want your own space."

"I hear you," Post said. "Anything else?"

"Endless pre-port lectures that don't apply to us... Group travel. PowerPoints. Sunday arrivals... The cow nibbling on a bag of shit in Varanasi... Feeling like I had to clean out my eyeballs after setting out on a rickshaw in Varanasi..."

"Okay. A little rough on the cow, I'd say. Next."

"Global studies…"

"Let's not impale ourselves on that one," Post said, glancing over at Anna. "Let's get it out of the way. If you had problems with that course, raise your hands."

It was almost unanimous with the sole exception being Tommy, who'd abstained from the start. Anna Cather was taking notes. *You never knew about taking notes*, thought Will Post, who'd taken plenty of notes in his time. Sometimes they were legitimate records of things that mattered. Other times, though, you took notes to convince the person you were talking to that what they said mattered. Especially when it didn't.

"Time's running out. Look over what you've got and give us your liveliest items."

"My fellow students acting indecent in port," said one of his students. "The fashion we had of visiting orphanages again and again. Sometimes there were more visitors than orphans. The video they showed us at the Cu Chi Tunnels, with the dead American soldier." From the next student: "Getting mugged in Vietnam. Luckily, no one got my purse, but my dress was torn in half… Getting stalked and chased by a Spanish Eddie Munster look-alike in Brazil."

"Actually," said Post, "if it happened in Brazil, he probably wasn't Spanish. Next." Now he was a conductor, pointing at one student after another. What a bunch of tunes! A final crescendo.

"PowerPoint irritations… Ship rumors and how they just fly… Not realizing what I was doing until I was done doing it… Group tours where the tour leaders would hold a flag so you always stuck out like a sore thumb… Minimal time in each country… Seeing peers act the way they did in port… Being rushed on almost every tour… Buying too much worthless crap… In Shanghai, not having the big dumpling with soup inside… Announcements, long ones… The smell of India… The trips that were really just trips so pictures could be taken. Or a service trip so you could say you made a difference when in reality you didn't… Putting up with the SAS holes in my boat… Not meeting any students in our 'university hosted' Beijing trip."

"Well, then," Post said. "There you have it. There are things I could say. And…Ms. Anna…you too could surely respond." As a matter of fact, Anna seemed to take that as an invitation to speak. Post rushed on before she could get out of her seat. "But I like the idea, just today, of letting students have the last word."

And then, in this final class, something happened for the first time. The shy, smart, self-effacing Darlene Tedrow raised her hand. Sure, he'd called on her earlier. But now, evidently, she had something to add. The last words were hers.

"Wow," Post said. "Go, Darlene."

"This voyage keeps on insisting that we're changing, growing, getting better. A day doesn't pass without a reminder of how terrific we are, how we're making a difference in the world. It all reminds me of when my parents put a mark on the garage wall every once in a while that showed my height and how I was growing, inch by inch. The date and the height. It stopped in my case at sixty-two inches. So they measured me. But they didn't measure me or ask me to measure myself every damn day!"

That led to another first—a round of cheers from the classmates who'd admired and resented her. Post applauded.

¤

HEADED TOWARD HONOLULU, MEGHAN was reminded of an old—and questionable—maxim about teaching: tell them what you're going to say, say it, and then tell them what you said. That's what was happening all around. Reflections, summing-up, valedictories, anything to convince the students they were extraordinary and their days on board were life-defining. Not surprisingly, fund-raising kicked in at the same time, pleas for donations as well as raffles with prizes and privileges: one student paid $1,600 to be first off the ship in San Diego. Meanwhile, here was Honolulu, where they were not permitted on shore. They docked at Aloha Tower, a return to America, sort of, like immigrants in old black and white photos starting at the Statue of Liberty. The immigrants, mostly, got to Manhattan. Not the students, who stood at the railing contemplating what was off-limits. They saw people shopping at Aloha Tower; a microbrewery was right in front of them. But the passengers were confined to the ship. All but one of them.

Meghan had trailed Beckmann since dawn, watching him drink coffee in the faculty lounge. She'd joined him and Post at breakfast, talked about how far away their meeting at a fish restaurant in Nassau felt. Post had found a letter on a seventh deck corridor; it had been taped on someone's cabin door. Post read the letter, of course. It was a petition—make that a declaration of war—against global studies, a course it claimed had "failed miserably" and was "a quintessential example of why SAS students do not take academics seriously." The course offered "insignificant" information about countries visited. It closed, Post said, with a suggestion that grades be reviewed for "this extremely flawed and inefficient course."

"Was it signed?" asked Beckmann.

"No way."

"It's quite well-written," Meghan said, looking at Post. "One of your kids?"

"Whoa! I had nothing to do with it. My hands are clean. But it wouldn't surprise me if it were one of mine. Or displease me."

"Oh well," Beckmann said. Then he remembered something and turned to Meghan. "Weren't you mulling over global studies for a while? Trying to make sense of it?"

"I *was*," Meghan said with a nod.

"No more?"

"I found something else to do," she answered in a way that didn't invite a question about specifics.

"But you did think about it…"

"It doesn't matter what I think. Or you. At the end, the passengers leave, the cabins are cleaned, the classrooms, the halls, the dining rooms are vacuumed and polished. And that's it. Our presence, our complaints, our suggestions are history. Also, our compliments. The ship fills up and everything—global studies included—begins again. Oh, I tried all right. But it was like striking a match on a bar of soap."

"Maybe they'll just kill it," Post guessed.

"You may be right," she said. "Anybody want anything else to eat?"

"Only if there are chocolate croissants," Beckmann said. Meghan walked off across the room and joined another table. But when Beckmann arose and made his way to the back of the ship, then up the stairs to the seventh deck, she followed. He paused at the faculty lounge to use the public restroom. Morning coffee. He reappeared and stepped outside to say good morning and goodbye to Honolulu. The watershed mountains beyond the city, the high-rises toward Waikiki, the sense—if not the sight—of Pearl Harbor to the west. Then Aloha Tower, where no one could shop or drink, the dock where no one would stop. Then he saw something that no one should have to see: love leaving you behind, Edith Stirling walking toward the terminal building.

"No one gets off at Honolulu," Beckmann said.

"I'm sorry, Professor," Meghan said. "She arranged it. She has a place here. A condo…"

"She never mentioned it."

"And a doctor. She thought it was time to see him again. Actually, she thought it was probably past time."

"When did she decide?"

"I can't say. But she contacted me—in confidence—in Keelung. She didn't want a fuss."

"I guess I'm the fuss," Beckmann said.

"The voyage is practically over. She's not missing much."

"It's what I'm missing," he said. Then she handed him an envelope. The inevitable envelope. The last, maybe second to last scene in a thousand treacly films. "You're the voice of the voyage, Meghan. Read it to me."

"I think you should."

"Stop it! I can't bear the thought of sitting in my room and opening that letter. Please, Meghan. You bear the weight of a million announcements, many fatuous and trivial. This isn't. Please."

"Okay," she said. Glancing down, he saw it wasn't much of a letter. More of a note about the length of a thank-you-for-a-lovely-evening. "'Dear, dear friend. Time for me to go, tests and checks and—I hate the word—procedures. Thank you, dear man, for everything. The good company. Undeserved. Unexpected. Thank you. Please press on with the project. It means the world to me. Edith.'"

"So…" he said. "It goes. Shipboard acquaintance." Now he pictured the way she'd walked away from the ship, away from him. Her step had a certain finality about it, a sense of a job—a mission—completed. Something she'd done in memory of her late husband. The last he'd see of her, he was sure.

"Listen, Professor," Meghan said. "You got lucky on this voyage. You may not think so right now. But you will." She rose up on her toes, then kissed him on his cheek. "At the start, I resented you. You were a fossil, a place of the past that refused to move out of the way… my way."

"Have I changed?"

"Maybe not. But I have."

"Well…" He was surprised, this coming from a woman he'd thought resented him. "Thank you."

XIII.

SAN DIEGO

"WHAT DO YOU THINK, Professor?" Will Post asked. "The end of the Yamamoto Run. I'd have to say the Japanese made more of an impact on Oahu than we did. We missed the target altogether and hit…envelope please!…Hilo! Wow!"

Beckmann had to laugh. Still, he couldn't help wondering whether Edith was sitting quietly on a pleasant lanai or wearing a hospital gown somewhere. He'd decided against email. And he would not phone. He disliked phone calls too much; they invaded, interrupted. Reach out and touch someone: a questionable invitation. He'd have to decide what to do on his own. What, then, about Post? So fast, so facile, so variously talented. Would he be scouting tourist traps forever? And Meghan, same question: *quo vadis?*

"What'd folks do in Hilo, anyway?" Beckmann asked. He hadn't done much. He walked to a roadside restaurant and had a Portuguese sausage omelet. He'd taken a taxi to Hilo, which felt like a left-behind place. Edith was on his mind. A kid again: she loves me, she loves me not. Do we ever grow up? He mulled over the work she'd implored him to take on. Sometimes it appealed, mightily. That was before she left. Now he had some doubts. He couldn't picture himself completing it. He also couldn't picture himself returning to the classroom back home. At home or away, loneliness confronted him.

"When we got there," Post said, "the students sang 'God Bless America,' and some were honked off. They wanted their passports stamped but got waved through. So they rented cars, drove to beaches, surfed, went to a Wal-Mart. And, down in Hilo, I saw a half-dozen girls on the sidewalk, outside a restaurant—this is around ten in the morning—peeking in the window, waiting for the waiter to open so they could go in and wallop mojitos."

Beckmann half-listened. His mind was elsewhere. Perhaps he'd go to just one of the places on his list, then another. See what came to him, what words and feelings. It sounded lonely, rummaging around like that. But what wouldn't feel lonely after such a voyage?

"Would you do it again, this voyage?" Beckmann asked. The question was epidemic. Everybody asked it. Well, not the students: they had college to finish. They might come back later, as life-long leaners, but the student incarnation was over. The staff and faculty were the ones who wondered about returning, more and more urgently the closer they got to San Diego.

"I'd consider it," Post said. "I'd never say never. On the other hand, it's a mistake to look too eager. You get a feeling they don't want people to get too familiar. But if they knocked on my door…"

"You'd take it," Meghan said, sitting down beside them. "If they asked you. And you hope they ask you."

"Wouldn't you?"

"No. This is my third voyage. If you asked me back in Nassau, I'd have said yes. Not now. Three strikes, you're out. I'm making other plans…"

"Wow!" Will Post said. "Other plans! Can you share them?"

She smiled, touched her lips with her finger and turned to Beckmann. "How about you, Professor?"

"Hard for me to answer now. But what I wonder is how long this will keep happening, this voyage. You've heard it all: dangerous world, high fuel costs, universities declining credit…"

"How would you feel about that?"

"Bummer," Post interjected. "I liked my classes. Doubt if I could feel the same on shore."

"Professor?"

"If God came down and ruled that all students should spend four full years in school, American education would probably gain. That junior-year vacation is pernicious. And it's the most crucial year. And, after all, how long is college? Four years? Not really. Thirty-two months of classes peppered with vacations. Please. That must be said. And I can understand why some places require total immersion in one country, one culture, one language. You can't go sailing around the world with stops of three and four days and not appreciate the benefits of a longer stay. But…"

"Aha!" said Post. "The long awaited 'but' clause. Our saving grace."

"I've loved this voyage," Beckmann said. "The teaching, the travel. The weave of life on board. There are a lot of things you can learn. It isn't required. It can't be. But it's there. We're still at sea and I've already started missing things. And people. The bright ones, the goof-offs. The troublemakers. And if this were to stop, if this were lost…I'd understand. I'd know why. But I'd be sad. It's not that they do everything well. But it's remarkable that they do it at all."

¤

NOW SAN DIEGO WAS all they had left, and, on this last leg, boredom yielded to sadness especially on the fifth deck, all those lively, irreverent kids were feeling blue. Lots of posing for pictures together, lots of hugs and "I love yous." They talked, some of them about the fun they'd have back home, but it didn't quite cut it. Others planned to rent a car in San Diego, start driving, not stop before they hit Las Vegas. Road trip. No one believed it, though.

"They're crying," Rosa Sanchez said to Post. She was dry-eyed, smoking a cigarette. "'We'll never see each other again,' they say. And I want to tell them, 'Hey, you live in the same country, right? You can talk on the phone, can't you? You can Skype? What's the big deal?'" She sat with Post, amiable and familiar, and he knew that he was in her past. Rearview mirror. No apologies, no regrets. It was what it was.

Underwood had said he wanted to talk to Post more about what he called "our project." Maybe he'd gotten a book contract. But Anna Cather intercepted him. They sat together at dinner which featured thin—quarter-inch—pork chops that looked as if they'd been sawed off a log, not sliced off a pig; and these chops, which were Florentine one night, Creole the next, teriyaki on the third, reminded him of Meghan's Taiwanese tribesmen changing clothes as they raced from one village to the next. Anna was annoyed when some faculty members asked to sit with them. She ate quickly, excused herself, signaling for Will Post to follow.

"I've got this meeting," Anna said. "Keep me company. After that, I want to talk with you."

It would have been wise to leave these last days and nights open and unscheduled: free time might lead to reflection, introspection, the kind of life-changing decisions that the program advertised. But these things weren't left to chance. Tonight was a recognition night where "absolutely fabulous people" who had made the voyage special were called up on stage and applauded. Almost all of the dean of students' staff and the living and learning coordinators turned out to have been absolutely fabulous.

Then it was the dean of students' turn. "Let's play a game," she suggested. She would ask a series of questions and, by way of affirmation, the people would be asked to stand. To stand was to answer yes. To sit was…well, never mind. So it began. Stand up if you had eaten something new. Stand up if you successfully bargained for something. Stand up if you had a meaningful conversation with a citizen of a country you visited. Up they popped and down they sat and up they popped again. Could a Stalinist party congress have been more dutiful? Stand up if you were proud, if you were humbled, if you were scared, stand up if you made a new friend for life or accomplished a personal goal. Stand up if you think you've grown as a person. (That unnecessary "as a person" made Post wince.) Stand up if you're looking forward to our last week on ship. God, what coercion. Pet therapy in convalescent homes was more impressive. But at the end of it all—actually, before the end—Anna Cather tapped him on the shoulder and they left the room.

"What did you think of that?" Anna asked.

"I was hoping you wouldn't ask me that," Post said. And then he admitted that he was angry. Couldn't the students for once be left alone and not subjected to an exercise that would embarrass a summer camp? Could you imagine anything like that happening at a college or university back home? Hell, stand up if you thought six port arrivals on Sunday were in your best interest, stand up if your field trips were well-run and fairly priced, stand up if you loved global studies, stand up if pre-port sessions actually prepared you for what you found on shore. "All I can say is I'm glad I took you to the class of mine," Post said. "That's where you heard what they think. I've had a lot of sessions like that."

"Have you made a list of your own?" Anna asked. "Like what you asked the kids to turn in?"

"No list on paper," Post said. He pointed to his head. "It's in here." And touched his heart. "And here. You'd hear lots of things, good and bad, that the kids mention. And one more. The teaching. I never minded stepping into that classroom. And I'm not even a professor."

"I admit," Anna said, "that…for sure…there are annoyances on board. But your complaints…and your students' are mostly about what goes down on shore. Am I right?"

"Right. It's kind of a mess. Monuments and malls. You want more?"

"Yes," she said. "A lot more. But not now. Listen, you've traveled all over. You know your tourist traps. You know what's a reward. What's a rip-off. We need someone to interrogate what happens on shore. The destinations, the guides, the faculty trips, the size of groups, the lengths of stay. We want to deliver what we promise. And change the promises, if we can't keep them. Is that something that you'd be interested in doing for us?"

"Yes."

"I'll see what I can do," Anna said. "Although my recent hiring is…" She laughed, looking for the right word. "Not impeccable. Definitely not. Peccable. But memorable." It came out on its own. No negotiation with Anna, no dialogue within. It just came out. And it didn't stop coming. Another opportunity knocking on his cabin door. Then Post waited for the steward who'd promised some cardboard packing boxes. Bit by bit, the voyage was being disassembled.

¤

POST DECIDED TO TAKE a seat on the deck outside his cabin and, as a last defiance, to smoke a cigar there. What could they do? Kick him off the ship in San Diego? He sat happily, blowing smoke rings that the wind caught and carried away. Then someone else was knocking on the door. He set down his cigar, returned to the cabin and found Leo Underwood standing in the hall.

"We need to talk," Leo said.

"That we do," Post said. "We've got to decide how to collaborate. My place or yours. And I'll need some money to pay for transcription of tapes. Hours of tapes. You'll be telling your stories more than once. I'm going to wear you out."

"No you aren't. It's not happening. That book."

"I guess we should sit out on the deck then," Post said.

Leo took a chair. Post relit his cigar and waited.

"I'm not feeling it," Leo said. "I'm not sure what I'm feeling. But that book feels like the wrong way to close things out."

"That's all you need to say. You don't owe me an explanation."

"I thought of all those books written by ex-presidents or a star who just got out of rehab or some lawyer…" His voice trailed off. "All that tell-all inside-story bullshit."

"I have to point out that there's money on the table."

"I know. But…remember Carla Hutchinson? Drowned halfway around the world? She keeps coming back to me. Eventually you have to leave the ship. The voyage ends and that's that. It was what it was and now it's over. Okay?"

Post stood and shook his hand. "I think you made the right choice. I feel better."

"So do I."

Will Post mulled over his future after Leo left.

¤

HE'D HAVE TO DO something about his travel blog. Bring in an assistant, possibly as a successor. Someone smart, sly, hardworking. Someone whose writing—whose very voice—could match his own. Someone he'd caught at a computer reading through his archived columns, years of them. Darlene Tedrow. She'd been half-apologetic when she asked about travel writing. Why not give her a shot? She'd do well for a while. She was smart. And then, he guessed, she'd find something else to do.

¤

BECKMANN DECIDED TO CONCENTRATE on places that were, one way or another, connected to the Vietnam War. Even that made for a daunting list. Saigon, the Mekong Delta, the Ia Drang Valley, Cam Ranh Bay, China Beach, and a dozen other places he didn't know the names of, but he'd find them. Then there were abandoned bases in the Philippines, Clark and Subic, that abandoned secret airstrip in Laos, threatened bases on Okinawa. So much work. So much travel. He might never finish. But maybe that wasn't the point. Oddly, though he felt Edith's departure was a huge subtraction, he'd savored crossing the Pacific where every sunrise and sunset, rainstorm, and moonlit night felt like a gift to him. Now the halls were filling with corrugated boxes and packing tape was in great demand. And another thing: cast-off toiletries, shirts, and running shoes were deposited in boxes for the crew to pick through. Students, faculty, staff, and adult passengers were summoned to the back of the ship for group photos. First you smiled, then you waved, then you jumped in the air.

As the ship plowed east—and it felt odd, traveling east to find America—you could sense that no more islands or straits, no rivers, no ports of call were waiting for them. Like a horse headed for a stable, the ship steamed ahead. Would he be on the ship again? Unlikely. But he was grateful for this trip and sad to see it end. Nothing but Pacific out there this morning. He thought of something that Francis Bacon said: "They are ill discoverers that think there is no land when they see nothing but sea." Beckmann thought, *I'll miss the sea.*

¤

LEO AND ANNA STOOD next to each other when the time to be photographed came. They declined to jump, consented to smile and wave. Some people cheered at that. Hatchets buried, *auld lang syne.* "We're lucky to have had you both," one sociologist said, shaking their hands and beaming, before walking away.

"Some guys'll do anything for a job," Leo said. "Want to talk? Now's the time or never." The past and present walked down to their office where Meghan sat at her desk, weeding emails.

"Hey," Leo said. "The first thing I have to tell you is that this is one great lady. Saved my ass many times. Listen, she's been working for weeks, trying to figure out what we should do for global studies. I'd recommend you listen to her, not just for my sake."

"No thanks," Meghan said.

"What's with you?" Leo asked. "You worked so hard."

"That I did. But right now I've got other plans."

"You do."

"A job offer, actually. Overseas. And I owe you for that."

"You do?"

"It's from Bobby Rummel," she said. Then she included Anna in the loop. "He's a kid Leo threw off the voyage. Maybe he deserved it. But I talked to him before he left. He's been following the voyage for a while. No interest in Hilo, though. It turns out his dad's the principal of an international school in Jakarta. That's where I'm headed. As a teacher."

Then…it was odd…they walked together to the railing. They weren't alone there. San Diego lay before them. There were students all over the place. The ship went slower and slower, it seemed, and when it stopped it was going to be over. Hard not for both of them to feel a sense of loss. And corny melodrama. On the dock, outside the terminal fence, parents stood waiting, waving, taking pictures, and it was a cliché all right, but it got to them anyway. Across the street from the terminal, sheets spray-painted with *Welcome Home!* hung out of hotel room windows. Post and Beckmann joined them and suddenly a girl with a cell phone started jumping up and down. It was Sanchez, Will Post's shipboard girlfriend.

"What's going on?" Leo asked. Sanchez was wearing one of those faces that might be expressing sheer joy or utmost grief. You couldn't tell.

"What's the matter?" Will Post asked. He hadn't stop caring, quite yet.

"My parents!" she said. "I called them. They're supposed to be in Lubbock! And I tell them I'm on deck and we're coming in to the dock and then they ask where I am and I say up here, seventh deck, left-hand, sorry, port side—and they say I should wave and I'm like, what? And they tell me they're on the dock and I wave and they wave back." She started crying. Post hugged her. For the last time, he supposed. "I'm losing it," she said.

"That," said Leo, "is a nice surprise. I'm losing it myself."

¤

THEY WANTED TO STAY longer. They wanted to be the first to leave. They glanced at empty cabins, worried about luggage that was waiting in the terminal. They left the ship. Some of them planned a meal that night—Mexican for sure—with parents, a pound of answers confronting an ounce of questions. Others had airport connections to make. They walked through the gangway, a roofed tube that fed them down to the terminal. And Leo watched them leave. Faculty and life-long leaners first, students next. Every minute was a subtraction, an emptying, and an ending. Fourteen voyages, Leo had always been the first off the ship. Now he would be the last. Somehow…he couldn't say why…it felt like the right way to leave.

AFTERWORD

THIS IS A WORK of fiction that draws upon two Semester at Sea voyages, one in 1993, the other in 2011. The experience of those voyages is complemented by accounts of other trips, as well as by imagined scenes that might, and in some cases—I hope—never will happen. My writing benefits from adventures and insights students shared with me. Teaching writing at Semester at Sea is a great pleasure. The Semester at Sea program—currently sponsored by Colorado State University—continues to improve. I believe it is a gift to sail around the world on a university ship. Shortly after this novel appears, I'll be embarking on my third voyage.